DIE BIRKEN

[THE BIRCHES]

D1615726

PAMELIA BARRATT

Library of Congress Control Number: 2019952163
Barratt, Pamelia
Die Birken

ISBN: 978-1-7341443-0-7 (trade paperback edition)

Cover photograph adapted from: *River birch tree on a snowy Saturday afternoon*; January 21, 2012; photochem_PA from State College, PA, USA

Published by:
Plowshare Media
P.O. Box 278
La Jolla, CA 92038

To our grandchildren:
Jack Jeffery, Milo Jeffery-Baum,
Alvaro Barratt, and Emma Barratt

CONTENTS

BERLIN

1933

On a clear May evening, two young men walked out of their apartment building in a hurry. Wolfgang, the taller of the two, zipped up his lightweight jacket as he rushed ahead. He was continuing a conversation: "I know we should be studying for exams, but this is an attack on German culture!" Andi listened to his friend's rant while trying to keep up. Although he wasn't German himself, he fully agreed with Wolfgang.

The two students were hurrying to catch a tram, but when they reached the stop, they found a long queue of people also wanting to go to Opernplatz. They took their place at the end of the line. A minute later, frustrated and impatient, Wolfgang declared: "It'll be faster to walk."

The cool air was invigorating and pushed them to maintain a quick pace—easier for Wolfgang with his long legs. Andi braced himself for what was to come. He dreaded knowing, yet had to find out how bad things were. By 9:00 on this May evening, the Berlin sky was already dark. Few streetlights lit their way. They walked briskly at first, passing by closed shops with apartments stacked up five stories above them. The upper windows were mostly dark. Are a majority of the residents down here on the streets marching with us, he wondered?

The sidewalks were filling now with men of all ages. There were some women and a few children. All were heading in the same direction. Andi and Wolfie had to slow down. Most people carried a book or two. After awhile, the crowd was so thick all they could do was follow the people in front of them. Later still, people were forced to walk in the streets. Vehicle traffic must have been diverted.

Wolfgang noticed the trees lining the street. Hawthorns, he thought, like those in his grandparents' garden. Insects, especially bees, love their white blossoms. But his attention was drawn back to the people around them, pursuing their mutual rush to get to the square.

He felt Andi nudge him, pointing out four people a distance ahead: three men and a woman, standing their ground, facing the crowd, and holding a placard above their heads so all could see. The sign was in the shape of a book and had a message in large black letters: OPEN BOOKS, OPEN MINDS. As the two of them got nearer, Wolfgang noticed how nervous these protestors appeared. Suddenly, five Brownshirts came on the scene. The placard was snatched and broken to pieces. The dissenters were pushed, thumped, and dragged to the sidelines.

"Hey," yelled Wolfgang, "you can't do that!" Andi grabbed Wolfgang's arm to lead him to the opposite side of the street. One of the Brownshirts eyed Wolfgang and then Andi. It seemed like he wanted to come after them, but the movement of the crowd quickly swept them apart.

Andi tried to calm his fears while the two of them pushed ahead toward Opernplatz. "We'll be lucky to get within four blocks of the plaza." An ironic choice of words, he thought. How can it be 'lucky' to witness the crumbling of the social order? Yet he was compelled to know for himself. Were his fears justified? He tried to read people's faces, to see which books they carried. It was impossible to make out the titles. The snatches of conversations he heard were not encouraging. Their eager voices, the spring in their steps, the smiles on their faces—all sickened him. It was hard to believe it had come to this. Many supporters participating in the march were university students—the educated, the elite.

Closer to Opernplatz, Andi pulled Wolfgang by the sleeve into a doorway. "We may not make it through this horde."

With furrowed brow, Wolfgang spat out: "Christ Almighty, this is disgraceful. Many of these guys are from our university!" Without waiting for Andi to reply, he pointed to the right, "Isn't that Heinz over there?"

"Yes!" Andi had already spotted Heinz. In fact, he noticed other students whom he recognized from various classes he had taken with them over the previous three years. "This is unbearable."

Andi would have much preferred to be back in his flat, but nevertheless stuck with his decision to verify what he feared. They stepped out of the doorway into the flow again and found they were almost pushed along. Suddenly, a thrust to the right tossed them smack into other people. No one was able to move. All eyes turned to the center of the street, where a legion of newly arrived students marched in formation toward Opernplatz. The crowd greeted them with a thunderous "Heil!" and arms raised in the Nazi salute.

"Oh, my God, I can't take this!" Andi said, just loud enough that only Wolfgang could hear.

A voice came over the loudspeaker: *...truckloads of books ...25,000 have been brought to the square*, Andi thought he heard. The voice continued: *...a pyre of 'un-German' literature....*

"A pyre of un-German literature!" Wolfgang repeated. "Jesus, Thomas Mann—un-German?"

The huge crowd became quiet. Andi whispered: "I think Goebbels is going to speak."

The era of extreme Jewish intellectualism has come to an end, and the German revolution has again opened the way for the true essence of being German....

"Such a tragedy!" Having just seen for themselves what the Brownshirts could do, Andi hoped Wolfgang would not draw their attention. Even without speaking out, Andi felt vulnerable. Should he have asked Wolfie to accompany him? Maybe that was a mistake. No, considering it further, he would not have had the courage to come on his own.

*During the past fourteen years, while you students had
to suffer in silent shame the humiliations of the Weimar
Republic, your libraries were inundated with the trash
and filth of Jewish 'asphalt' literati.*

Wolfgang burst out: "Lion Feuchtwanger, trash? Einstein,
filth? Ridiculous! How can anyone believe such nonsense?"

Andi hadn't ever seen this side of Wolfgang. Usually, his
friend was calm and soft-spoken. Now, his volatility could draw
attention and get them in trouble.

Goebbels went on:

*Surrender to the flames the evil spirit of the past. Jewish
intellectualism is dead. You students have the right to
clean up the debris of the past.*

Goebbels wrapped up with:

*…the Reich and the nation and our Führer, Adolf
Hitler—Heil!*

The sky lit up and sparks flew as the loudspeaker announced
that Brecht's and Freud's works were being tossed into the fire.
The crowd broke out in rapturous singing of the Nazi Party
anthem. Andi caught a glimpse of Heinz again. His voice could
not be heard above the others, too many were singing, but by
seeing his fellow student's gestures and erect posture, Andi could
feel Heinz's pride as he sang with full throat.

It was almost 1:00 A.M. when Andi and Wolfgang walked back
down Hoffmannstrasse and into their apartment building. They
called it "Die Birken" for its stand of birch trees in front. Like other
students, they gladly put up with fifth floor accommodations just
to be close to the university. A bed, desk, and a lamp were all any
of them needed.

Should Andi have chosen to study in Berlin? He could have
gone to university in Budapest, where his home was, and where
he was known as András. But Budapest restrained him, in part,
because it was home. He knew he would love Berlin more.
The city had a reputation for culture, edgy satire, gay bars, and
cabarets. How was he to know that within three years Berlin

would fall to Nazi fervor? What had brought this about—the Great Depression? Many people were bitter about having lost their life savings. Who wouldn't be? But it was more than that. Was it fear of communism? Why didn't people understand the difference between social democracy and communism? In his opinion, German conservatives tended to lump the two together.

Andi loved this city, but what was happening to Berlin, indeed, to Germany? He couldn't explain it. At home in Hungary, people were just as accustomed to authoritarian rule as Germans. There, too, anti-Semitism was commonplace, as it had been throughout Europe for centuries. Nazi leaders seemed to be masters at using propaganda, and Hitler was a powerful speaker. His simplistic rhetoric fulminated untruths, such as blaming Germany's problems on Jews and communists, while boosting anglo Germans' pride by telling them they were the superior race.

Andi remembered that in his freshman year, fellow students thought goose-stepping Nazis were ludicrous. Now, he was dismayed that so many of his classmates were followers.

Andi had first met Wolfgang doing laundry in the basement of Die Birken, where they realized they were in the same German literature class. Wolfgang was German and had read German authors extensively. Andi spoke other languages and was able to compare German novels with those of other cultures. They met sometimes over coffee for just such conversations.

Occasionally, their discussions ran late into the evening. Not tonight! The emotional strain of witnessing the book burning had exhausted Andi. Four flights up, one to go! Wolfgang was already at the top. He looked toward Andi again and said: "Wherever they burn books, they will also, in the end, burn human beings."

Andi recognized the words of the 19th-century German poet. "Heinrich Heine," he called out. Wolfgang smiled and bade him good night.

Although Andi was grateful for their friendship, he couldn't stop his spirits from sinking. The thought of burning to death made him shudder. For days, he had been having trouble sleeping, worrying about what to do. Tonight would be no different. Should he try to make it through his senior year so he could graduate? He would be safer living in Budapest with his parents. Damn these Nazis! They are spoiling everything.

BAUER FARM

SPRING 1940

A brisk wind funneled through the valley, blowing loose soil over the furrow Wilma had just plowed. She was finding it difficult planting the potatoes on her own. The sets were already prepared. Cutting up the larger potatoes so that each piece had at least two eyes—that was easy. Two nights before, sitting with Grandpops in front of the fire, he said: "By the time those pieces have healed, Goran will be home to help you with the planting."

But two days later, Goran had not returned, and she had no choice but to start the planting by herself. The snow had melted, and in its place, edelweiss dared to show their white, wooly faces. Definitely, it was time to start planting. The growing season at their high elevation was short enough as it was.

Placing the sets a foot apart, cut side down, she thought about her brother. All he had to do was take their fifteen sheep to high pasture as they did every spring. It used to be her job, but since the war started, both Goran and her grandfather decided it was too dangerous for a woman to do shepherding.

"If a German soldier saw you on your own, who knows what he would do to you. You can't count on your German ancestry to protect you. Each time a soldier kills, it is easier for him to kill the next person."

The Bauer family had lived on this farm in Poland for 80 years. It was tucked in a small valley in the High Tatra Mountains. Their nearest village, Szaflary, was twelve kilometers away. A kilometer in the opposite direction was the nearest farm. Wilma hoped they were too isolated for the soldiers to bother with them, but why hadn't Goran returned? Her family had a hut up on the high pastures. Sometimes it was so wet in the spring that she herself had spent a few nights there, waiting for the rains to stop before making the descent back home. But it hadn't rained on the farm for a week, and by now, Goran would have eaten all the food he took with him. And what about Olga? She wouldn't come back without Goran. She must be starved. As loud as her bark was, the pasture was too far away for it to be heard.

Wilma's weathered hands picked up the hoe again, this time to cover the potato segments with the soil that she took from both sides of the furrow. It would be a balmy day, she thought, possibly 10 °C, if it weren't for the wind. Periodically, she stopped her work to scan the hills abutting the mountain. She knew where he would first appear. There was only one path up. She envisioned him bounding down the last slope without a drop of perspiration to show for it.

They had a peculiar relationship—somewhere between sister-brother and mother-son. Wilma had been eight when Goran was born and eight when her mother died, a time of both joy and sorrow. Over the years, her resentment diminished and was replaced by a multifaceted love. It wasn't just Goran's strength and his help with potato planting she missed. It suddenly occurred to her that he might never return.

Every now and then, Grandpops came out to the field to help her, but at close to 80 years of age, he didn't have much stamina. Should she go up and look for Goran? "No," said Grandpops. "Not yet!"

In the early afternoon, Wilma thought she saw some motion far up on the trail. A speck of white! "Olga," she called out. The speck got closer. It could be Olga. There seemed to be a figure further back, following. A minute later, she was sure it was Olga, and it seemed that Goran was following. She was so relieved, and ran to fetch Grandpops.

Wilma and her grandfather rushed up the hill, but before

Olga reached them, she knew something was wrong. The man was dressed like Goran, but was not Goran. Wilma froze. "What's wrong?" asked Grandpops, whose eyesight was not that good anymore.

"I don't think it's Goran," she said. The two of them stood and waited for the man to approach. Meanwhile, Olga went crazy barking. When the dog reached Wilma, she got behind her and nudged her, then ran back up the path, looked back at Wilma, and repeated the whole process.

Wilma's disappointment was overrun by fear. What did this mean? Who is this man?

The stranger spoke first. His speech was distinctly German, educated German, and he was clearly dressed in Goran's clothes. She recognized her patchwork on Goran's trousers.

"Hello, my name is Günter. I believe your dog's master has been killed."

"Killed?"

"Yes, shot by soldiers."

"But why? Why would anyone want to kill Goran? Oh, my God…. Oh, my God!" Wilma turned toward her grandfather. From his expression she knew he grasped what had happened. She hugged him and started weeping. Grandpops, who normally was so tender, stood rigidly still, eyes fixed on the young man.

"I'm sorry to bring you this bad news."

"Why are you wearing his clothes?" The question was no sooner out of Wilma's mouth when she noticed the hole in his shirt. "Dear God, he was shot?" She paused and looked fiercely into the man's eyes.

"He had been shot already when I found him. He was definitely dead, I'm sorry to say. Yes, I took his clothes."

"Why? Why would you want to wear a dead man's clothes?" she asked with disgust.

He lowered his eyes and didn't answer her. Finally, he said, "I'm so sorry," and started crying. He collapsed on the ground. Neither Grandpops nor Wilma knew what to do. While standing there, staring at the man, they saw he was falling asleep.

Olga kept rubbing against Wilma's leg. She bent over to pet her, but the dog ran to the house, stopped at the door, then turned around to look at them. Wilma realized the dog was probably famished. "I'm going to go in and feed Olga." She took her grandfather's arm and led him to the house.

The two of them sat at the table and watched Olga eat, not knowing what to do about the man. Having gobbled down her food, Olga started scratching at the door to go out. Wilma followed Olga out. She wanted to see what the man was doing. Grandpops came out too. The man was motionless, still lying on the ground, fast asleep. Olga sat next to him.

Wilma wondered if it was just the smell of Goran's clothes that attracted Olga. She shrugged her shoulders at Grandpops and told him she was going back to planting the potatoes. She thought she might as well keep planting while grieving over their loss of Goran. As she worked, they discussed the impossibility of retrieving Goran's body. The two of them didn't have the strength to carry it down the mountain. It was too dangerous to try to bury it up there with German soldiers around, but to just leave his corpse there exposed, to be ravaged by animals, seemed so heartless.

By late afternoon, the man awoke and walked out into the field. Wilma clutched the hoe, not knowing what to expect.

"May I help?" he asked.

She thought about it and decided that he could make it go quicker. She had just finished covering a row, but there were three more furrows ready to be seeded. She showed the man how to put the potato pieces in, face down. Then she followed with the hoe to cover them with soil. She knew better than to let him have the hoe.

When he bent over, Wilma could see the back of his shirt. She gasped to see a bigger hole than that on the front of the shirt. She knew that meant Goran had been shot in the front. There was dried blood around the larger hole. Oh dear Goran!

They carried on with the planting until the sky was darkening. Grandpops came out and said he had dinner ready. He offered food to Günter and said he could sleep in the barn that night. The next day, he would show him how to walk to Szaflary.

In the morning, the wind had died down. Wilma went out to get some eggs from the hen shed for breakfast. Günter was already out in the field, planting potatoes by himself. At breakfast, he thanked them again for the food and the place to sleep. Grandpops told him the way to Szaflary. "Thank you. I will go if you want me to, but I would appreciate working for you, for food."

Wilma looked at her grandfather. He took her aside and asked her what she thought. While they tried to reach a decision, Günter bent over to pet Olga. Olga liked it. They decided to try him out.

GERDA

Gerda's daughter, Renate, had been gone since January of 1944. Many young German children living in big cities like Berlin had been sent to safer homes in rural areas to escape British and American bombs. An army social worker had explained the arrangements to Gerda. "Because of your daughter's lovely blond hair, we have found her a good Nazi home. She will be living with Herr and Frau Wiesenhuber on their farm outside of Bamberg."

Gerda was given the address but she could only get herself to write Reni three letters while she was gone. What could she tell her—that she was the lucky one? Just last night, Gerda had to help dig people out who had been buried in the rubble. At times, she was so overcome with fear that sweat would bead on her forehead, her mouth would go dry, and she would start to tremble. Sometimes, when the sirens went off, she could barely make it down the three flights and into the nearby shelter. Once down inside, she felt she was in her grave. Reni was the lucky one.

Before Renate left, food was definitely in short supply. The government had already begun issuing ration cards. It seemed with each passing month, the rations decreased. A neighbor complained that they were now receiving no more than 750 calories a day. That number meant nothing to Gerda, but she had no doubt that she was on a starvation diet. She assumed Renate was being better fed on the Wiesenhuber's farm. She wished she could join her there.

Would Renate be glad to be back home when she returned

from Bamberg? Is this really still a home? Die Birken was now in shambles. There was a hole in the wall that made their living room visible to people on the street! Even worse than living in a fishbowl, the hole let in cold air. The building had an inner staircase that wound around the courtyard as it rose to the fifth floor. A bomb had gone into the courtyard and taken out the banister. Gerda could now get up to her third floor apartment only by keeping far to the inside. There was nothing to hold on to. The debris from the explosion covered the ground inside the courtyard, making it difficult for the first-floor tenants to get to their apartments.

Fortunately for Gerda, she had been waiting in line for bread when the bomb hit Die Birken. The building suffered other damage. Water didn't come out of the faucets anymore. There hadn't been electricity for months.

Before the war ended, ethnic Germans living in Eastern Europe began migrating to Germany. They came from far and wide: East Prussia, Pomerania, Poland, Czechoslovakia, and even Hungary. Some were forced to leave communities where they had been living for generations. Their neighbors associated them with Nazi terror and wanted them gone. Once the German Army was in retreat, German civilians left Eastern Europe for an additional reason: fear of Russian retaliation. Many of these expatriots didn't speak a word of German, but Germany was the only country that would tolerate them. Gerda had noticed many strange people on the streets recently, speaking languages she couldn't understand.

One day, Gerda found a young woman camped out behind the closet door in the basement. Amazingly, the door still opened and shut. The woman was filthy. Her hair was stringy with dirt. Gerda told her that she couldn't stay there. The woman's German was barely understandable, halfway between Polish and German. The next day, Gerda found the woman sweeping debris off from what was left of the stairs. She must have found that old broom in the basement. The woman kept asking Gerda about a man whose

name was Gounter, or Günter, maybe. Too tired by the third day
to shoo the woman off again, she decided to just let her stay in
the basement. She feared there would be others who would try to
squat in the building. Refugees continually passed by, struggling
to pull their carts through the rubble.

Finally, a time came when the bombing stopped. That was no
reason to celebrate, she was told, for it meant that the Russians
were close to the city. She heard Russian soldiers liked to rape
German women. Gunshots were heard far away, then tanks rolled
in and there was shooting right in the neighborhood. Everybody
stayed inside. Who was left to fight off the Russians? The Führer
ordered whatever soldiers were still around to fight to the end.
Boys as young as fourteen were drafted.

Gerda would always be grateful that Renate was still with the
Wiesenhuber family during those first terrible months when the
Russians started occupying the city. At least Renate was spared
from seeing women assaulted. How would Gerda be able to
explain it all?

The rhythm of daily life at Die Birken immediately changed.
Most of the building's occupants were women and children, with
a smattering of elderly people. By four o'clock in the afternoon,
they barricaded themselves in their apartments as best they
could and kept quiet. The Red Army supplied its soldiers with
an evening allotment of vodka. In May, daylight reached up to
8:30 at night, allowing many tipsy, armed men in uniform to
roam the streets while they could still see. Solicitations became
commands, "Komm frau," and ended in rape. Fortunately, most
soldiers never went above the second floor in Die Birken. The
condition of the steps was too precarious for a drunk.

Every morning at sunrise, while the soldiers were sleeping it
off, the women in Die Birken braved going out together, carrying
empty buckets to a hosepipe 100 meters down the road. Gerda
saw the cellarwoman helping a woman named Frau Fritz carry
her bucket upstairs to the fourth floor. She then went to the
aid of an old couple living on the same floor. Gerda knew the

cellarwoman's number. She was trying to get in their good graces so she could move upstairs.

At night, a week later, Gerda heard screams from the basement. The cellarwoman was probably being raped. Gerda covered her ears as best she could with her pillow. The next day, Frau Fritz carried her bucket herself but took it down to the basement. A few days later, Gerda realized that the cellarwoman had successfully 'conned' her way up to the fourth floor and was staying in Frau Fritz's apartment. Eventually, she learned the woman was a Polish refugee named Wilma.

When the Nazis rose to power, they discouraged women from working, insisting that they should be homemakers, raise a family, and give birth to babies. As the war started, Gerda noticed young boys were assigned jobs that women could easily do. With no husband and her only child removed to a safe locale, Gerda resented having to just stay in her apartment all the time.

After the war ended, in August, Renate was finally brought back to Die Birken. Gerda had been dreading her daughter's disappointment when she saw their building, but Reni greeted her enthusiastically, with smiles and hugs. "Where are the birch trees?" she asked.

"They were cut down. People needed to keep warm. All the trees are gone."

Reni's sweet smile surprised Gerda. "They'll grow back, won't they? At the farm, everything grew back the next year." She took her mother's hand, trying to pull her into the building.

Gerda never knew for sure what Renate was thinking. Is her father a quiet man? Is someone who didn't reveal his thoughts? He's probably not still alive. If he's alive, will he come back here looking for Renate? She only knew he had entered the army in 1939 and was immediately sent to Poland. Reni was born just before the war had started. She knew Renate couldn't remember him. He had been gone from Die Birken for 6 years.

The first night that Renate was back, Gerda could only offer her a piece of bread for dinner. She wasn't willing to burn a candle, because it might attract the soldiers' attention. Every night, a few lingered outside the apartment building. Reni quickly understood it was important to be quiet. Thank goodness for that! With nothing else they could do, Gerda proposed they get into bed. At least that way they could keep warm. Renate suggested they tell stories to each other.

Renate did most of the talking. She made it clear to Gerda that she didn't like living with the Wiesenhuber family. "The children were mean, especially Hans, who changed into his Hitler Youth uniform as soon as he got home from school. Then he'd order me and his younger sister around." On days when her own children were in school, Frau Wiesenhuber kept Reni busy doing tasks like dusting, weeding, and washing clothes. She criticized Renate for not knowing how to darn socks.

The problem was, Gerda thought, that Renate was tall for her age. Frau Wiesenhuber might have thought Renate was older than she really was. Caught by her own thoughts, Gerda was not concentrating on what Reni was telling her. She found herself saying: "Your dad was probably tall." Renate's confused look forced Gerda to focus on their conversation. "I know, dear, you don't remember your dad," Gerda went on: "He's a brave man fighting hard for Germany. You do remember the photo I have of him, don't you?"

"Yes, a man with a hat on his head wearing a soldier's suit, a…ah, what do you call it? A uniform? Should I call him 'Daddy' when he comes home?"

"Yes, of course." Good God, Gerda thought, what do I do then?

"What happened to Dolly and my jump rope?"

"Dolly got smashed into many pieces by a bomb, and I've been using your jump rope as a clothesline."

"Oh," Renate said, looking away. A minute later, she asked about her picture books.

"They were destroyed, except for *Little Peter's Journey to the*

Moon. I keep it in a special place."

"Thank you, Momma. That's my favorite." A little later, Renate added: "I'm hungry, Momma."

"Yes, I know, dear. Let's just try to go to sleep. I can give you something more in the morning."

The next morning, they went out together to fetch water as usual. Once a day, they had to pour some water in the toilet to flush it. At least the drainage pipes still worked.

Later in the day, they walked to some distant fields, hoping to find dandelions or nettles for soup. On the way, Gerda noticed some dirty children out on the street..."up to no good—orphans!" she commented. Once back home, Gerda was too tired to do anything else, so she went back to bed to recoup her strength. Renate peeked out the hole in the wall and watched the goings-on while her mother rested.

"The plumbing is supposed to be fixed in another month," Frau Fritz told Gerda one day.

"How do you know?" Gerda questioned.

"Wilma hears a lot of news." After a minute or two, she added: "She's working as a rubblewoman, you know."

Gerda hardly ever talked to Wilma, but she had seen lines of women passing buckets of rubble from one to another in an effort to clear a path or remove debris around buildings. In fact, there were crews of women engaged in this work wherever she went.

"She gets a little more rations for doing that," Frau Fritz explained.

"More rations would be nice, but all that work!"

"She has a baby on the way, you know."

Good God, thought Gerda. She turned around and walked away.

On another day, Gerda overheard Wilma and Frau Fritz talking about the memorial that the Soviets had built immediately after the war. Gerda hadn't seen it, but she knew it commemorated

Russian soldiers who died in the battle to liberate Berlin.

"They keep saying that they liberated us," Wilma said. "Give us food, rebuild our homes, that's what we need, not a monument."

"It ought to be called: 'The Tomb of the Unknown Rapist,'" Frau Fritz quipped. Both women burst out laughing.

Gerda hadn't heard people laugh in such a long time, it seemed out of place.

She knew Berlin was now divided into four zones and that Die Birken was definitely in the Soviet zone. In some respects, there was less chaos than when the soldiers first arrived, certainly less raping now. You didn't hear the screams at night. The Red Army had taken charge of its troops, engaging them in other tasks, which Gerda didn't understand. Frau Fritz told her they were dismantling factories and sending equipment to Russia as reparations payments. "Aye, factory equipment, machines, metals—anything of industrial value—they just rip it out of the place and put it on trains to be sent to Mother Russia."

Gerda was starting to agree with Frau Fritz. The Soviets were not interested in rebuilding Berlin.

Renate kept asking to go outside. She wanted to play with the other children she saw in the street, but Gerda was leery of giving her permission. There were orphans out there, wild and filthy, using the piles of rubble as a playground. Some were only a few years older than Reni herself! Gerda couldn't stand looking at them, and always held Renate's hand whenever they came within sight. She had heard that some of them played with grenades. For sure, they pilfered food, and not just food—it was said that they broke into apartments in the middle of the night. Well, that's easy to do! Someone told Gerda that a woman had had her blanket stolen right off her while she was sleeping!

As the weeks passed, Gerda became aware that more and more refugees, mostly women and children, were arriving from the east. The streets were crowded with those darn garden carts, each piled high with belongings. One woman she saw was so exhausted she slept standing up while leaning over to rest her head on the heap in her cart. "What would make them want to come here?" Gerda asked the woman in line behind her waiting to pick up her new ration cards.

The woman gave a little laugh and answered bluntly: "Gunpoint!"

"What? The war's over."

"Yes, but everyone—Poles, Hungarians, Czechs—none of them want Germans living in their countries. From what I've heard, these people are the lucky ones. They made it here and are still alive. Yeah, you haven't heard? They are forcing Germans everywhere in Eastern Europe to leave. Germany is the only place they can go to. Believe me! These people are forced to come here."

"Where will they live?"

"Who knows? Somewhere in Germany. Some are being kept in concentration camps, the same ones our government used for Jews."

"Do you believe those stories about what the Nazis did?"

The woman took a deep breath and stared at Gerda while she asked slowly: "What they did to Jews?"

"Yes," Gerda confirmed.

The woman answered very quietly. "Yes, I believe it."

Gerda wanted to continue their conversation and ask the woman why she believed such stories, but she was finally at the head of the line and eager to pick up her new ration cards.

Gerda looked forward to the end of the summer. She had been told that Reni could start school in September, and that the school was not very far away. Reni was to be in the morning shift. Gerda heard that the classes were huge and that the same teacher had to teach both shifts. There simply weren't enough teachers. Gerda couldn't wait for September to come. Recently, Reni had become clingy. She wanted to know what Gerda's life was like when she was young. She only wants me to entertain her, Gerda thought.

"Did you have electric lights?"

"Yes, and flush toilets...on Sundays, we would gather in the parlor where we had polished furniture, starched curtains, and soft chairs. We had a cook box, with an insulated sealing lid. The vegetables or soup would be brought to a boil on the stove and then inserted in the cook box. The food would simmer in its own steam." Gerda realized her mistake, talking about food. Both she and her daughter were continually hungry.

"What kind of vegetables?"

"Mostly potatoes with some bacon grease. If we had meat, it was usually sausage." She tried to stop, but she couldn't. "For Sunday supper, we would have a pork roast, or goulash, or a pot roast with vegetables and potatoes."

"Did you have dessert?"

"No, only on holidays."

She had already told Renate that she grew up in Lemgo, a town in the center of Germany, that her father was a baker, and that her mother was very frugal.

Another night, Reni asked her mother if she had friends when she was little. "Oh yes, six or seven, constantly. We played hopscotch, marbles, walked on stilts, and rode bikes."

"Was there anything that you didn't like?"

"Yes, chilblains. Every winter I had chilblains on my hands and feet."

"Oh, I've had that. Isn't it terrible?"

"Yes, and I didn't like the scratchy, woolen stockings I had to wear in the winter."

"Mine aren't scratchy. Frau Wiesenhuber gave me some she was going to throw out."

"That's because they are worn. Now they're smooth."

"And now they're too small."

Reni asked one day: "When did you learn to sew?"

"Not until I was 10."

EVE OF WAR

In 1934, as soon as Andi graduated from the university, he left Berlin to go home to Budapest. He lived temporarily with his parents, who were delighted to have him home again. Kind and loving as they were, Andi felt he was in a straight jacket—there were feelings he couldn't express, experiences he couldn't talk about. Nonetheless, he was thankful to them for his upbringing. A common practice in his family was to engage other people with stories. Andi had learned that skill. He was also grateful that they had trained him to be well-mannered and charming in social situations.

Two months later, he was offered a low-level diplomat's job with the Hungarian embassy in Poland, which was located in Warsaw. Getting any assignment in the diplomatic corps was difficult. In the past, much had depended on who you knew and even family background. Andi attributed his success to his fluency in German and having spent the last four years living in Berlin. But there was more to it than that. Most Hungarian politicians viewed Poland as unstable. The country was reconstituted as a nation only after World War I, and since 1918, it had engaged in several border wars. Working in the embassy in Poland was not a job most diplomats sought. The Polish government saw its greatest enemies to be the German Nazis and Stalinist Russia. Both those countries had a history of partitioning Poland.

In Warsaw, Andi tried to curb his homosexual mannerisms. That was not always easy. The fact that he was short, with a frail physique, didn't help. He was not the sporty type, either as a participant or as an observer. He kept his interest in theater and the arts to himself until he felt a friendship was secure. Over the next four years, he came to love his work at the embassy and could tell that he was appreciated.

On the eve of Hitler's invasion of Poland, he was asked to step into the ambassador's office. "Andi, we want you to be well, and you won't be safe here when Hitler's forces arrive. We will help you get to Sweden, but there will only be this one opportunity. Can you get yourself to Pier 1 at the harbor in Gdynia by 6:00 tomorrow morning?"

Andi was shocked and had to digest what his boss was saying. "Yes," he finally articulated. His mind was whirling. *What does he know about me?*

"Good. Pier 1—it's the pier furthest to the south. Take nothing with you but the clothes on your back. Someone on the dock will approach you. Just follow his directions. Here is your salary to date." The ambassador handed Andi an envelope. "Please leave now. Don't take anything from your desk. Just go! Appear relaxed as if you are doing nothing out of the ordinary. Don't try to contact anyone. Just go! And Andi, thank you for the fine work you have done at the embassy. We will miss you."

Andi couldn't keep his eyes from welling up. "Thank you," he said, barely able to look the man in the face. Grateful that the ambassador cared for his safety and embarrassed that he was 'out,' he wondered how long his boss had known about his homosexuality, and who else knew.

Andi went directly to his apartment to double up on underwear and shirts. On top, he wore a sweater and a jacket. Fortunately, it was a cool day. He wished he could call his parents, but he had been instructed not to contact anyone. He would have to call them from Sweden. He wrote down some telephone numbers and addresses and took his passport. He was about to take his checkbook, but realized it would be useless in Sweden. He'd have to go to his bank and turn his money into traveler's checks. While he was at it, he might as well return his library books. What to do about his apartment? He wrote a letter to his landlord, terminating his lease and included an extra month's rent for leaving his apartment in disarray. Before sealing the envelope, he would insert the key, once he had locked the door.

Andi had some lovely works of art that he would have to leave behind. The photographs of some attractive men he decided to put in the trash bins outside. Once he was ready to leave, he again checked the rail schedule. There was a train for Gdynia leaving at 5:00 that afternoon.

By the time he arrived in Gdynia it was dark. After getting a bite to eat at a small restaurant, he began walking towards the sea. The salty breeze must be coming from the Baltic, he figured. He walked a good three kilometers before he reached the port. By then, he was emotionally and physically exhausted. He found Pier 1 and its adjoining warehouse. Everything was locked up tight, not that Andi would have tried to go inside. No one was around. That helped Andi to relax. He went over to some bushes, crawled under one to lie down, hopefully out of sight, and tried to go to sleep.

Several hours later, some noises awakened him. Voices. It was still dark but he could see a few people on the pier, so he crawled out from under the bushes and walked over to join them.

As he approached, a man quickly came up to him: "Follow me."

Andi was ushered into the warehouse. A flashlight revealed several wooden crates, each about a cubic yard in size. It was then he saw the ambassador's wife, dressed in a fur coat, wearing several jeweled necklaces. She got into a crate. Two men turned it right side up and started to nail on its top. Andi's turn was next. He got inside, for once thankful for his small size. His crate was also nailed shut and then shoved somewhere. A voice from the outside warned him in a low tone, "Don't make a sound."

After a couple of hours passed, Andi heard what he imagined was a large door opening. Several men called out to each other.

All of a sudden, the crate Andi was in was lifted up, possibly by a machine. He heard other crates being moved. He was jostled. His crate was suddenly turned upside down. He quietly tried to flip himself over so all the blood wouldn't rush to his head. Another crate was placed on top of his and more around him so that now, the men's voices were muffled. Claustrophobia rose to the top of his fears and stayed there all the time the ship was moving.

After three hours, he adjusted to his cramped position and fell asleep. When he awoke, he realized the ship must have moored. There was no light, so he couldn't check the time on his watch. He was painfully aware of his need to pee. His thirst ran a close second. He heard men's voices. Crates were being moved. Now he could discern that the voices were speaking a different language: Swedish. Andi became hopeful. There was more jostling of his crate. "Upp och ner," Andi heard. Just as he figured out what that probably meant, his crate was put upright. He squelched the urge to yell out. His extra clothes buffered his body from bruises, but again, he had no protection on his head. There followed an hour of voices shouting, crates moving, then all was quiet, Oh my God, are they going to leave us here?

He started to panic again. For some reason, Andi recalled the voice of his old friend from Berlin University. It was Wolfgang's, Wolfgang Morgandal. What did he tell me to do? "Sit quietly, close your eyes, and just wait!" Andi almost burst out laughing. What else could he do? Oh yes, Wolfie would also say: "Way will open." Andi cried quietly. Wolfgang was a good friend.

About three hours later, Andi heard muted voices. He thought he heard crates being opened, possibly with a crowbar. Yes, definitely, crates were being opened. When Andi was lifted out by two huge men with blond hair, he broke down with sobs. He saw the ambassador's wife. There were four or five other people, who must have also escaped. Andi recognized another—the young man who cleaned the Embassy at night—Aron Jaworski. He was Jewish.

RETRIEVING SHEEP

1940

Initially, Wilma was highly suspicious that Günter had murdered her brother Goran for his clothes, or some other reason. Yet each day, Günter was ready to go to work even before breakfast. At first, he slept in the barn. Grandpops gave him a heavy woolen blanket to keep him warm. In spite of the relentless heat during the day, the temperature at night could drop very low. Günter repaired the fence around their extensive vegetable garden. When finished with that, he fortified the hen shed, as a fox had been spotted nearby three nights in a row.

Several weeks following Günter's descent from the mountain, Wilma started to feel comfortable around him. Grandpops kept apologizing for having no money to pay him for his labor. "I'm happy just to stay here and work, if you don't mind feeding me," Günter always said.

At night, after he retired to the barn, Wilma and her grandfather would talk about him. "He doesn't seem to want to go anywhere," Wilma noted.

"When he said the other day that he was from Berlin, I wasn't surprised. You can tell he's been educated—no slang, crisp pronunciation."

"I asked him if he wanted to go back to Berlin after the war ends. 'It depends on how it ends,' he said."

"Yes, that fits." Grandpops stroked his chin. During the summer, he kept his beard trimmed. The stroking gesture meant that her grandfather was about to say something he had thought hard about. "It looks to me that he deserted the army when he saw his chance to put on Goran's civilian clothes. He probably wants to lay low until the madness is over."

"Do you think he killed Goran for his clothes?"

"Could have, but somehow, I doubt it. He loves our Olga." More beard stroking. "He doesn't seem like the killing type. Olga ain't a bit frightened of him."

Another week went by and finally, Günter was allowed to move into Goran's room.

By the end of the summer, Grandpops asked Günter if he would help shepherd the sheep down from the mountain. "Wilma will go with you to show you where they are likely to be. And of course, Olga will be a big help."

Wilma noticed that Günter looked nervous, perhaps scared. That worried her.

"Goran's body will probably be torn up by animals by now. That will upset you," he said to Wilma.

"Yes, I've thought of that," she said. "It will be horrible, but I'll have to face it." She turned to her grandfather: "We should take a shovel with us, to bury what is left of him."

"What about the soldiers?" Grandpops asked Günter. "Do you think there will still be German soldiers up there?"

"I don't know, but now that winter is approaching, I would expect they would not want to stay at such high altitude. There are too few people to warrant guarding the area. But of course, I could be wrong."

Wilma wanted to get up there before it snowed, so the sheep would be easier to find. She dreaded it, but on the other hand, she wanted to get it over with.

"Do you think the soldiers would have killed the sheep?" Grandpops asked Günter. By this time, Wilma and he were convinced that Günter had gone AWOL, even though Günter hadn't actually come out and said so.

"I think it's very likely."

None of them had recent news about the war. In the fall of 1940, Wilma and Grandpops made the long trip to Szaflary to sell their vegetables and buy winter supplies. They hitched Roza, their old horse, to the wagon filled with potatoes and other items they hoped to sell in town. Günter chose to stay back at the farm. Once in town, they learned that Hitler had invaded France, The Netherlands, and Belgium. They heard a German soldier brag that Denmark and Norway had been conquered. A man in the market told them that Switzerland, Sweden, Spain, and Portugal had all remained neutral.

On the bumpy ride back to the farm, Wilma told her grandfather that she worried that soon the trip to town would be too much for Roza. Probably by next year, they would have to buy a new horse. She and Grandpops talked about what they could swap to help pay for a younger horse. Such a big expense!

They arrived back home with the supplies they hoped would carry them through the winter in case they got snowed in, which was often the case. Wilma was tired from the trip, so she went to bed right after eating the supper that Günter had prepared. Tomorrow, the two of them would hike up the mountain with Olga. Günter had gathered all the items they needed to take with them, even the food.

As she went to sleep that evening, Wilma realized she was always thinking of Günter. She liked his quiet manner, as well as his ability to work hard. He was thorough. He wouldn't leave a task until it was completely finished. She liked that about him. Both Grandpops and she could count on him. He would make a wonderful husband, but she didn't allow herself to think along those lines. She wouldn't be suitable for him. She had only completed the eighth grade.

It was not easy going to school while living on the farm. They took turns with the other family in the valley taking the children into Szaflary. This worked out reasonably well until Wilma completed the eighth grade. Wilma's father, who had suffered from depression ever since Wilma's mother died, decided to leave the farm for good, abandoning his family to the care of Grandpops. This coincided with the neighbor's youngest child graduating from high school. At that time, Goran was old enough to start school. Grandpops couldn't take them into town each day and still manage the farm work, so he arranged with a distant relative, living in Szaflary, to have Goran stay with their family during the week while he attended school. Wilma remained at home to help Grandpops with the farm work, and thus her formal education ended.

Being two years younger than Günter was of little advantage. She was plain looking, her skin already looked weathered, and her hands were mannish. She was not likely to find someone to marry. She had to face it. At least she had experienced some aspects of mothering while helping to raise Goran.

Wilma was having trouble getting to sleep. She dreaded finding Goran's mutilated body when they reached the high pasture tomorrow. She and Günter could be good friends but nothing more, she figured. Günter was educated, university educated. In the three months that he had been with them on the farm, he had read every book in the house. Their conversations revealed how little she knew about geography. He seemed pleased to sit down with her to teach her…about some faraway mountains and rivers…. Finally, Wilma fell asleep.

The next day when they climbed up to the high meadow, it was windy and cold. Wilma wanted to find Goran's body first thing, so they went to the hut. There was no body. They went outside to look for a mound of dirt. Perhaps someone had come along and dug a grave to bury Goran, but the earth was compacted everywhere they looked. Why would someone carry the body far away to dig him a grave? She couldn't help herself. She started feeling suspicious of Günter again. Had he told them the truth?

"The only explanation I can come up with is that the soldiers found Goran's body and took it to bury in one of their ad hoc cemeteries."

Or to show their commander that some soldier had deserted,

Wilma thought. Günter went pale as if he had read her mind.

After several minutes of looking around the hut for any clue whatsoever, Günter said: "Well, let's collect the sheep and get back down to the farm."

The good news was that they came down off the mountain with healthy sheep. None had perished. Their fleeces had recovered from the summer's shearing and were thick enough now for the cold months ahead. She and Günter had seen no sign of German soldiers.

STOCKHOLM

After the two men lifted Andi out of the crate, he thanked them and watched them go on to their other business. Overwhelmed by the sudden rush to leave Poland, he'd had no time to think about what he would do if he did make it out. Now that he was in Sweden, he asked himself what he should do. He spoke no Swedish. He wasn't even sure where he was. He had no Swedish money, and he couldn't think of anyone he knew who lived in Sweden. Maybe an idea would come to him.

It was then that he noticed a lady with white hair walking towards him. She introduced herself as Kerstin and said in German, "You Andi?" She took his arm and led him outside the warehouse. "You ride bike?" Was that a question or a command? "I take you to home," she said.

Andi was relieved to stretch his legs, be in fresh air, and feel a cool moist breeze on his face. He had barely registered the overcast sky when the lady, Kerstin, pointed to a bush and said: "Pee!"

That, he was sure, was a command, and he gratefully complied by turning his back to her and aiming at the bush. When he finished, he turned to face her. She directed him to two bicycles. They each mounted a bike and she led the way. He tried to keep up with her, but he was weak and still stiff from being crammed in the crate for seven hours. The last food he had eaten was bread and sausage in Gdynia.

The port was extensive. As they peddled by the sea, Andi

noticed many watercraft, from large ships down to family sailing boats. Passing by fishing boats reminded him that the Swedes love pickled sweetened herring. Best not to think of food!

Then Kerstin turned away from the water and led him onto some busy streets. Andi figured they were in the downtown area. Five minutes later, Kerstin made some zigzags into a neighborhood of mixed apartment buildings and shops. Every time Kerstin looked over her shoulder to see how he was doing, he tried to smile. Good heavens, this woman is peppy, he observed.

It took them twenty-five minutes to reach Kerstin's destination. Andi thought they were in the suburbs. Kerstin stopped in front of a small house, small in the sense that it was narrow, only one room wide, but four stories high. It was sandwiched between two larger homes. They parked their bikes in a rack next to the front door. A blue plaque on the outside wall had only one word that Andi understood: Quaker.

The door opened directly into a small living room that was filled with people. By the time Andi and Kerstin stepped over the threshold, nine adults and two children were standing, eager to shake Andi's hand. "Välkommen!"

Herr Swenson, the owner of the house, spoke some German. He served as the translator. They obviously knew Andi was coming and were clearly excited to have him there. Anticipating Andi's hunger, they sat around a ridiculously small table and had a wonderful dinner together. Andi wanted to know what the meat was they were eating. Herr Swenson didn't know the word in German, so the two children spread their fingers out on top of their heads and pretended to ram each other, one almost knocking over his glass of milk. "Deer or venison?" Andi guessed.

"More north," Herr Swenson said. Andi eventually learned he was eating reindeer stew, juniper berries, and mashed potatoes.

Andi lived with the Swenson family for the next three years, sharing a bedroom with their seven-year-old son. In addition to the Swenson's home, the small building also served as the

Meetinghouse for Quakers (Religious Society of Friends) in the area. In those three years, Andi learned to speak Swedish reasonably well, and became appreciative of the Quaker way of life. Equality and simplicity guided their behavior. He helped with a few of their projects. The one in which he was most effective involved reconnecting conscientious objectors with their families abroad. Andi's language skills were so useful that the Swedish Quakers introduced him to the work of the American Friends Service Committee (AFSC).

This committee, although based in the United States, had projects in various conflict zones in the world. The agency learned about Andi's fluency in several languages and was especially interested in him when they discovered that he had lived in Berlin. They began consulting Andi on plans for aid projects in Germany after the war. This was very satisfying to Andi. He had long felt guilty that he had avoided the war's pains and hardships. He had a strong love for Berlin. The happiest days of his life were spent living there during the Weimar Republic, before Hitler rose to power.

Then one day he met Mark Brant in downtown Stockholm. Having lunch in a crowded cafeteria, they were forced to eat at the same table and fell into conversation. By the end of the week, they had become good friends. Mark had left Germany in the same year as Andi, only Mark went to Norway and Andi to Hungary. They both made their way to Sweden from different directions, but for the same reason.

Mark was originally Karl Sneider. He grew up in the north of Germany in a poor family. Although he went to Berlin to enter the university, he soon joined the Nazi resistance. One evening, while enjoying a stein of lager in a beer hall, a stranger brushed by him and Karl felt something land in his lap. It was a note that warned him he was about to be arrested by the SS. Two days later, Karl had made his way to Norway. "Don't ask how I got there," he always said when telling his story. Once in Norway, he changed his name to Mark Brant. There, he finished his university studies and even became a Norwegian citizen. But in 1940, Hitler's troops invaded Norway, so Mark, once again, had to escape. This time he chose his destination wisely: the neutral country of Sweden, where he intended to remain until the end of the war.

Even in Sweden, neither Mark nor Andi felt entirely safe. It was well known that there were Nazi spies lurking about. Sweden allowed the Wehrmacht, the German army, to use Swedish railways to transport German infantry, weapons, and ammunition from Norway to Finland. Also, German soldiers on furlough from Norway were allowed to pass through this neutral country to go home to Germany. On the other hand, Sweden offered asylum to 8,000 Danish and many Norwegian Jews.

Andi and Mark became lovers within a year of meeting each other. Andi had not had a romantic relationship since living under the Weimar Republic. Before Hitler rose to power, he felt reasonably safe going into Berlin's gay bars. There were gay bars in Sweden, and although he was always discrete when he was in public, he was fairly sure that the average Swede was considerably more tolerant regarding sexual orientation than the average German. By 1944, he was proven right when Sweden passed a law legalizing homosexual relations.

REFUGEES

As the war years continued, the Bauer farm thrived. Food became so scarce in nearby urban communities that they could sell as much as they brought to town, and townsfolk still wanted more. Some Poles from Szaflary even made the long trip to the farm to buy what they could, sometimes bringing their family heirlooms for barter. All was not rosy, however. The three on the farm noticed an increasing coldness and formality, even among some old friends. Was it jealousy? No matter how much Grandpops and Wilma tried to be charming, recalling pleasant mutual experiences, their buyers' expressions were becoming more frozen, their eyes cast downward.

Günter usually left the talking to the other two. "My German accent is not welcomed."

Last month, an old friend from her school days had said to Wilma, "Being German, you probably don't mind Poland being occupied."

It got worse when the German army started to retreat. By 1944, townspeople said things like: "You must be terrified by the Russians coming," and "If I were you, I'd head back to Germany now, while you still can."

"We've lived in Poland for 80 years, and now they're thinking of us as German," Wilma complained later to Günter and Grandpops.

"You can't blame them for hating the Nazis, but they shouldn't take it out on you." Later, Günter added, "It's a shame there is no electricity here at the farm. We can't listen to a radio. I wonder if the attitude in Szaflary is the general attitude all over the country."

In another month, they realized it was, indeed, the general attitude all over the country. When Wilma was in Szaflary, she also heard stories about the Red Army and its reputation for raping women. Reverberations of such stories reached countries long before the army actually arrived. Evidently, Germans who had settled in Belarus were already passing through Poland to get to Germany.

In March of 1945, after much debating and regret, they decided that Grandpops and Wilma should leave the farm for Germany. Günter would stay and farm as best he could. Safety, for him, was nowhere to be found.

Günter drove the wagon through the snow to Szaflary with Grandpops and Wilma aboard. Their new horse, Misnk, seemed to enjoy the exercise. A wind straight from Siberia pushed them along. They were all dressed in their warmest clothes. Wilma looked up the slopes of the valley, cherishing the scenery, knowing it might be the last time she would ever see it. She pointed out a chamois to her grandpops, whose eyesight was steadily getting worse. "See him, stepping out from behind that spruce?"

Around another bend was where Wilma remembered marmots could always be seen in summer. Now, they were hibernating through the winter. Would she ever see them again?

She and her grandfather boarded a train in Szaflary that would take them northeast to a town called Miedzyrzecz. She had never been there, but they were told that from Miedzyrzecz they could connect with another train that would take them near the Oder River.

For Grandpops, this must be especially difficult, Wilma thought. His whole life has been dedicated to the farm and the family. Wilma, on the other hand, saw her life not as ending, but possibly as beginning. Maybe she could get more education in Berlin, maybe find a man to marry. Of course, she would miss the farm, the beautiful High Tatra Mountains, and the animals, especially Olga!

It was hard to say goodbye to Günter. "When you get to Berlin, go to Die Birken on Hoffmannstrasse, 141 Hoffmannstrasse," he told them for the ninth time. "Someday, I hope to go there myself. We'll be together again." After almost four years, Günter had become family.

They were able to get on the train, but just. There was no place to sit. People were pressed against one another. Fifty kilometers from the Oder River, the train stopped again. Both Wilma and her grandfather got off to relieve themselves. It was supposed to be a 25-minute stop, but by the time the two of them got back to the platform, the train started to take off. Wilma could have run to get on, but she knew her grandfather couldn't make it. "We'll catch the next train," she reassured him.

They waited on the crowded platform for several minutes when Wilma noticed people had stopped talking. Heads were craned to the east. "Plane!" someone called out. People fled the platform for cover as it flew overhead. Wilma saw the Red Star insignia on its side. Three minutes later, they heard a mighty explosion. Word soon got back that the train they had missed had been hit, many people had been killed, and the track was a mangled wreck.

Together with everyone else, Grandpops and Wilma started walking along the road that led to Berlin. Occasionally, German army trucks passed. When they had to slow down to drive around rubble or go off road to avoid pits caused by bombs, Wilma could get a good look at the soldiers that filled the backs of the trucks, some sitting, but most standing. Many were bandaged and wearing torn uniforms. They looked exhausted. She wondered how long they had been travelling. Rarely did she see one smile. The trucks never offered anybody a lift. How could the driver choose which civilian to rescue? They all needed help!

When she and Grandpops stopped to rest, they would often hear stories from other refugees. Some had been robbed when they slept at night—some beaten by locals who hated all

Germans. Refugees who had been walking for months admitted, without shame, that they had stolen food from passing farms whenever they could. A woman told Wilma that, a week ago, a fourteen-year-old girl had been dragged off the road and raped by some local thugs.

When they reached the Oder River, soldiers wouldn't let them on the bridge until all the army trucks in the vicinity had crossed. Due to previous bombing raids, only one lane of the bridge was functioning. Refugees had to line up to wait their turn. Precedence for crossing was given to Army trucks, then soldiers, and finally refugees. All were afraid planes would come to finish the destruction. When they were finally given a chance to cross, people ran to get to the other side. Grandpops started to panic that he wouldn't make it. He began to hyperventilate. Normally, Wilma would have suggested that they sit by the side of the road for a while until he got his breath back, but that was impossible. More Army trucks had gathered and started to cross the bridge. Soon, only Wilma and Grandpops were holding them up. A soldier jumped out of the back of the nearest truck and ran to pick up Grandpops. He carried him to the other side. He put Grandpops gently down at the edge of the road and ran back to hop on his truck. Wilma waved and shouted, "Thank you!" He waved back and gave her a broad smile.

Every time planes buzzed the road, people ran to crouch in the ditches. Usually, someone was killed or wounded with each strafing or bombing. Being missed or hit was the luck of the draw. It was almost worse if someone was wounded. There was little people could do to help.

In such a raid on the second day, Grandpops was hit by shrapnel. He started bleeding profusely from the neck and abdomen. Wilma tried to put pressure on both areas, but it was hard to do. He lost consciousness and soon died. She lay down beside him, not wanting to leave him. What a wonderful man he had been to her and Goran, more like a father than her real father. She stroked his beard, apologized for not burying him, and kissed him goodbye.

Now, Wilma was completely on her own, scared, not knowing what was coming next. She took her grandfather's food and pressed on. After the stories she had heard, she definitely wanted to walk in the company of other people. She passed by a few families and started walking beside a woman who was also travelling on her own. She was pulling a handcart. She smiled and seemed friendly, but she didn't say anything. Maybe she's mute, Wilma thought. To make her feel comfortable, Wilma tried communicating with her hands. When it got dark, she suggested they stop and spend the night in a ditch. It reminded Wilma of playing charades. The woman smiled again and nodded in affirmation.

Having a handcart was a disadvantage. She couldn't take it with her into the ditch. Left on the road, it looked unattended and tempting to steal. Wilma took off her scarf and tied one end to a wheel and gave the woman the other end. They spent the night together, both under their blankets, back-to-back, to conserve heat.

The next day they ate a morsel of their food, packed up, and started to walk again. They got through the day without being hit and slept another night, cold, but in peace. The following day, Wilma figured that they would reach Berlin before dark. The woman still hadn't uttered a word, but when a plane was suddenly upon them strafing the road, she yelled, "Oy gevalt!" in a thick Yiddish accent. Wilma dove into the brush, but because of her cart, the woman wasn't so quick to get off the road. She was fatally hit in the chest.

Wilma was trembling with terror, but was also grateful that she hadn't been wounded or killed. She pulled the woman's body off the road and went through her pockets to find her name. What could she do with a name, anyway? Deep in one pocket she found a little notebook. She put it in her own pocket to study later. She had to keep moving. Her friend's cart—why not take that too? She could always leave it, if it became a problem, or give it to someone else. Right now, she had to get to Berlin. People were already passing her that she had passed yesterday. She had to get to safety. Did safety exist?

She had lost a friend—although only briefly a friend, a friend nonetheless. Wilma would try to remember what she looked like. She had a long pointed nose, dark eyes, and black curly hair. Pulling her cart was not as difficult as she had anticipated. It was piled high, but with what had to be lightweight stuff. As she walked along, Wilma wondered why the woman had hesitated to speak to her. And, if she was Jewish, why did she want to go to Germany? From the stories Wilma had heard, that would be the last place a Jew would want to go.

By around 2:00 P.M., Wilma was at the outskirts of Berlin, asking directions to the borough of Friedrichshain. Some cars and more bicycles went by, weaving in and out to avoid piles of rubble. Women and small children were everywhere, most looking homeless and as disoriented as she felt. Buildings were heavily damaged, some bombed out completely. When people told her she was in Friedrichshain, she was shocked. So many buildings were only shells. After several inquiries, she learned it had been an industrial center. That explained why it had been a frequent target of British and American bombing campaigns.

On streets away from the factories, there were buildings still standing. In one of those areas, she finally found her way to Hoffmannstrasse. The buildings there were heavily damaged, but were definitely structures with apartments where people were living. There wasn't a birch tree to be found. Every now and then, a building showed its number. In front of what Wilma thought might be 141 was a woman sitting on the step to the front door. "Pardon me, but is this building 141?"

"Yes, it is." The woman seemed to mutter with a wry smile, "Would it matter?"

"Is it called Die Birken?" Wilma asked, obviously confused. "I was told to come here by a friend named Günter."

"Some friend!"

"He used to live here before the war."

"Well, I never have known all the people who lived in the building, and I know fewer now. They keep changing. What's your name?"

"Wilma, Wilma Bauer."

"Where are you from?"

"I lived on a farm in the High Tatras."

"Do you come with family?"

"No, not now. They're all dead."

The woman muttered something like, "Jesus, this is the beginning of the end." She looked aside for a minute, then stood up and said: "Welcome, Wilma, to Die Birken. My name is Frau Fritz. I'm sorry the better apartments are already spoken for, but I can offer you a space in the basement. Would you like me to show it to you?"

Wilma wasn't sure if the woman was sincere or just being sarcastic. Probably both! But she was dead tired and just wanted to collapse anywhere. "Yes, please."

"To get your cart down there, we'll have to enter from the alley behind the building," Frau Fritz explained. "It would be too hard for us to get it down the stairs from the courtyard to the basement. I'll help you pull it around the block to the back side. It should be fairly easy, it's mostly downhill from here."

Except for the obstacles presented by random piles of rubble and some deep potholes, it was relatively easy for the two women to maneuver the cart the half-block to the next cross street. Turning left at the corner, there was a gentle grade down to the alley that ran behind the building. Turning left again, they pushed the cart the half-block back to the rear of Die Birken.

Because of the slight grade down from front to back, the building's basement at the rear was at the same level as the paved alleyway that ran behind it. Thanks to a bomb or artillery shell that had exploded behind the building, a portion of the basement wall was gone and they could enter directly from the alley. Wilma moved some rubble out of the way so they could pull her cart inside through the hole. Though there was a double door exiting the basement to the alley that was wide enough to accomodate the cart, they didn't need to use it.

Wilma was immediately aware of the stench inside the basement, but growing up on a farm, she felt she could abide it. She'd put up with anything for a place to sleep where she would be safe. "People come in off the alley to do their business where they can have some privacy. Fortunately, the drain in the floor is still working," Frau Fritz explained.

Wilma tried to see something good about the piles of shit.... She couldn't think of anything.

"Come back here…" Frau Fritz motioned her further into the space, "people don't seem to come back this far…and maybe few are aware that there is a closet…originally for the janitor to store his supplies…I haven't looked in here since the war began."

Underneath the stairway that descended from the first floor was a closet. The door faced the back wall of the basement. Frau Fritz pulled the door open. There was only a broom inside.

"The space is wide enough for my cart," Wilma noted.

"There's no key to lock the door, I'm afraid."

"Thank you. This will be fine." As soon as Frau Fritz left her to ascend the stairs to the first floor, Wilma rushed to the two zinc-coated sinks to turn on the faucets. No water came out. She was so thirsty.

There was still enough light in the day to see into the closet. She swept it out as best she could, then backed the cart inside. She wanted to flop down on it, but she thought she should make it more comfortable, so she took out a few of the lumpy items and placed them in the back of the closet.

She heard someone come in off the alley, so she didn't make a sound. When the person left, she continued to make a bed out of her friend's belongings. The woman's sweater became a pillow and her canvas tarp, Wilma's blanket. She shut the door to the closet and climbed aboard the cart. It was a little cramped, but in spite of hearing people coming in and going out of the basement, she got her first fairly good night of sleep since leaving the farm.

The next morning, Wilma's thirst and hunger were over-whelming. She closed the closet door, peed at the front, and then went out on the street to look for water and food. Two blocks away, she found a hosepipe, drank water, and rinsed her face and hair as best she could before she had to give others a turn. Refreshed but weak for lack of food, she retraced her steps to where she had passed a grocery store the day before. She went to the back of the store, where the daily delivery was made. She stayed there hoping she could pick up something that fell off the truck. This accomplished nothing.

A truck did pull up to the back entrance. Milk containers and a few dozen eggs were unloaded. Then empty containers were put in the bed and strapped down. The driver went into the store, perhaps for his payment. Wilma climbed into the back and laid down so she couldn't be seen. The truck took off. Wilma tried to cushion herself from the bumps by lying on her tummy and resting her head on folded arms. Three-quarters of an hour later, the truck stopped. The driver got out of the cab and went somewhere. She heard a door shut. Wilma hopped out of the bed and started walking down the road as if she belonged there.

She was on a farm. She was walking toward the fields. She could see some women who were perhaps planting a new crop. Being early spring, there wouldn't be any mature plants growing yet. She saw ahead to her left several fields allowed to go fallow. She walked into these meadows and started selecting plants that she knew were edible. She stuffed her shirt front and back with greens. Now she had the problem of getting back to Berlin.

She turned around to look at the rest of the farm. There was a long building that appeared to be a barn at one end and a family home at the other. The truck was parked in front of the house. She decided to look into the barn. There were empty cow stalls. The cattle must be out to pasture. She heard chickens, but other than that, nothing else seemed to be going on.

Walking outside again, she noticed a bike leaning up against the wall. If she stole it, she could get back to Berlin. Fortunately, she was distracted from that possibility. A second truck drove into the farm and up to the house. Might this truck have food in the back? The driver was an old man. Another old man came out of the house. "Hello Tomas, I drove the milk and eggs in already. We have nothing more to go into Berlin."

"OK, I'm sorry I was late today. I have no help at my end. The last two boys were drafted yesterday."

"Not Stephen?"

"Yes, Stephen. He's only 13."

"Oh, my God! Where are they sending him?"

"To Berlin. The Red Army will be here in a few days they say. They need everyone they can get their hands on to defend the city."

"God help us. I'm sorry, Thomas."

"Helmut's but a year older. They took him, too. He's my sister's boy, you know."

"You know what I wish, but we can't say it."

"I know, so don't say it. God bless you, Wilhelm."

"And you. So long, Thomas."

While this conversation was going on, Wilma approached the truck from the passenger side. She stepped up on the running board and prepared herself to hold on for dear life. The truck took off. The vehicle was rickety and made extraneous grunts and groans. It seemed it couldn't go very fast. Thank goodness! When it arrived in Berlin, it stopped at another grocery store, Wilma hopped off again, but this time, she was spotted by the grocer.

"Hey, what are you doing?"

"Just hitching a ride," she answered, pretending it was an ordinary procedure. She walked calmly away. She had no idea where she was. She heard shooting far, far in the distance. She was told she could take a tram to Friedrichshain. She had no money for the tram, but by walking along the tracks she was back at Die Birken by three in the afternoon. The same woman, Frau Fritz, was seated on the steps. Wilma offered to share her greens with her. Frau Fritz led her up to her apartment on the fourth floor to make a soup. Going up the steps was tricky. Half of each step was missing and they were covered in a dirt and plaster mixture. Tomorrow she would sweep them.

"Are you sure you can eat this?" Frau Fritz asked, holding up a plant unknown to her.

"Oh, yes. That's...ah...I can't remember what it's called in German."

It was in late March when Wilma first spoke to Frau Fritz outside of Die Birken and was led to the basement. Three or so weeks later, the Russians took Berlin. Wilma, like most people, wished Germany would surrender—get the inevitable over! It had become a common sight to see a body hanging from a lamppost, since there were no trees anymore. They were German deserters who refused to continue fighting to the bitter end.

Finally, there were explosions and guns were fired in the neighborhood of Die Birken. Red tanks and convoys of troops drove by their apartment building. The end was at hand. The Russian conquerors were also in poor shape. Many a Soviet soldier had no boots, but merely rags wrapped around his feet. Their facial features and body structures varied immensely, depending on the part of Russia they came from.

During the day, the soldiers had specific duties to fulfill. When evening came, they were given food and vodka, after which the Soviet authorities paid no heed to their behavior. Raping and plundering were considered 'well-earned compensation' for having liberated Berlin.

Wilma stayed in her closet from four o'clock in the afternoon until morning. She hoped that the odor of excrement would deter soldiers from coming into the basement. It didn't. Many entered the building through the broken front door. Women in apartments on the first and second floor were victimized. The building had been so damaged that several doors couldn't be locked. The soldiers were too drunk and the stairs too precarious to climb higher than the second floor. They got into the basement easily, either from the alley or, once in the building, they could descend the stairs from the first floor.

Wilma knew to lie still and was prepared to cover her face with the tarp if someone opened the closet door. For the first couple of weeks, she was not discovered. But one night, the door was opened and Wilma felt the cart being poked by a hand. Then the door was shut again. A couple of hours passed. Wilma heard nothing more outside the closet.

She figured the soldiers had returned to their posts when the door slowly opened again, and the tarp was snatched off her. A man grabbed her legs. Wilma started screaming as loud as she could, knowing full well it would do no good. The man grabbed her, lifted her out of the cart, and slammed her upright against the outside wall of the closet. He pinned her arms behind her back and pressed his body against hers so hard that she could barely breathe, let alone free her arms. One hand covered her mouth to stop her from screaming while the other pulled down her underpants. He entered her. The pain was excruciating. Wilma was a virgin. The smell of his breath made her nauseous. When he was finished, he picked her up and laid her back on the cart. She was sobbing. He covered her with the tarp and shut the door. She tried not to cry loudly, in case there were others nearby who would like a turn at her. She finally got to sleep, and only woke to find Frau Fritz calling to her through the door.

CARETAKING THE FARM

1945

Günter's gratitude to Wilma and Grandpops was boundless. By entering their life, he had regained his feeling of self-worth. He had forgiven himself for the people he had killed during the war. Being isolated for the last four years, living with two kind people, and having an abundance of hard work, had been a blessing. The irony was that now that his moral compass was functioning, there was nowhere to go; nowhere that was safe, anyway. He couldn't go back to Germany because he had deserted. He would be shot. Would the townspeople want to drive him west out of Poland, or would the Russians capture him and send him to a Russian labor camp? Or would they simply execute him as an enemy?

He would wait out his fate, enjoying farming in this beautiful valley with the little time he had left. What had happened to his baby girl? Would he ever see her again? Was she still alive?

Could he avoid being found by the Russians? He assumed they would enter the valley the same way he did. They would have high-powered binoculars and would see him long before he saw them. He had already been letting his beard grow and was accustomed to wearing old dirty clothes with patches. Both made him look less Germanic. Thank God, his hair was a dull brown. By now, he knew how to speak Polish. Would the Russians pick up on his German accent?

The snow was three-to-six feet deep over the grassy meadows where the sheep grazed each summer. It would obliterate the path down to the valley. Maybe they won't come from up there after all, but from the town of Szaflary. Would they bother with a farm that was ten kilometers away? The Nazis would, but would the Soviets?

Four months later, the Russians still hadn't come and it was time to drive the sheep up to the high pastures. Günter dreaded going up there, but he had to do it. Would Olga be up to the task? She was getting to be too old for this work. He set out early in the morning, hoping to avoid spending the night in the hut.

Things went well. He was able to start the descent around 3:30 in the afternoon. He hoped he and Olga could make it home before dark. He had forgotten to bring a flashlight. As he started the last steep decline, in the darkened sky, he could just make out the shape of the house. He thought he saw a light flickering. Olga had already run ahead. Her persistent barking must have startled the soldiers. Three of them rushed out of the house and one shot Olga dead. Then, spotting Günter, they kept their riffles aimed at him while they stumbled up the steep slope.

Günter raised his arms and shouted out a word that he hoped meant 'surrender' in Russian. Tears welled up but he didn't dare wipe his eyes. He kept looking at Olga. One soldier circled behind and nudged Günter with the barrel of his gun, forcing him to continue down the path to the house.

At the house, a fourth soldier emerged saying: "Where vodka?"

Günter said: "No vodka. I will cook you a chicken dinner."

One of the other soldiers came in after a quick trip to the henhouse. He threw a dead hen on the table and said: "Cook."

Three of them lay down on beds wearing their wet boots, while the fourth watched Günter cook, holding his rifle. Günter put potatoes on to boil and asked if he could get some beans that Wilma had canned last summer from the cellar. They didn't understand his words, but once Günter raised the trap door, they recognized the promise of what could be stored in a root cellar.

They ate every last morsel of the meal Günter prepared, leaving a miniscule portion for him. Two of them seemed to be boys, around 15 years of age. One of them helped Günter with the washing up. Günter was then tied to a chair with his hands and ankles bound. He had no trouble falling asleep, nor did the others. In the morning, Günter was untied and told to make eggs and tea. By 8:00 A.M., they wanted to leave. Günter hitched up Misnk to the wagon. The chickens were thrown in a basket with a lid. The cellar was cleared out of all the canned goods. A box of stored tubers, bed linens and blankets were all put in the wagon. Candles, utensils, frying pan, plates, cups, and tea were added. Günter drove the wagon to Szaflary, with the soldiers all piled on top. Some slept. Günter could tell they were in good spirits. He turned around to take what he was sure would be his last look at the farm.

Once in Szaflary, Günter was immediately ordered to stand on the railroad platform with a group of men who were surely prisoners. Minsk, the wagon, and the soldiers who escorted him to town disappeared. When the train arrived in the station, he was pushed on to it. He travelled the rest of the way in boxcars with other men of many descriptions. Seldom was there enough room to sit on the floor. One corner of the car was reserved for excrement. No one wanted to be near that. The desired location was next to the slatted walls of the railroad car, where passing scenery could be glimpsed. The scenery itself was depressing; bombed-out buildings, people walking with bundles, pushing carts, hobbling along. It wasn't the scenery that was treasured, but the fresh air.

Günter lost his sense of time, but he thought a week went by before he reached the camp. He had only been given something to eat three times since he left the farm.

The camp was located close to the border between Poland and Belarus. Günter never knew which of the two countries he was in. He eventually learned his logging job was in the Bialowieza Forest.

The Russians had sectioned off a large square area of the forest. Surrounding the square was a clear-cut area. If you tried to escape, you would have to cross the clearing. They had erected four observation towers at the corners of the square. Armed guards staffed the towers 24-hours a day. Evidently, Stalin thought it best to require work quotas. The size of your ration depended on the percentage of the quota you were able to deliver. The men slept in barracks with no heating. The work was brutal, especially on an empty stomach. Günter wasn't even a war prisoner. He had been kidnapped to do slave labor.

No matter how much he produced, he was never fed enough. Diseases in the camp were rampant. All night long, he heard men coughing. In his fourth year at the camp, Günter became aware that he, too, had tuberculosis.

NEW BEGINNINGS

Wilma moved into Frau Fritz's apartment, 'so to speak.' Actually, there was nothing to move but herself. She left the cart in the basement closet.

"Just call me, Fritzy. Frau Fritz brings back bad memories."

Fritzy fetched a bucket of water, hauled it up the four flights, just so Wilma could wash. There was no running water, but the drain in the tub allowed some of Wilma's filth to disappear. Once cleaner, Wilma forced herself to go out with Fritzy to look for food.

Days later, Wilma decided to join others, mostly women, to help clear Hoffmannstrasse of debris. She learned that she would be rewarded with extra food rations—the equivalent of an extra slice of bread a day. From Hoffmannstrasse, she moved to other streets. Picking up bricks or stones and putting them in a bucket was one job. Another was taking part in a human chain where each full bucket was passed on to the next woman in line. The buckets were dumped in high piles off the streets.

Serving as a 'rubblewoman' helped to distract Wilma's thoughts. It would have been easy to dwell upon what she had lost: Grandpops, Goran, Günter, the farm, her home. If she weren't so hungry all the time, she could think this work easy compared to that on the farm. Day after day, she worked with one team or another. This gave her the chance to meet other women and hear their stories of what they had been through. It helped keep Wilma from dwelling on her own losses.

When she realized she was pregnant, some women on her team told her she could get an abortion. So many women had been raped, the hospitals offered to terminate anyone's pregnancy. Wilma thought about it, but put off making a decision. In time, she became excited that she was growing another human being within her. Even when she started having spells of morning sickness and resented anything coming out when it was so difficult to find anything to put into her mouth, even then, she didn't want to give up her baby—a new life seemed gloriously hopeful, especially when surrounded by the destruction of war.

Gradually, Wilma realized she would be living in the city for a long time. Would she ever get used to it—the gray skies, lack of trees and birdsong? The air never seemed fresh. Buildings were in ruin or barely liveable. At least she was relatively safe living on the fourth floor, as drunken soldiers rarely climbed up so high.

That first winter in Berlin was bitterly cold. On the farm there had always been wood to burn for heat. The snow packed around the house insulated them from the wind. This building, Die Birken, was far from tight. Even in Fritzy's apartment, where all the walls were intact, the wind still found places where it could whistle its way in.

Her labor started around 1:00 A.M. on February 4, 1946. The contractions were far enough apart that Wilma thought she could last until daylight before making her way to the hospital. She had heard stories of Russian soldiers even raping pregnant women. At dawn, she and Fritzy headed out. The pains were twenty minutes apart by the time they arrived. Three hours later, an angry little baby emerged with fists clenched and wailing. Such a display of determination inspired her name: Ursula.

Over the course of the war, Andi attempted to stay in contact with his parents in Budapest. Realizing Germany was going to lose the war, Hungary had tried to make a separate peace with the Allies. To prevent this, Germany invaded its own Axis partner. The Soviets quickly pursued and laid siege to the capital for some 50 days. Fighting took place in the sewers as well as on the city's elegant wide boulevards. Seven monumental bridges over the Danube were destroyed. Budapest finally surrendered. Its fall served as the prelude to the Battle for Berlin.

On Christmas day, Andi's phone call from Stockholm to Budapest failed to go through. Three days later, the news on Swedish radio told of the siege. In February of 1945, Andi knew that the city had surrendered to the Soviets. In April, he received a letter from his aunt which told him that both of his parents had been killed during the siege.

He hadn't seen them for six years. Now Andi only had Mark to relate remembrances dear to his heart. He never told his parents that he was gay. They probably knew, but he didn't want to confront them with a reality that might cause them anguish. They were kind and good people who had always shown him love, but sadly, this issue had kept them from being close.

Andi felt the need to talk with Lars Swenson. It had been several months since he had gone to Quaker Meeting. The following Sunday after Meeting, Andi chatted with old friends. Finally, he had Lars to himself. Birgitta, his wife, sensing their need for privacy, went into the kitchen. Lars asked about Andi's family. Andi's eyes welled up, but he was able to explain what had happened.

"I'm sure you made them very happy."

Andi knew he could trust Lars, so he explained the sadness he felt of not being able to tell his parents who he really was.

"That must make you feel lonely. Thank goodness you have Mark."

Andi told Lars how he and Mark had talked endlessly about where they should live once the war was over. Now, there was no point for Andi to move back to Hungary. "Mark is happy to stay in Stockholm," he explained.

"You're able to live together here legally. That must be a great help."

"Oh yes, it is, but I feel guilty that I never did anything to resist the Nazis like Mark did. I just moved away."

"Well, you were a student when they came into power."

"Yes, but I only thought about my own safety. I've never been a very brave person."

"There are many ways to serve and to do good."

Lars suggested that Andi revive his connections with the American Friends Service Committee. "Maybe you could do relief work for them in Germany."

Six months later, in October, Andi finally made arrangements to travel to Berlin to see how bad the conditions were. He didn't want to make any commitments for the long range. He simply planned to check in at some schools where AFSC was providing lunches.

What current knowledge he had of the city came from newsreels and newspapers. They did not prepare him for the devastation he was to see. He had assumed only some pockets had been destroyed, but he found huge swaths of Berlin had been leveled. The mere number of people in the streets—mostly refugees from Eastern Europe—was oppressive.

He decided to try to find the apartment building he lived in while at the university. He exited the train station, itself very damaged. From there, he spent more than an hour to find his way to the Friedrichshain district. That would have been a twenty minute walk before the war. Friedrichshain had been an industrial area. Now only some of the housing was still standing. A few weird landmarks gave him clues as to the direction he should take, like the fountain in Boxhager Platz. He came across a small church he had always loved, back in his student days. It was still standing, although missing one tower. From there, he knew how to get to Hoffmannstrasse.

Once on Hoffmannstrasse, he had trouble determining exactly where he was. He was looking for number 141. There were many apartment buildings, but all were damaged, some totally ruined. He mistakenly kept looking for the birch trees which had lined the front of the building, but, of course, they were gone. One building looked right, but it had the number 14, even though it was on the side of the street with the odd numbers. Maybe the last numeral one fell off, he thought. He could see some holes in the exterior walls and some broken windows.

He went in the door, which didn't quite shut. Only half of the stairway going up around the courtyard was still attached to the wall. As he stood there looking around, a woman was in the process of descending. She kept her steps close to the wall. My heavens, he thought he knew her. Oh my God, it's Frau Fritz. She looks twenty years older, and so thin. Once down on the first level, Fritzy gave Andi a good looking over.

"Are you Andi? You're Andi, aren't you—one of the students from before the war?" They spent several minutes catching up. "A few students still live here. Some were killed in the bombing. Oh, remember your friend Wolfgang?"

"Sure. Do you have any news of him?"

"No, but his wife has a flat on the third floor."

"Really?" Andi's spirits perked up.

"Yes, she has a little girl, Renate. They have the apartment that faces the street. I don't remember the number." She looked up the stairs. "Ah, here's Wilma."

A woman was making her way down the steps. Andi watched her descend carefully. She was skinny, too, but he noticed her protruding stomach and wondered if she was pregnant. He started to go up to help her come down. Wilma started laughing. "I'm alright, but thanks. I do this every day."

"Wilma's going to work," Frau Fritz explained. "Wilma lives with me up on the fourth floor."

Andi shook Wilma's hand. It was a thin hand with rough skin, but her grip was strong. Wilma had said just enough that Andi could identify her Polish accent. She continued out the entrance. Frau Fritz explained that Wilma worked as a rubblewoman.

"That's hard, in her condition. I mean she looks pregnant. Is she?"

"Yes, raped." Andi winced. Frau Fritz went on to explain that they got more food rations with Wilma working.

"I've heard the number of rapes was horrible."

"You can say that again. We made sure we were home in our apartments by late afternoon," she explained. "In fact, we still do, although now the Russian soldiers have been brought under control...supposedly."

Later, Andi navigated the tricky steps up to the third floor and knocked on what he thought must be Wolfgang's wife's door.

He heard a female voice say: "Don't answer the door." The request was too late.

A young girl opened it and said: "Hello."

Andi was taken aback, the resemblance to Wolfgang was remarkable, or was that what he wanted to see? "Hello, I wonder if I could speak to your mother." A half of a minute later, Gerda came to the door visibly disgruntled. She was ready to shut it in Andi's face. He had to think fast. "I'm a friend of your husband, Wolfgang."

"Oh, yes?" She looked Andi over skeptically.

The woman had an attractive face, blond hair, but something wasn't right. "Are you Wolfgang's wife?" he asked.

"Supposedly!"

"I'm Andi Szabó. Wolfgang and I went to the university together. In fact, we used to live in this building. Is Wolfie back yet?" No sooner were the words out of his mouth than Andi realized his blunder. It could be that Wolfgang was dead.

"I haven't heard from him since 1940," she replied grimly.

"Oh, that must be difficult for you. And what is your name?" Andi noticed the little girl hadn't taken her eyes off him.

"You're a friend of my daddy?" Reni asked before her mother responded.

Gerda gave her name while frowning at her daughter.

"Do you wear a uniform and a hat, too?" Reni asked, looking fondly at him. Andi laughed, but Reni's question reopened his feelings of guilt. He wondered how Gerda was able to pay her bills. Were all veteran payments suspended since the war ended?

After the door shut, Andi reviewed his exchange with Gerda. She never asked him inside. In fact, she still seemed suspicious of him when they said goodbye. Rather than leaving the building, Andi carefully climbed up to the fifth floor to find his old studio apartment. The door appeared to be ajar, but when he knocked on it, it practically fell over. It was not hinged to the door frame and it was too small. It wasn't the original door for this room. No one was there. He didn't want to pry, but he couldn't help but notice the sparse furnishings—a cot with a rumpled blanket and not much more. Next, he went down to the basement. As students they did their laundry there. Descending the stairs from the courtyard, a disgusting smell overpowered Andi. Holding his nose he looked around. A gaping hole in the wall gave access from the alley. Jesus! People come in here to shit! The sinks were on the opposite wall. There people were camping out—squatters! How could they stand it?

An idea started to percolate in Andi's mind. He climbed the stairs again and found Frau Fritz by calling her name. He didn't remember which apartment was hers. After their twenty-minute conversation, Andi knew how he could assuage his feelings of guilt.

Before returning to Sweden, he made the rounds of the schools to which AFSC was providing a hearty soup each day for the children. The schools were very appreciative. Andi had been told that the U.S. government had refused to let charities provide food to Germany. Evidently, President Roosevelt, before he died, felt that the Soviets would cite such charity as proof that the States supported fascists. That was another thing Andi liked about the Quakers—they refused to let politics keep them from doing what was decent.

Back in Sweden, Andi told the Swensons what he hoped to do. They contacted a Swedish group they knew that had immigrated to Minneapolis, Minnesota, in the U.S., sometime after WWI. Their community was a mixture of Quakers and Lutherans who, over the years, had kept in touch with the Swensons. After six months of letter writing, a decision was reached to provide the money to repair Die Birken. Andi would oversee the work and take photos of each project, from start to finish.

Andi realized that the AFSC's promise to help finance the repair work was useless without permission from the building's owners. It took weeks to establish that the owner was deceased. The new government in the Russian sector of Berlin had no interest in having the building's ownership passed on to a living relative. When Andi menioned he had funding for repairs, he was appointed its manager. The city's chaos and desperate need to provide housing worked to his advantage.

He started by paying some rubblewomen to remove the debris in the courtyard. Now the melted snow and rain could go down the drains. It was no longer a haven for rats. Andi made a ground-floor apartment suitable to live in, to make it easier for him to manage the repair work.

By early 1947, running water was coming out of the pipes again. The basement and first floor were the next projects. Once they were done, the building could be closed at night. This increased the tenants' sense of security.

Fixing the stairs going up to the fifth floor was a big job. Andi had to hire a firm in the American sector to do the work. Their prices were greatly inflated. The company didn't want to do work that would make an improvement in the Soviet zone. How ridiculous! He asked the AFSC to put pressure on the firm until they brought their price down.

Andi could only occasionally afford to return to Stockholm to see Mark. When he got a chance to go, he tried to look his best. His shirts and trousers were pressed properly. He asked Frau Schmidt, who lived on the fourth floor, to cut his hair, trim his beard, and shave the back of his neck. With polished shoes, he set out for the hour walk to Tempelhof Airport in the American sector. He hoped to be neat and stylish, at least, even if not quite sporting the Humphrey Bogart look in *Casablanca* that he aimed to achieve.

THE ORPHANS

1947

The building was now functioning again: doors could be locked, water ran out of faucets, and the stairway was whole again. Many tenants had pitched in to get some jobs done. Disabled neighbors were especially grateful for the improvements. Herr Schoen, who was practically blind, always took an interest in the other tenants. "I haven't felt so safe in years." He shared an apartment with Frau Schmidt, who had had her right leg amputated from the knee down. She could get around fairly well using one crutch and the new banister.

Reni was now nine years old, but her mother still wouldn't allow her to go outside the building on her own. She latched on to Andi, loving to hear his funny stories. He was an adult she could talk to. She assigned herself as Andi's helper, offering to run messages for him or climb up to the fifth floor to fetch a tool. She questioned him on every aspect of the repair work and reported to him what she saw the orphans doing outside from her third floor apartment. Eventually, Andi started teaching her to play chess. She didn't care about strategy or even winning. She just wanted to spend time with Andi.

Reni was the first person to point out to Andi that the same three orphans often slept on the front step to the building—two boys and a girl. He had occasionally heard other tenants complain about these neighborhood waifs. Every time a hammer or saw went missing, they all thought one of the orphans had probably stolen it and sold it on the black market.

Andi had been so absorbed with the repair work that he paid little attention to Reni's updates about the orphans. When she reported for the fourth time that they were sleeping on the doorstep, his conscience woke up. He could no longer dismiss them as urchins. But what could he do? All he had to offer was the building and the work that had to be done on it. Maybe some of the tenants could help. Could the children possibly live in the building without causing havoc? They were scrawny, filthy, and rumored to be ill-mannered and foul-mouthed.

He considered the tall one, Klaus. He was about 13 years old. When they played tag or hide-and-seek among the piles of rubble—the world's best playground from a kid's point of view—Klaus dashed around and jumped with agility. Could he do some work on the building? But before anyone could tolerate his proximity, he'd have to be cleaned up. Andi went up to Fritzy's apartment and asked her if she could cut his hair and let him take a bath.

Fritzy winced and said, "I don't want to get near him because of the lice, although the boy doesn't seem all that bad. He even offered to help me once."

Wilma must have been listening from the other room. She joined them carrying her little Ursula, who was quite a handful. "I agree, he's not a bad boy. The tall one loves it when I bring Ursula out with me. He smiles at her. Yes, I'll help clean him up, but I agree with Fritzy—first he's got to be deloused. On the farm we had to deal with pigs, manure, and the like. I'm used to it, but not lice. He's got to be deloused first—that's what they do to all the refugees when they arrive."

"Why haven't they gone to an intake center themselves?" Fritzy wondered aloud. "They would have been placed in a temporary shelter of some kind. They must know that."

"Yes, they probably do know that," Wilma agreed, "but they don't want to be confined. Those kids have probably had some awful experiences and prefer their freedom."

"I think they might be willing to be deloused, if they go

together as a group," Andi speculated.

"That could be, but they'll be snatched up by the authorities, who will insist on registering them and sending them to one of the barracks. The bureaucracy will take over."

Andi thought Wilma had a point. "They are all missing the chance to go to school." He went back to his apartment to think it through. The children must have a place to live. What if he could promise the authorities that he would serve as their guardian? To the tall one, Andi could give the vacant studio on the fifth floor. It was a wreck, but eventually it would be repaired. Maybe the girl, Sabine was her name, could stay with Gerda, if she'd be willing. On second thought, he would probably have to pay Gerda to do it.

In bed that night, Andi continued trying to determine what was best to do about the orphans. The other boy was a problem. Renate said his name was Walter and she didn't like him. Andi was curious as to why. He looked about 12 and was extremely handsome—perfect features, although much too skinny, with blond hair, and a beautiful erect posture. He had heard him speak the other day and it sounded to Andi that he spoke German with a slight Polish accent. Had Wilma noticed this, he wondered?

When he asked her about it the next day, she thought for a minute before replying: "I wonder if he's one of the 'beautiful Polish children.'"

"What do you mean?"

"The rumor was that the Nazis kidnapped 'beautiful specimens' like Walter and sent them to Germany to be raised. They were considered 'racially valuable.' They could help 'purify the master race.'"

"Iyee!"

"It's possible that Walter was separated from his Polish family and now has lost his German family."

After a couple of weeks, two of the three orphans had settled into living in Die Birken. Klaus liked his fifth floor room and eagerly helped with repairs. Sabine seemed to be content living in

Gerda's apartment, sharing a bed with Reni. Both she and Klaus started attending school. Walter, however, remained a problem. Andi first arranged with Herr and Frau Lange to take him in. They lived next door to Wilma and Fritzy on the fourth floor. The Langes were in their seventies. Although they themselves had been unscathed, all their children and grandchildren had been killed during the war, in one place or another. When Andi asked them to take in such a gorgeous little boy, they readily agreed.

All was well for a day or two, until Herr Lange's watch went missing. Every night, he took it off and placed it on the dresser before getting into bed. The next morning, after washing up, he would buckle it on his wrist again. He and his wife spent a long time looking for it. They emptied the dresser of their few belongings, even taking out the drawers.

He no longer thought it was necessary to hide it under the floorboards like he had immediately after the war ended, when Russian soldiers could be seen on the streets with several watches strapped to their arms. But maybe he had hidden it there without thinking, so he lifted up the floorboards to check. It was not there, either.

The Langes tried not to think that the beautiful boy living with them would do such a thing, but when their silver-framed family photo went missing two days later, there was little doubt about Walter's guilt. At first, they were heartsick to think that the photo was gone, but weeks later, they found it between the pages of a book, without the frame.

Wilma, Fritzy, and Andi tried to figure out what to do with Walter. Putting their heads together, they realized there had been other mishaps in the building, the cause of which had been incorrectly assigned: like Frau Schmidt's crutch mysteriously hanging from the coatrack inside the building's front door. "He probably couldn't sell it, so he just hung it up there to get rid of it," Fritzy said. Around this time, Wilma and Fritzy started referring to Walter as 'Gorgeous Little Shit.' Eventually, they would leave off the 'Gorgeous.' The one thing that was clear to Andi was that he could not allow the boy to stay with the Langes any longer. Walter would have to come to live with him, where he could keep a closer eye on the boy, until he could find somewhere else to put him.

That night, Andi thought again about Walter's possible Polish origins. There were many Nazi survivors around who who had lost their children in the war. Perhaps some might still be concerned about 'racial purity.' An idea began percolating in Andi's mind. Perhaps Walter would be just the kind of child a Nazi would want to adopt. His thoughts went to Heinz, one of his classmates at the university. He recalled how enthralled Heinz had appeared during the book burning fourteen years ago. Is Heinz alive, living in Berlin? Such a long shot!

The next morning, Andi took a break from managing the building's repairs to walk to the University of Berlin. When he was a student, he used to enjoy this walk every day. Then, the the buildings were whole and the streets were lined with trees. Although Germany had also lost World War I, there had been no carpet-bombing then, and the victors had not divided and occupied the country, as they had now.

Unlike many structures he walked by, he found his former history classroom building had not been damaged. But once inside, he noticed the atmosphere had changed. Classes were going on, but there was no longer the buzz of excited voices. He ran into his former French History professor, Conrad Krüger. He recalled this professor had been new to the job back in 1933. That's probably why Andi remembered him. All his other professors had been much older. Herr Krüger didn't recognize him at first, so Andi reminded him of a particular class in which an argument ensued over the Dreyfus Affair.

"Oh yes, I remember that class, and now, I remember you. You were an excellent student. You helped to calm down the students. Thank you for that." Then he said in a low voice: "I wish we could have such lively disputes now."

"Why can't you?" Andi asked naively.

Herr Krüger deflected and talked about other aspects of student life. Andy realized he wanted to be sure of Andi's attitude before he actually answered the question. Finally, he said: "We are expected to instruct along Party lines. We are told what to teach. There is only one acceptable answer to every question."

Andi commiserated. "Critical thinking is so important, though. Do students have debates?"

"They are completely phony. Only certain topics are open for discussion, and the students know what points they should make." He lowered his voice almost to a whisper: "Several of us are thinking of quitting."

Later, Andi was able to speak to some people in the university's administration. He learned that Heinz Mayer had developed an interest in cryptology and was now living in the American sector. That fits, Andi thought. A hard-core Nazi would be more afraid of the Soviets than the Americans. Cryptology; that was curious. What would he do with such an interest? Andi had recently learned that the U.S. had formed a new bureau for espionage that they called the Central Intelligence Agency. Maybe that would be a place to look next for Heinz.

Two days later, Andi found the CIA headquarters and asked if a Heinz Mayer worked there. Of course he wasn't going to get an answer right away, if ever, depending on how secretive Heinz's work was, but the search intrigued him.

First, he was escorted down a hall and into an office where a stone-faced man sat behind a desk on which some telephones and an intercom were sitting. The man asked questions and recorded Andi's answers. He then called in his secretary and handed her a note, showing no expression nor offering any explanation to Andi. Such lack of grace would have immediately disqualified him for diplomatic work, Andi thought.

Then, a 'Harry' (no last name was given) joined them in the room. Harry was all smiles, but nonetheless, threw Andi another barrage of questions—questions to do with Andi and not with Heinz Mayer.

"What languages do you speak?"

It was beginning to sound like a job interview. "Where were you during the war? What was your work with AFSC all about?" Smiling Harry jotted down Andi's answers. He then requested that the first man take a note somewhere.

The first man finally re-entered the room with yet another man, who introduced himself as George, George Goggin. George must have had a higher rank, because Harry rose from the desk to turn over his seat to him. Andi was about to give up looking for Heinz, but when George asked him how he had escaped from Poland, Andi had no trouble expounding in detail. He loved to tell that story. A nudge from George got the stone-faced man to leave the room. No longer impatient, Andi expanded his descriptions. The telephone rang. George looked annoyed and said quietly into the receiver: "Sapo."

Andi knew what Sapo was. It was Sweden's espionage agency, comparable to the CIA. Were they checking up on Andi's story? Yes, he was sure they were. They kept him talking for another hour; his work in Sweden, his reason for coming to Germany, etc. Andi was enjoying himself. Finally, George stated rather dramatically: "Well, András Szabó, we would like you to come work for us."

Andi smiled and said he was very flattered, but he was involved in a project that he felt obligated to finish.

"Of course, that is, after you have finished repairing Die Birken."

Andi had never mentioned the building, specifically. Were they trying to impress him? He told them again that he was completely taken by surprise and was greatly honored.

"Think about it. You don't have to say anything now. When you're ready, please come back and we can talk about the terms, if you're interested. Now, let's get to your question about Heinz Mayer." He held up three photos of men who were similar looking. "Do you recognize one of these men as being Heinz Mayer?"

"I haven't seen him in fourteen years, but I believe this is him," Andi said, pointing to one of the three pictures.

George told him that Heinz Mayer might currently be visiting the local beer hall, two blocks down the street to the south. "Please don't mention our conversation if you find him there," he concluded, rising from his seat and shaking Andi's hand with a sly smile before exiting the room.

WALTER

1948

Wilma had been in Berlin now for two years and things were settling into place, thanks to Fritzy and Andi. Rations were slowly increasing. Although she was still very thin, she wasn't always thinking of food. Ursula brought her so much happiness. She disrupted Fritzy's life, but Wilma knew her roommate loved Ursula too.

Just about everyone Wilma knew had lost someone dear to them in the war. For her, it was Grandpops, Goran, and Günter. Maybe Günter would show up some day, you never know. Or maybe he was still living on the farm, with Olga and Misnk. She could picture him with his long legs and disheveled hair. He was a strong man. She remembered how easy it was for him to lift up a sheep. She smiled, just recalling the first time he tried to shear one. He was so awkward. Grandpops said that it would take him five days, at the rate he was going. Eventually, he picked up the skill. She hoped that wherever he was, he was all right.

She still hadn't learned much about Fritzy's prior life in spite of all their fun conversations. They both loved to talk with Andi. Every now and then, Fritzy mentioned her work at the library. She had been a librarian for years. Her library had stayed open during most of the war, even though parts of the building had been severely damaged. One night, Wilma thought Fritzy was about to tell her and Andi about 'Herr Fritz.' They waited, holding their breath, for what seemed to be a whole minute, but all she ended up saying was: "He was a bastard." They both hoped she

would expand on that, but no, it was all she offered. Wilma was
fairly sure Fritzy had never had children.

One day, Wilma asked her age. Without a moment's hesitation,
Fritzy answered, "Seventeen."

"That's about right. The war's made everybody look twenty
years older," Wilma quipped.

Unlike Fritzy, Wilma's background had not put her on guard. She
had never suffered any negative consequences from talking frankly
to the people she met on the street, or to other rubblewomen.
This enabled her to learn quickly from people about what was
going on, where to find things, and to discover her way around
the city. She openly spoke to others about her life on the farm in
Poland.

About two weeks prior to his monthly visit to Sweden, Andi
was listening to Wilma talk about farm life. An idea suddenly
occurred to him. He asked Wilma if she would like an allotment.

Wilma looked unsure how to answer. Andi explained: "I
know you can get one near the airport, Tempelhof Airport. Do
you want me to look into it?"

"What does that mean?"

"You would have a plot of land for growing vegetables. It
would be fenced, I think."

Andi not only arranged for her to have an allotment, but was
able to procure some used gardening tools. The plot was in the
American sector, which was about an hour away by foot. Wilma
was pleased to learn it was a quarter of an acre. Of course, that
was much less land than she had on the farm, but she could do a
lot with a quarter-acre.

She hoped to prepare the ground for seeding as soon as
possible, and asked Klaus if he could go with her to help with the
work. Klaus, like Sabine, was now enrolled in school, so Saturday
was the first day Wilma could get his help. That was just as well,
because Fritzy couldn't babysit Ursula until the weekend.

Klaus wanted Sabine to go too, but he couldn't coax her away
from her studies. Wilma suspected Klaus was sweet on Sabine.

Reni said she wanted to help, too. She complained that Sabine spent all her time studying. "I think Mama would let me go out on the street to play if Sabine would go out with me, but she only wants to do schoolwork."

Wilma would love to have Reni come with them, but would Gerda allow it? On the Friday before they planned to go, Wilma knocked on Gerda's door. Within seconds, Reni opened the door. The nine-year-old moved so quickly her blond pigtails had to dance to keep up. Such an enthusiastic smile, Wilma thought. Who did Reni remind her of?

"It's Wilma, Mom," Reni called over her shoulder.

Wilma had a brief chance to peek into their living room. The hole in the wall had been fixed and plastered, but was not yet painted. In front of the window, Sabine sat at a table strewn with books and papers. She didn't even look up to greet Wilma.

Finally, Gerda emerged from the other room looking pale and lethargic, taking her time to approach the doorway where Wilma waited. When the Russians took over, Gerda had been forced to take an office-cleaning job. That and shopping were all that made Gerda leave her apartment. In fact, Wilma thought, it was quite likely Gerda was unaware of the events going on in Berlin. The Soviets had closed all rail, water, and road links to the West. Berlin was now an island in a Soviet sea, completely cut off. If Wilma told Gerda these things, she probably wouldn't let Reni go with them to the allotment, so she said nothing about it.

After minutes and minutes of explaining what they were intending to do the next day, Gerda finally consented to let Reni go. Was Gerda convinced that Reni would be safe, or did just having a conversation with someone else wear her down? In any case, Gerda agreed.

Wilma's next job was to get the handcart emptied so she could use it to carry a watering can and tools to the allotment. Going to the basement was always difficult for her. The cart was still in the closet. She tried not to think of what had happened to her there, but now, she had to face it. At least he hadn't raped her on the cart. Forcing the memory to the back of her mind, she opened the closet door and pulled out the cart to go through her friend's belongings. She would take the tarp to the allotment. It would be handy for hiding whatever she wanted to leave at the plot.

She thought of her dead friend. Living or dying during a war was so arbitrary. As a survivor, Wilma felt grateful but undeserving. Remembering her friend relieved her guilt in some small way.

The blanket under the tarp was now moldy. She stacked the sweater and other items of clothing in a neat pile at the back of the closet. Opening a wooden box revealed a letter and some photos. The letter was addressed to Frau Frieda Liebermann at a Warsaw address. One photo was of her and a man and two children around five and seven years old. Wilma assumed this had been her family. Wilma was happy to think that she had had the love of a man and the opportunity to raise children.

Why only one letter? Maybe they hadn't been separated long. If she lost her family, how did she escape? A wooden object was also in the box. It was strange, like nothing Wilma had ever seen before. She replaced the items in the box and took it up to Fritzy's apartment for safekeeping, along with the small notebook she had taken from Frieda's pocket three years prior. Wilma could think of nothing she could do to honor Frieda's existence. Before leaving the farm, Wilma had never had a female friend. How lucky she was to be living with Fritzy now.

Upon leaving the CIA building, Andi walked in the direction of the local beer hall. After a couple of blocks, he spotted benches and umbrellas down the street. Even from that distance, he could smell stale beer. The customers were noisy, mostly men chatting with their buddies before going home after work. Andi walked around looking for Heinz, nervously jingling his key and coins in the pocket of his trousers.

At Berlin University, Andi often sat behind Heinz in class. He remembered staring at Heinz's cowlick on the back of his head.

Otherwise his hair was blond and straight. He spotted a large blond-haired man wearing a traditional, v-neck wool sweater over a long-sleeved shirt talking to another man sitting across from him. As he got closer, he recognized the cowlick. Andi went up to Heinz and stood beside him to wait for a break in the two men's conversation. "Excuse me, aren't you Heinz...?" pretending not to remember his last name. He hoped Heinz would recognize him.

"Oh my God, if it isn't little Andi—Andi, the star pupil. Which of your many languages are you speaking today?" He winked at the man across the table. "Andi, this is Reinhold Zellweger. Rein, Andi Szabó, right, Szabó, isn't it?"

"Yes, that's right. Nice to meet you, Rein," he said, but Andi was thinking how irritating Heinz still was. He kept his smile going, in spite of his thoughts. Fourteen years later, and this guy still feels superior, even after losing the damn war. Groomed for diplomacy, Andi had no trouble disguising his true feelings. "So, you're still living in Berlin; what are you doing these days?"

"Business, and you? Did you ever get married?"

Andi saw him give the other man a quick glance. "Not yet. What about you?"

"Yeah, I tied the knot ten years ago. So what are you doing? I thought I heard you became a diplomat."

"Yes, I suppose. I did a spell in one of the embassies. Do you have children?"

"Not yet." Heinz looked down.

Andi ordered a beer and sat down, joining the two. The conversation was tricky because Andi could not get into questions about what Heinz did during the war, or really what kind of work he was doing now, so he asked Heinz and Rein what they knew about reconstituting German football clubs—a subject Andi knew little about and cared about even less—to get Heinz talking. Rein eventually left to go home.

Hoping to lure Heinz to stay longer, Andi ordered some pretzels with mustard. He maneuvered the conversation to the lack of housing in Berlin, and finally, he explained about the repair work he was engaged in on an apartment building in the Russian sector. From his jacket, he brought out some photos that illustrated the early stages of repairs. The orphans were in a few of the pictures. Heinz took the bait.

"Orphans you say?"

"Yes, I'm trying to find good homes for them."

"What is that one like?" Heinz pointed to Walter in the photo.

"His parents were both killed. Let's see, he's neat and orderly. He must have had a strict upbringing."

After more discussion, Heinz said: "My wife and I might take a look at him. Could we come over this weekend? Don't let him know why we're there. I would hate to disappoint him."

When Andi returned to Die Birken that evening, he went up to talk with Wilma and Fritzy, explaining to them that Walter may possibly be adopted. "The couple wants to see him this weekend."

"It can't be soon enough," Fritzy commented. Wilma related Gorgeous Little Shit's latest bad behavior to Andi. Then they noticed Reni standing in the doorway to the bedroom.

"Oh," Wilma said, "you've gotten Ursula to fall asleep."

The three adults were embarrassed that Reni had heard their discussion, but before they could think of what to say, Reni spoke: "He reminds me of the boy in the Wiesenhuber family. That's the family I had to go live with during the last part of the war. Whenever he came home from school...well, no, not from school, but some group he went to after school..."

"Hitler Youth?" Fritzy suggested.

"Yes, that was it. Well, he would boss his sister and me around. He was so mean."

"That's interesting, Reni. Oh, and thanks for helping with Ursula. But you had best get back downstairs. Your mother may be worried about you," Wilma said.

"Oh, and Reni, it would be good not to tell others what we

were talking about," Andi added.

"OK, but Klaus calls Walter Little Shit, not Gorgeous."

Amused, the three of them waited for a few minutes to be sure Reni was gone. Fritzy was the first to speak: "Maybe what Walter needs is to feel important."

"Would a uniform help?"

"It could."

"He needs a job," Wilma added, "a job where he thinks he's helping; no not helping, necessarily, but where he thinks, as you said, he's important. Like the boy Reni described. Maybe Walter would like to be in charge of other people."

The others agreed. "I bet I could find the makings of a uniform like the Hitler Youth wore, without any insignias, arm bands, and the like. Nobody in their right mind would wear such a thing now, so it shouldn't cost much. You know—just a brown shirt with a black scarf or tie. I think I know where to find one," Fritzy said.

"Yes, but what could he do?" Andi asked.

"I've got it," Wilma said. "Have him check people in and out of the building, recording the date and time they leave and come back, what apartment they live in."

"Yes, that should do it. I'll find a notebook. We'll call it a record book. Tomorrow, hopefully, he can start the job."

The next Saturday, Klaus, Reni, and Wilma walked to the allotment, pulling the handcart with the tools and tarp atop. As they walked, they began to hear the sound of airplanes. When they actually reached Wilma's plot, the sound made by planes landing and taking off was constant—deafening and relentless. It was quite exciting to see, though they had to nearly yell at each other to be heard.

"Why so many planes?" Reni asked.

Wilma and Klaus looked at each other, but neither had an answer. Klaus surmised that a lot of stuff was being unloaded. "Trucks are being filled and then driven off to the terminal. While the workers are unloading, it seems a tanker truck is putting fuel into the plane. Then that plane goes to another runway and takes off. It looks like another plane is landing about every two minutes."

The three of them were mesmerized. They just stood and watched planes for a half hour. Klaus tried to name the nationality of each. "That one's French. There's another American plane, now, two British, one right after the other."

"Do they do this every day?" Reni asked.

"My goodness, I think they're bringing things in for Berliners," Wilma guessed. "They have been saying that we'll run out of food and there won't be coal to heat our homes this winter if the Russians continue to blockade Berlin."

"Why are the Russians doing that?" Klaus asked.

"Andi says the Russians want the Americans, the French, and the British to leave Berlin. He calls it a cold war."

Hard as it was, they finally tore themselves away from the noisy spectacle and started to work, preparing the vegetable garden. The days were getting long in late May, so they were able to work well past 6:00 P.M. They left the handcart filled with the tools and covered with the canvas. The ground had been cleared and grass removed from half the plot. They managed to get ten rows planted of carrots, peas, courgettes, onions, and beets. Wilma had heard that some people lived on their allotments, although it was illegal. If she lived here, she could raise chickens. But that thought was barely completed when another plane landed, causing her to reconsider. No, she would never want to live with so much noise.

When they arrived back at Die Birken, it was getting dark. Reni went straight to her apartment. Wilma went immediately to relieve Fritzy, who had taken care of Ursula all day. "Did Heinz and his wife come to look at Walter?" Wilma asked her.

"Oh, yes, I was coming down the stairs with Ursula when they came to the door. Walter asked to see their papers, to prove that they were who they said they were. Can you believe it? While

they were engrossed with Walter, I got a good look at the man—
Heinz Mayer. I knew him years ago. The jerk was enthralled with
Walter. The wife didn't seem convinced. I turned around and
went upstairs, in case he might recognize me. Andi told me later
that after an hour or so talking with him, the Mayers took Little
Shit home with them, still wearing his uniform."

"That was gutsy of them!"

"Let's hope we never have to see that Walter again." Wilma
went to bed thinking it had been a perfect day. She ran into Andi
the next morning, eager to tell him about the planes. But Andi,
who was usually so pleasant, was in a foul mood. Wilma had
never seen him so upset. "What's wrong?" she asked.

"Something's missing."

"What's missing?" she asked.

Without answering her, he went into his apartment and shut
the door.

Wilma caught Fritzy just before she left for the library. "Andi
is really upset about something...."

"Hmm, I'm sorry. He's usually so chipper at the end of the
month. Have you noticed how he always gets his hair cut just
before he leaves for Sweden? I bet he is seeing a friend there."

"You mean 'that kind' of friend?"

"Yes, of course, but what is missing that upset him so?"

MARK

Andi was cursing himself during the entire flight to Stockholm. He and Mark had been so careful. They were quite sure nobody in Stockholm had caught on to their relationship, even though living together there was no longer illegal. They had engaged in certain behaviors to put off people who might be suspicious. For instance, Mark never met Andi at the airport. Andi had his own key, which he always kept in his pocket. He didn't bring a suitcase with him, he just kept some clothes at Mark's apartment.

"It is good that we decided not to put return addresses on our envelopes."

"Yes, and you hadn't signed it 'Mark,' so I think you're in the clear. But you remember those lovely things you said referring to sheets." They both smiled, recalling the memory.

"Was it obvious that a man wrote the letter?"

"I'm afraid so…"

"Oh yes, I talked about whiskers, didn't I? Oh dear!"—more smiles. "Well, we can't undo that letter."

Later that weekend, Mark and Andi discussed Mark's future. He wanted to move back to Berlin. Andi knew Mark had always wanted to get involved in politics. He had spent ten years of his life waiting for the chance to help his country get back on the right track. Not that those ten years were wasted. He had become a newspaper columnist in Stockholm, who was frequently interviewed on the radio.

"Where do you think you'll live?" Andi asked.

"Oh, in the American zone, for sure! But it doesn't matter

where I live, because we can't live together, sadly. Germans have heard so much Nazi propaganda against homosexuals it will take decades for them to accept gay couples. It may be three years since they lost the war, but I'll wager many Germans still believe they are the master race."

Andi was quiet. Even though they saw each other only four days a month, here they could live together and almost lead a normal life. Soon, they'd have to give that up. Andi agreed to the idea, though, and didn't complain or express regret because he wanted Mark to be happy.

"Now, we'll be able to see more of each other," Mark reminded Andi, "but we'll have to be more careful about not being noticed as a couple." Mark let out a big sigh. Andi knew what Mark was feeling. There were so few places in the world where there was no prejudice against homosexuals.

Later, during that same visit, Andi read one of Mark's articles written for his newspaper:

The Berlin Blockade
By 1945, the German Reichsmark was almost worthless. People were resorting to the black market, bartering, and using cigarettes for currency. It became increasingly obvious that the Soviets and the West had different goals for Germany.

Russia would just as soon run its former enemy into the ground. To that purpose, they took factory equipment and resources from East Germany and sent them back to the Soviet Union. They devalued the currency by excessive printing of the Reichsmark, not caring if, by so doing, they were producing inflation.

The Western occupiers came to think that Europe could not recover from the war if Germany remained weak. They wanted to give Marshall Plan grants to Germany, but such money would soon be devalued if they continued to use the Reichsmark. Without forewarning

*or consultation with the Soviet zone authorities, they
created a new currency for the Western zones of Germany:
the Deutche Mark. To avoid being devalued, all Marshall
Plan grants were to be given in Deutche Marks.*
As Andi kept reading his article, he could feel the strength of
Mark's interest in German politics and government. No wonder
he wants to live in Germany.

*The communist powers in East Germany responded
by creating their own currency—the East German Mark.
Furious that the Western allies had acted on their own
and in unison, they were determined to take control of
Berlin....*

*The West countered the blockade with an airlift...
The blockade made the Cold War officially a war....*

Later in the day, Andi told Mark how much he appreciated
his analysis of the blockade. "Don't you think that Germans are
now being seen by the West less as former Nazis and more as
allies?"

"Yes, I do." Mark went on to tell Andi that he had some
interviews set up in the following weeks with government
agencies in West Berlin. "Hopefully, a job might come from one
of them."

Andi reminded Mark about the CIA's offer to hire him when
the repair work on Die Birken was completed.

"Maybe we could at least live in the same building," Mark said
smiling.

Just before going to bed, Mark asked: "Didn't you say that
Heinz, Little Shit's father, works for the CIA?"

"Yes."

"A former Nazi in the CIA, Jesus!"

Andi started worrying again. What if Little Shit shows the
letter to his father?

GÜNTER RETURNS

When Günter arrived back in Germany, he was missing five teeth, had TB, and was emaciated. His ribs and back bones stuck out so far they could be counted visually, there was no need to feel for them. Somehow, he had managed to survive five grueling years in a Soviet forced labor camp, better known as a gulag, where he worked 15-hour days, slept in an unheated barracks, and was fed wretched and insufficient food.

The Soviets felt no guilt for abusing these men. Russia lost 27 million people during the war, and something like 37,000 towns had been completely destroyed. To industrialize quickly, the Soviets had to collect resources from wherever possible. This required manpower. Forced laborers weren't just prisoners of war. Punishing the people who had obstructed Soviet goals was part of it, but they needed more still, so civilians were taken. Germans being expelled from Eastern Europe were fair game, but able-bodied civilian men from anywhere could fall victim. Other prisoners included kulaks (prosperous peasant farmers who rebelled against Stalin's collectivization program), political prisoners, victims of Stalin's other whimsical purges, and intellectuals, as well as common criminals.

For five years, Günter was made to cut down lovely old oak trees in the most beautiful forest he had ever seen. He resolved that if he ever returned to a normal life, he would plant trees wherever he could.

Life in the labor camp entailed exhaustive work, little food, little sleep, and no privacy, but Günter found it did provide him one opportunity. He learned how to discipline his thinking. At certain times of day, he gave himself the assignment of reflecting on his life. He forced himself to recall incidents in his life, whether significant or trivial. With nothing to read, no materials to use for writing anything down, his thoughts became his source of entertainment. They helped to distract him from his gnawing hunger. He had various tricks. A favorite one was to combine reflection with fantasy, such as when he imagined being interviewed by Orson Wells:

Wells: *Today we are so honored to have on our program Wolfgang Morgandal, survivor of the notorious Soviet labor camp in Belarus. Wolfgang, I think our listeners would first like to hear about your life growing up.*

Wolfgang: *I grew up in the Charlottenburg section of Berlin, the only child of Adrian and Anneliese Morgandal. I never really knew my father, because just when I was born, Germany entered the Great War. My father was a devoted speaker for the German Peace Society. The society publically committed to fulfill patriotic duties, but it refused to demonize Germany's so-called 'enemies.' It urged Germany to negotiate a peace, condemned annexations such as Alsace-Lorraine, and advocated for a government that was fully democratic, one that permitted women's suffrage. He was imprisoned for promoting these ideas. He died in prison, not because he was tortured, but from neglect. The prison conditions were unhygienic, to say the least.*

Once my father went to prison, Mom and I went to live with her parents. My mother was Anneliese Huber before she was married. Her parents were well-to-do and made sure I was given the best education. They were very critical of Dad. In fact, they were ashamed of his attitude and stance. As a young boy, I became bitter that he had abandoned us for the sake of peace issues.

Wells: *Do you still resent your father today? Compare your situation with that of your father's.*

Wolfgang: *No, I am not as resentful as I was. Our situations are similar, yet different. I admire my father for having strong principles and sticking by them, but Dad could have avoided fighting without going to prison....*

As for the similarities: I was anti-Nazi, as you know. Had I refused to fight, I would have been beheaded. Also, I knew how awful it was for a child to grow up without a father. I didn't want my daughter to experience what I had experienced. So, despite being anti-Nazi, I decided to fight in the Wehrmacht. That was a foolish decision. I was young, an academic, and thoroughly obsessed with German literature. I should have just left the country....

Another trick Günter used was to recite poetry that he could remember. There were four poems he went over in his mind at least once a week. Every now and then, he tried to create a limerick. Another goal was to see how many prime numbers he could identify, but that became difficult without pencil and paper. And yet another trick, perhaps his favorite, was to make up a skit in which he was some kind of hero. Just making it up made him feel good, and when it became too absurd, there was the benefit of making him laugh at himself.

Günter was fortunate in the sense that he was released in 1950 and allowed to return to Germany. There were others that left at the same time. Maybe a new influx of slaves was about to arrive so they got rid of those most worn out or likely to die.

He was given a pass that permitted him to ride trains back to Berlin. As a shell of his former self, he made it to Berlin with just the clothes on his back and an empty belly. His hair and beard were long and home to lice. His clothes were ragged and filthy. People on the trains avoided being near him, if they could. Every now and again, someone took pity on him and gave him something to eat. Without that generosity, he probably wouldn't have made it back.

Once in Berlin, he was so exhausted from lack of food that he only made it outside the train station before he had to sit down. Some others were sitting on a broken concrete slab, serving as a bench. He joined them. The man he sat next to moved off when

Günter had a coughing fit. He knew he was unwelcomed, but he had no strength. He sat on the slab for some time, looking around, trying to figure out which buildings he recognized from before the war. So sad! He remembered his grandfather telling him that after World War I, the Germans didn't think they had lost the war. Oh my God! They sure as hell must know it this time!

By 1950, most of the rubble had been removed. Trams were running. There were a few cars and more bikes on the streets. Most people were walking. Many spots had just ruins of buildings surrounding huge bomb craters. By early afternoon, Günter had at last found his way to Hoffmannstrasse. Many of the buildings there were damaged, but most were still functioning. He came to the familiar corner grocery. It must be still operating. There was a line of women waiting in front. When a clerk came out and announced that there was no more bread, eggs, butter, or milk, many women left the line.

Günter continued down the street, taking small steps. He was trying to remember buildings he had passed so often ten years prior. He counted on spotting the birch trees, until he realized that, of course, the birch trees would be gone. When he did recognize his old apartment building, a joy filled his spirit. The joy wasn't evidenced by a quickening of pace or a smile on his face. He was too tired and weak to be so demonstrative. But there it was, Die Birken, no doubt about it, damaged but still standing.

Another coughing fit made him look for a place to sit down again. He was just lowering himself onto a front doorstep when he recognized the woman who walked by him holding the hand of a little girl. My God, it's Wilma! "Wilma," he said out loud in a raspy voice. He had to cough. "Wilma," he called out again. She turned around and stared at him. He smiled his toothless grin and tried to get up from the step. He saw Wilma's face wrinkled up with cries and gasps.

"Günter, is that you?"

He gave her a toothless grin. "Yes, Wilma it's me."

"Günter?"

"Yes, yes, I'm Günter. I'm so happy to see you."

Wilma stared and then started crying. She made a gesture that she wanted to hug him, but he wouldn't let her. "I'm lice-ridden. I'm so glad to see you made it here." Günter looked at the little girl, who started to cry. "How's Grandpops?" Günter asked, looking back at Wilma.

Wilma was still sobbing, but managed to answer: "He's dead." There was a pause. She needs more time to take in what she was seeing, Günter thought. She finally spoke again: "I'll tell you all about it, but let's get you home first. You're almost there, follow me."

He struggled to lift himself off the step, not taking his eyes off Wilma. She was the loveliest person he had ever known. He had to sit down again. He tried to make small talk: "I hardly recognized the street," he managed to say before his next coughing fit consumed him.

"You should have seen it five years ago."

Another try to get up was more successful. He was able to follow her until they reached the doorstep of Die Birken. A young man loped through the door and came to an abrupt stop when he saw Günter. "Hi Klaus, I want you to meet an old friend of mine: Günter. Günter has just come back from...where were you, in Poland?"

"Yes, in a labor camp...in the mountains, either in Poland or Belarus. I'm not sure."

Klaus went pale. "In a labor camp?" Klaus asked.

Wilma asked Günter to sit on the doorstep while she fetched him something to eat and drink. "I know you're weak." Klaus sat down beside him while they waited for her to return. Günter had another coughing fit.

"I'm sorry. I can't stop sputtering."

"Would you like me to take you to the intake center?" Klaus asked hesitantly. "That's where they'll get rid of your lice." He paused then spoke faster. "That's what I had to do five years ago.

I think we can stop by the church next door and get you some clothes. They're second-hand, but clean. I'll wait for you so you'll know how to get back."

Günter was touched, crying and smiling simultaneously: "Thank you. That sounds good. I think I'll rest for a minute first." His crying stopped when he was overcome by another coughing fit.

Wilma returned with some potato salad, followed by Fritzy and the same little girl, whom they called Ursula. Is she Wilma's child? His thoughts were jumbled. He dozed off. When he awoke, they were all staring at him. He realized they were horrified at the way he looked.

Klaus went inside to fetch Andi. When Günter saw Andi, it took him a minute to realize who he was. Have I died? Is this heaven? Günter asked himself. His toothless grin turned into another coughing spasm.

"Wolfgang, Wolfgang Morgandal?" Andi burst into floods of tears. The two men stared at each other. "Oh my God, what you must have been through!" Andi said.

"Morgandal?" Fritzy asked slowly.

"Wolfgang Morgandal?" Wilma repeated.

"I believe your wife is living on the third floor," Andi informed him.

Everybody was silent.

"No. It can't be." Another coughing spell overtook him. "My little girl?"

"Renate? Yes, she's here, too."

"I want to see her." He started to try to stand.

Andi assumed leadership on this one: "No, I think you had better get cleaned up first, Wolfie."

"Wolfie?" repeated Wilma.

Hours later, Günter had been deloused, bathed, hair and beard cut, and was dressed in clean clothes. He was still emaciated, weak, and coughing. Andi insisted that he rest first and made him lie down in his bed. He woke up five hours later. Wilma brought him a light meal and stayed with him until he was ready to go upstairs to Gerda's apartment. Andi accompanied him.

Gerda opened the door and stared: "Good God!" She slammed the door shut.

"Perhaps she didn't recognize you," Andi said, trying to ease the situation.

"I don't know, but that woman is not Gerda!"

TREATMENT

Much had happened in the five years since World War II ended. The Soviets detonated their first atomic bomb in 1949, elevating the stakes in the Cold War. The democratic West and the communist East waged their ideological battle via propaganda and espionage. During the airlift, the Soviets broadcast on the radio that the Americans had dropped beetles over the Soviet sector to destroy the potato crop. The Americans told the world they were saving the West Berliners from Russian entrapment. But now, added to such propaganda was the possibility of using a deadly nuclear weapon. Fear and tension heightened.

In the same year that Günter returned to Berlin, 1950, the East German government took two important steps. It created a new agency called the Stasi, which was charged with both internal and external security (a secret police with an espionage wing). Secondly, the GDR held its first 'election.' The ballot had a list of candidates placed there by the SED, the communist party. Voters were expected to put their paper ballots into a box. If you chose to vote against the party's list, you had to take your ballot to another room, where there was a box for dissenters. Reportedly, and to no one's surprise, 98.53% of East Germans voted and 99.9% of those were in favor of the party's list.

At this time, East Berliners could still work in West Berlin. Crossing the checkpoints would become increasingly difficult as time went on.

Andi was horrified at the difference in Wolfgang. It was hard for him to accept that the intervening years could have brought about such a change. Wolfie was now emaciated and consumed by TB. His rare smile displayed several gaps in his teeth. Far more disturbing to Andi was the change in Wolfgang's spirit. No longer outspoken, his friend rarely ventured an opinion on anything now. Except for his coughing, you would hardly be aware of his presence.

By 1950, a new drug, streptomycin, had been shown to be effective with 50% of tuberculosis patients. Before Wolfgang could be entered into a program to treat him for TB, he had to decide on his name. Should he be Wolfgang Morgandal or Günter Beck? With all the personal tragedies that the war had brought about, it also offered opportunities. Some people could and would change their identities. Many inveterate Nazis downgraded their military backgrounds. Other people, with dead or missing relatives, homes bombed out, could invent more glamorous pasts, pasts with higher status, in other areas of the country. This might give them a foot in the door to a new type of life. There was always the worry, with the high level of recordkeeping that Germans were noted for, that the truth would come out. But that could take years, and after enough time had passed, who would care if Ernst, the brick layer, was now Helmut, the owner of a construction company.

Who did Wolfgang want to be? As Wolfgang Morgandal he would be the father of Renate Morgandal. That he wanted. But he would also be the husband of Gerda Morgandal—not the Gerda Morgandal he married, but some other strange woman who was impersonating his dear wife. As Wolfgang Morgandal he would be a former soldier in the Wehrmacht. Wolfgang hated that identity. He felt that he was more Günter Beck, a captured Polish farmer who served five years as a slave laborer in a Soviet forest camp on the Belarus border. By living in the same building as his daughter, he could watch over her. That would allow him to be as much of a father as he could be at this point, so, yes, he would be Günter Beck.

Andi enrolled his friend Wolfie, now Günter, in a clinic to treat him for TB. He was kept in isolation at hospital until he could be treated as an outpatient. Fortunately, Günter improved and showed no resistance to the drug. Upon his release, Andi got a cot so Günter could sleep in his apartment. He, Wilma, and Fritzy took charge of his diet, with Andi procuring an extra supply of meat in West Berlin that the grocers in East Berlin rarely had available for purchase.

Over six months, Günter added thirty pounds in weight. At first, he rested all day long, but as time went on, he was able to spend much of the day off the cot. He wasn't interested in reading. That was shocking to Andi, who remembered Wolfie as a university student completely devoted to literature. Back then, he had even started to write a novel. But now, he spent many hours sitting quietly, thinking about what? When he did talk, all he seemed interested in were trees. One day, he told Andi he would love to plant new birch trees in front of the building. "I know what to do, but where could we get them?"

A couple of weeks later, Klaus went with Günter to a nursery. Together they rolled Wilma's garden cart home with the crowns of seven little birch trees brushing their shoulders. Günter dug the holes himself. While appreciating Klaus' offer to help, he made it clear that he wanted to do the planting. Klaus later told Andi that Günter became talkative at the nursery. He even asked if they needed to hire someone. On their way home, Günter suggested that they go out of their way a bit so they could visit Tiergarten. Klaus said that Günter was close to tears when he saw that there was hardly a tree standing.

"You are probably too young to remember this park before the war."

"Well, yeah. I really never got out of my neighborhood much as a kid, but I do remember hearing that it was beautiful. Didn't it used to be where kings hunted?"

"Yes, that's right, but that was centuries ago."

"I was told that during the war, Berliners were so desperate to keep warm that they cut down all the trees for fuel."

Klaus was currently enrolled in an apprentice program with a master carpenter. He also went to regular school one day a week. Andi used him to make repairs in the building. Stories about his childhood slowly seeped out. Günter learned that Klaus' father had been a carpenter and his mother, a school cook. Klaus had a little sister that he took care of for years in the mornings, before she went to school, and in the afternoons. The bomb that killed his family and destroyed much of his neighborhood had missed Klaus as he stood in line for bread a few blocks away.

"That probably explains why Klaus is so good with Ursula," Wilma said to Andi. She compared Klaus with Sabine, who was living in Gerda's third floor apartment. "At first, I had hoped to lure Sabine into some babysitting so she could give Fritzy a break. The time I asked her for help, Sabine climbed the one flight of stairs carrying her notebook, text, and pencils to babysit Ursula. When I came home, Ursula ran to me and clung to my leg until Sabine left."

Andi was aware of Sabine's disinterest in Ursula. One day, he overheard her remarking to Klaus: "She's such an ugly girl. Those slanted eyes and round face make her look Mongolian." Andi hated Sabine's racism. He could, however, easily visualize round-faced Ursula riding a small horse on the Gobi Dessert. Her father must have been a soldier from the east of Russia.

When Klaus turned eighteen, Andi offered him the opportunity to live in the basement. It would save him the long trek up to the fifth floor. There was still a lingering odor from the war years when immigrants, desperate for some privacy, had entered the basement through gaps in its wall and used the floor as a toilet. Although the wall had been repaired a few years back, the basement had no windows. Only when the doors to the alley behind the building were open could fresh air help to flush out the foul smell. Andi suggested that Klaus construct his own nook in the basement for a bedroom.

"I have another reason I'd like you to live in the basement," Andi added. "I was thinking we could make part of the basement serve as a carpentry workshop. We could have a table with a circular saw." Andi noticed Klaus' eyes light up. Encouraged, Andi went on: "...And a workbench. We could keep our tools safe." Lumber was one supply that was again becoming plentiful. Germany had many forests. Klaus had already started doing jobs for people in the neighborhood. He and his customers knew to keep quiet about such informal arrangements. Free enterprise was not allowed in the communist system.

Of the three orphans, Klaus had blended in best with the other tenants. Sabine was an excellent student and was definitely headed for the university. Andi wondered if she had a true interest in academics. Maybe she was subconsciously trying to pay homage to her dead parents, who had both been university professors. The truth was, however, Sabine lacked warmth. She had little interest in other people. As for Walter, the third orphan, Andi shuddered to think. Hopefully, Walter had settled in well with Heinz and his wife. If Andi ever started working for the CIA, he hoped he and Heinz would be working in different areas.

His thoughts were interrupted by a knock on his door. It was Reni, who, ever since she was nine, paid a daily visit to Andi's apartment.

Reni had many reasons for stopping in to see 'Uncle Andi.' She had to further their chess game along by making a few more moves. Her main reason to visit him, though, was to give him her latest news: what had happened in school that day, and what was going on in Die Birken that had, perhaps, avoided Andi's notice.

When Günter started living in her uncle's apartment, Reni was afraid of him. He was scary looking. Her mom had told her never to go near him because he had TB. Many people had TB after the war, kids too, so she was used to hearing people cough. One day, she asked her uncle how his 'patient' was doing. For some reason Uncle Andi didn't like her question, even though she had whispered it so as not to awake the man on the cot. Uncle Andi said that one day she would grow to love Günter, as he was a very good man. What a weird answer. Uncle Andi was rarely in a bad mood, but since he was that day, she left his apartment to go to Fritzy and Wilma's so she could play with Ursula.

LISE

The Nazi obsession with promoting the Aryan race had deadly repercussions for Jews, homosexuals, Roma, and Slavs. This same obsession had the side effect of marginalizing German women. To decrease unemployment before the war, the Nazis encouraged women not to work. Female judges, doctors, and teachers were dismissed. The number of women in higher education decreased by 85%. Instead, Nazi propaganda elevated a woman's role as a wife, mother, and homemaker.

The emancipation of women was invented by Jewish intellectuals and was clearly associated with Marxism. Women need to leave the workplace and return home.
—Adolph Hitler 1934

But statistics also showed that SS men were not doing their part. Germany needed to increase their average number of children from 1.1 to 4, in order to propagate the 'master race.' So the Nazis secretly established SS stud farms and maternity homes for single mothers. They even tried to raise the status of illegitimate children.

Lise Weger grew up in the city of Lemgo, in the heart of the Lippe region of Germany. Her mother was a high school teacher and pushed Lise to do better in school, but Lise's personality was more attuned to that of her father, who was a baker during the day and rested in the family's one stuffed chair in the evenings. Lise joined the German Girls League (BDM) in its founding year. It gave her some reprieve from her mother. She felt accepted in the league and was pleased to be chosen to lead the girls whenever they marched down city streets. Their ordinary uniform, a dark blue skirt and white middy blouse with tie, didn't hide her curvaceous figure. She was tall with lovely blond hair, which she wore in braids that could wrap around her head.

Lise became increasingly disrespectful of her mother. Frau Weger criticized the BDM leaders for grooming girls to simply become wives and mothers. In speaking to other parents, she found that many were suspicious that the BDM leaders were even encouraging the girls to have illegitimate children. About that same time, Frau Weger was dismissed from her teaching job.

Lise never told her family that she had passed inspection by the Reich Ancestry Office. She didn't tell her mother that she wanted to produce as many fine children for the Führer as possible. At age 18, Lise went to the very first Lebensborn home. It was in Steinhöring. There, she was paired with an SS man of equal Nordic stock. She signed papers renouncing her claim to any children she gave birth to.

When she arrived, there were about 40 other girls already there. They each were given single rooms. Nobody knew anyone's name. Lise had to wait until the tenth day after the beginning of her period before she was inspected by a doctor. When they said she was ready, an SS man visited her at night. He was nice but he hurt her a little. He had already performed his duty with another girl earlier that day. Of course, Lise didn't know his name. He paid her a visit for the two following nights. He was very good looking but somewhat shy.

Once it was determined that Lise was pregnant, she was given the choice to go home to her family or to a maternity home. Lise did not want to go home, for sure. The birth was not easy. She was encouraged to have a natural delivery. "No good German woman should need relief from the pain of delivery," she was told.

Lise nursed the baby for two weeks and never saw it again. They gave her eight months to recover at home. That was difficult because she hadn't told her parents anything about where she had been. Her father kept her busy working in the bakery. That was a blessing. But she suspected her mother knew what had happened. She couldn't wait to return to Steinhöring in the following spring. A year later, she had given birth to another baby. A different SS man was the father.

When she was ready to return to be impregnated for the third time, the BDM had another plan for her. They were pleased to be able to give her the opportunity to be a mother. This would be such a service to the Reich! She was offered an apartment and living expenses in exchange for becoming the mother of this child.

"Where would I live?"

"In Berlin."

"How old is the child?"

"Eighteen months."

Lise was relieved to hear that. She didn't really know how to take care of a newborn. During the two weeks that she had nursed her babies at the maternity home, she had never even changed a diaper. In fact, she had never been eager to be a mother, but the chance to be supported, and live away from her own mother, was very appealing, and she would get to live in the capital.

"Is it a boy or a girl?"

"A girl. You would have to take the name of the mother. All the legalities have been taken care of."

"Where is the real mother?"

"She has left for good. She was an enemy of the Führer. You will be providing the Reich a great service. Every German child is important. Another reason you were chosen for this honor is that you look like Renate, the little girl. Your name will be changed to Gerda Morgandal."

READING BOOKS

During her first three years in Berlin, Wilma worked as a rubblewoman, had a baby, and helped Andi with odd jobs repairing Die Birken. Her indebtedness to Fritzy went well beyond having a roof over her head. Fritzy cared for Ursula as if she were her own baby. As much as Wilma loved her, after three years of living with Fritzy, Wilma felt she knew little of her past, except that she had been married to a 'bastard' and the marriage ended in divorce. Fritzy skillfully changed the subject when anyone questioned her further.

By 1948, Wilma knew it was about time that she started pulling her own weight. She wanted a job that brought in money, but all she knew how to do was farm. With only an eighth-grade education, what kind of work could she get? When she started looking into the opportunities, she was surprised to discover that the City of East Berlin would train her for several types of jobs, and furthermore, her lack of education did not hamper her chances. Having working-class status proved an advantage under a regime run by communists. Childcare was free, readily available, and, until Ursula was of school age, Wilma needn't work more than six hours a day. That would allow her sufficient time to be home with her daughter.

She wanted a job that would eventually let her be outdoors. She thought post office work would suit her best. She first learned how to sort the mail and spent a year doing that. Compared to the others, she was able to learn new procedures quickly. She was usually the first to finish a task. After working inside for that year, she longed to be outdoors, so she asked to be switched to delivery. Her employers found that if they had to have someone fill in for another, Wilma would be the best person. After a year delivering mail in many areas of the city, she became accustomed to urban living and felt comfortable getting around. Eventually, the post office saw to it that she learned how to drive, with the anticipation of putting her on truck deliveries.

All of this was satisfying, but in 1950, when Günter walked up the street to Die Birken on Hoffmannstrasse, Wilma's life took on a new dimension. She became devoted to getting Günter well. When she and Fritzy were able to get meat, Wilma gave him half of her serving.

Imagine his real name being Wolfgang! It sounded so Prussian, and Wolfie, equally ridiculous in the other direction. She visited him every afternoon in Andi's apartment. At first, she restrained herself from asking many questions, but over the course of several weeks, the story came out about the farm and his capture by Russian soldiers. When he told her that they shot Olga, his eyes welled up. Wilma reached out and held his hand. He smiled at her.

"It's so good to be back with you." He shut his eyes for a brief moment, then, withdrawing his hand, added: "You must wash your hands. I'm still contagious."

The doctors at the clinic said Günter should rest in bed as much as possible. A half year later, Andi realized Günter was starting to read again. He read any book Andi laid around. On Wilma's suggestion, Fritzy started to bring him books from the library where she worked. Fritzy explained: "Our building was hit in several places. We lost half of our collection, but now, the library is functioning properly. With the new GDR government gearing up, however, I expect it will soon stop people from reading books like this. It was just published, so maybe the authorities haven't figured out yet that it could be a satire on Stalin."

"Good grief!" Wilma exclaimed. A little smirk was Günter's only response.

"So far, I haven't been instructed not to let people read it, so I took a chance and brought it home. This is just between the three of us, OK?" After nods of agreement from Günter and Wilma, Fritzy started reading George Orwell's *1984*:

> It was a bright cold day in April, and the clocks were striking thirteen....

Wilma was mesmerized. She wished she could read as well as Fritzy. She watched Günter out of the corner of her eye. He seemed to be paying close attention, but after a half hour, he nodded off, so they quietly left Andi's apartment to let him sleep, taking the book with them.

That night, after Ursula was asleep and Fritzy finally went to bed, Wilma stayed up and read ahead in the book. The next day, Fritzy stayed late at the library, so Wilma took the book with her when she went for her afternoon visit. Günter appeared bright and enthusiastic about seeing her. Was it because she was alone, without Fritzy? No, she mustn't start thinking that way, she said to herself. "Would you like me to read further in the book?"

"Yes, but will Fritzy mind if we go ahead without her?"

"I don't think so. She's probably read the book already." Wilma, shamefully, had no idea if that were true. "As you probably remember from the farm, I don't read very well."

He smiled and asked her to please read to him. He closed his eyes, but made little comments every now and then, so she knew he was listening. When she came to the end of the chapter, he opened his eyes and asked her about it. They discussed, among other things, the possible meaning of 'doublespeak.' That evening, when she was back in Fritzy's apartment, Wilma could not stop smiling. Then she realized Fritzy, too, was smiling and looking at her.

The apartment building known as Die Birken at Hoffmannstrasse 141 was listed with the city as having five floors and 24 apartments. As was true everywhere in the Soviet Zone, rents were frozen at the level of the Weimar Republic. Andi followed suit. He charged his tenants such cheap rents that the income only covered operating expenses. There was no money left over to make repairs. Without the AFSC money, no improvements could have been made.

Of course there was no elevator, but Andi, with Klaus' help, hoped to restore the dumbwaiter. There was a shaft still, but its wire rope was missing. Its pulley and weights were also gone but those were easier to come by. Klaus figured 200 feet of continuous wire rope would be needed. It was not cheap, nor was it even available in East Berlin. Andi had to shop around to get it, but it was worth the effort. The dumbwaiter helped tenants get heavy loads upstairs.

The door from the street was unlocked until 7:00 P.M. Andi had a spring attached to it so that it would automatically close. During the day, the postal carrier had access to the stairs in the courtyard. Each apartment had a mail slot in its door.

By 1950, Andi felt he had accomplished his original goal. Thanks to the money from the American Friends Service Committee, which footed the bill for the large items—the stairway, electricity, plumbing, etc.—the building was fully operational. Once he had Günter enrolled in a TB clinic, comfortably sleeping on a cot in his living room, and being looked after by the very capable team of Wilma and Fritzy, Andi felt he could move on with his own life. He accepted the job that the CIA had offered him almost four years prior, but he decided to continue to live at Die Birken. BOB (the code name for the CIA) gave him fake papers, so he could easily travel from East to West Berlin.

BOB also informed him of the pitfalls of living in East Berlin, where Moscow's Ministry of State Security (the MGB) was in full control. But there was also the local secret police and espionage agency, the Stasi, composed of East Germans, to take into account. "There may well come a time when the Stasi competes with the MGB for dominance. Wouldn't that offer interesting possibilities?" his boss, George, posited.

Andi had hoped that by working in West Berlin, he would have greater access to Mark, who was now an aide to a West Berlin city councilman. Both Mark and Andi were fully occupied during the day with their jobs. They tried to set one night aside every week. It was usually a Thursday, but not always, as any pattern needed to be avoided. Typically, they would both register into the same bed-and-breakfast or hotel at different times and check out at different times, always careful not to be seen together. This situation was unsatisfactory, but what could they do? Mark was a high flyer and very visible. He knew he definitely wanted a career in politics. Andi wanted to stay in Berlin and use his linguistic abilities to help maintain peace in Germany. He knew the CIA would fire anyone who was a known homosexual.

Andi wondered what had happened to Wolfie's real wife? When he tried to talk to Günter about it, he remained silent. And who is the imposter, Gerda Morgandal? Poor Renate, he thought, to be left with a mother like that lump in apartment 302. He so enjoyed the girl's daily visits. He bought books for her to read. Over the years, he had become like a father to her, at the very time her real father was right there, on a cot in his living room. Günter didn't want to face this issue. He enjoyed watching and listening to Reni, but seemed to have lost the self-confidence to claim her as his child. Oh, God, why can't life be simple?

Maybe the real Gerda Morgandal is alive somewhere, living far away or in prison. Maybe she thinks Wolfgang is dead, so she doesn't look for him. Maybe she's dead and her death went unreported by mistake or by design. Wolfgang didn't seem very concerned about it. That was strange, too. Perhaps, if he were to show concern, he would have to act like Reni's father and doesn't feel capable of that, at least not now. Andi realized that he should not have so many expectations of his friend. He's going to need much more time to get back into his stride.

FRITZY

With the new currency established in West Germany, the economy there stabilized. As Mark had reported, people now rarely made purchases on the black market nor used cigarettes for cash. What would come to be known as the 'economic miracle' had begun. In East Germany, the situation was quite different. General Secretary Ulbricht eliminated all opposition there. The country was run by a one-party government, the SED. Wages were low and stagnant. Supplies were minimal.

East Germans were fully aware that the economy was better in the West. If they had the money, they would shop in the West to compensate for what they found lacking at home. On the other hand, West Berliners could save if they made a purchase in East Berlin, where some items were subsidized.

When, in 1953, Stalin increased factory workers' production quotas by 10% without a commensurate pay raise, over a million workers demonstrated and rioted. The uprising began in East Berlin, but quickly spread to other parts of East Germany. Much of what the workers produced already went to Russia, without benefitting the GDR. The East German government called it an emergency. The Red Army moved in with tanks and put down the revolt.

1953 was also the year when significant world leaders changed. The death of Joseph Stalin was cause for universal celebration, although not outwardly expressed within the Eastern Bloc. Khrushchev, a more moderate communist, replaced Stalin.

During the 'Khrushchev Thaw,' most forced labor camps were shut down. Eisenhower replaced Truman. The U.S. held tight to its containment policy. The Korean War ended in a stalemate. The West wanted Germany to rearm.

For the last two years, Günter had been working in Tiergarten, the huge park just west of the Brandenburg Gate, where he was being paid for planting trees on land denuded by the ravages of war. By this time, he had regained his former weight and he no longer coughed, although he still wasn't the extrovert Andi knew at the university. Was it his teeth (or lack thereof) that made his friend unusually quiet? Perhaps he was self-conscious about what missing teeth did to his looks. Yet, many men Andi saw on the street had impairments: a pinned up shirt sleeve, crutches, an eye patch, were all common sights. Maybe it's me, Andi thought. Working in the West, I've become accustomed to a faster pace. I'm expecting change to occur quicker. Günter's been through a lot and needs more time to adjust. I should just accept it.

Andi had decided to wait for Günter to speak to him about his wife before he tried again to find out where she was, and why. But after three years of waiting, he could see that Günter, unprovoked, was never going to say anything, and damn it, Andi wanted to know. Is it working for the CIA that makes me suspicious of everything, he asked himself? Have I changed? To be fair, he couldn't talk about his work or his personal life with anybody, so he could hardly blame Günter for being closed-mouthed.

Where should he start? The obvious person to ask was Heinz. But Heinz was the last person he wanted to deal with. Just yesterday, Andi overheard a mutual acquaintance say that Heinz's son, Walter, was causing him a lot of grief. Andi remained silent. Evidently, Heinz had said something like: "When the boy turned 16, I thought he was going to break up my marriage!" Andi didn't like Heinz, but he would never want to damage the man's marriage. By keeping his distance, Andi hoped to minimize

Heinz's memory of his connection to Walter. Little Shit could easily turn into Big Shit.

It's just that Heinz was the only person Andi knew who was a former Nazi. He had to get someone else to inquire for him. Andi now had an office of his own and an assistant, but he thought it best not to get the CIA involved in the inquiry about Günter's wife. The only other person who he was sure must know some former Nazis was Fritzy. She had lived in Berlin all her life.

"Oh yeah, I know some ex-Nazis. I'll see what I can do," Fritzy said. She wanted to help Andi, and she, too, thought Günter's situation with his marriage should be resolved, but she had problems of her own that she couldn't reveal. 'Bastard' would know exactly how to find out, but she wouldn't have anything to do with him. First, she planned to do a little investigation on her own. After all, she was a librarian.

Fritzy was one of the first people at Die Birken to realize that the Stasi had informers, just like the Gestapo had, but she suspected the Stasi had more of them. There were official Stasi who wore gray uniforms, but they were not the ones doing undercover work. The latter dressed just like everybody else. She had noticed the administrators at the library were increasingly concerned with protocol, protocol in tune with the Party line, that is. In fact, some people had been recently hired who probably had never read a book on their own. She had to be more careful and no longer joked with fellow librarians.

She shuddered at her temerity to have brought *1984* home three years ago. Günter and Wilma liked it so much that she even risked taking home another book by George Orwell: *Animal Farm*. That one, everybody knew, was banned. If caught, she would have had no excuse. Günter and Wilma wanted to be read to every afternoon. She decided she could risk books with a storyline that occurred before Karl Marx. *War and Peace* was the next book she brought home. That took a couple of months to read. She returned it each day to the shelf, but such regularity might be easily observed. Eventually, she had to tell Günter and

Wilma that she could no longer take such chances. But by that time, the seed had been sown. Wilma's interest in books had sprouted, and Günter was starting to talk more.

Andi complained to Fritzy: "He doesn't talk about anything else, like his former wife, Reni, or the war—just trees and books."

"Yes, he loves them. I've found that he is especially delighted with American authors. I don't know why."

"He majored in literature, but in the early thirties at Berlin University, that meant you studied mostly German and European authors. American literature is new to him."

"Well, now Wilma is wound up too. She just asked if I could get a copy of *Fahrenheit 451!*"

Andi wanted to help, so he began purchasing books in West Berlin. Surreptitiously, he brought them home to his apartment. He asked Klaus to make some shelves for them that could be hidden behind a panel.

Klaus was not political, but he was fully aware of the hazards of living under a communist regime. He had heard stories from fellow workers at the factory where he was apprenticed. He understood the need for discretion. It took a few weeks for him to find enough time to finish the job. Andi or Günter, whoever was last to leave the apartment in the morning, made sure a chair was placed in front of the panel, so it looked like it was part of the wall. He warned the rest of them that he had heard that Stasi agents would go into your home without your knowing it. The five of them used a code word when there was an alert: "BB" (standing for Big Brother).

Before she asked for help with Andi's inquiry from a Nazi acquaintance, Fritzy decided to research certain avenues on her own. Since Reni was born in 1938, she looked up the record of births in Berlin for that year. Sure enough, she found Renate Morgandal born on October 27, 1938, to Gerda and Wolfgang Morgandal. Great, this may be easier than she thought. Gerda's maiden name was listed as Gatzel. Since Andi said he went to university with Wolfgang, she thought maybe Gerda went to Berlin University as well. Again, she was lucky. Gerda Gatzel was two years behind Andi and Wolfgang. She majored in literature, and graduated in 1937. Wolfgang was conscripted in 1939 and was sent to Poland. Reni must have been just a baby. When exactly were they married, was the next question. With little difficulty, she found they got married right after she graduated. So far, everything was typical.

Wolfgang had mentioned to Andi that he had received only two letters from her. Wilma had told Fritzy that Günter showed up at her farm in March, 1940. Had Gerda already died by then? Maybe that's why he had only received two letters. But once he deserted, he wouldn't receive mail delivered to the Army, so she could have been alive for years. "Oy!" Fritzy said out loud in the library. It felt good to be able to say 'oy' again. During the war, nobody dared to use a Yiddish expression. Oh my God, what if Gerda was Jewish, she thought? Maybe she was arrested and taken to a concentration camp and then put on a train for extermination in Poland.

By eight years after the war, there was data. There were extensive lists of people who died at each type of camp: concentration, extermination, and labor. Gerda Morgandal was not on any such list, nor was there a Gerda Gatzel. Morgandal was an unusual surname, but not so with Gatzel. There was a Mertyl Gatzel, an Ute Gatzel, a Giselle Gatzel, but no Gerda Gatzel. Of course, this woman could have slipped through the cracks. If Fritzy couldn't find her death listed anywhere, she may still be alive. That would make it really difficult to find her.

Wait a minute. How could it happen that another woman took charge of Reni all of the sudden? And that woman has Gerda's name. If Gerda had suddenly died, Fritzy could see how the state would have another woman adopt Reni. But usually, in such cases, Reni's name would change to that of the other woman— but here, some woman has purposefully taken the name of the real mother. With Wolfgang away, no one would guess that the other woman wasn't the mother. Why would the state allow that, unless it wanted to cover up the real mother's death? If the real mother was a criminal, they wouldn't have to cover up killing her. Maybe the real mother did something that the state wanted to be kept secret, so they had to kill her. Let's see. We Germans are notorious record keepers, so her death would be recorded, but how? Maybe she was a resistor. Maybe she was executed, with no trial. Sure enough, Fritzy found a record of people who were executed for treason in the year of 1940. On February 10, there was a Gerda Morgandal, guillotined for delivering anti-Nazi leaflets. Jesus!

THE ESSAY

1955

Following the 1953 uprising, the GDR tried to somewhat appease industry and construction workers. General Secretary Ulbricht ended price hikes and made consumer goods more available, although work production quotas were not lowered. By 1955, the Stasi had the East German population under constant surveillance. Border crossings were increasingly difficult. By the mid-fifties, the only way East Germans could get to West Germany was through East Berlin. Every day in East Berlin, there were people with suitcases on west-bound public transport. Once someone reached West Berlin, they could get to West Germany.

This exodus was of great concern to the GDR authorities. Their youngest and brightest citizens were choosing to leave. To stave off this westward flow, East Berlin authorities offered their citizens some of the same attractions that were enjoyed in the west. To this end, the city opened a zoo, which they named Tierpark, to rival the world-famous zoo in West Berlin located in Tiergarten Park, which had been established in the 1700s.

By 1955, Günter had worked for four years planting trees at Tiergarten. Evidently, he was well thought of by his supervisor, because Tierpark Zoo wanted to hire him as a landscape planner. Günter's new job was a jump up in responsibility, although the salary was equivalent to that of his old job, when the value of the respective currencies was considered. At the time, the East German Mark was 1/5 the value of the Deutche Mark in West Germany.

Tierpark was located in Friedrichsfelde, on the grounds of the old Friedrichsfelde Palace. The zoo used the palace for its entrance. Soon, new buildings went up to house animals of all varieties. In stark contrast to the palace, they were made of concrete slabs—functional, but without grace. The management decided not to have an aviary, as the one in the West Berlin zoo was world famous and they wanted the East Berlin zoo to be distinct. Tierpark would have mostly large mammals: rhinos, hyenas, lions, and elephants, to take advantage of its ample space.

It was the grounds that excited Günter. They covered 400 acres, with few trees. All this room to plant trees, he thought. Indeed, his first assignment was to plant trees, but why just pines and only at the far end of the park? Günter initially thought the pine trees were to be planted there to delineate the zoo's boundary, where the property backed up to a road that marked the edge of Berlin. Here, construction of a large building had already begun. Two months later, the building was almost finished. Günter could not understand its purpose. There were no windows. If it were to house large animals, wouldn't it have to have ventilation and light coming in from the outdoors? Maybe there were skylights.

"What is the building for?" Günter asked the manager one day.

"Oh, it's just going to be a warehouse."

That made sense. The zoo had a lot of large equipment that should be put away, especially during the winter months. But then, a day later, it occurred to Günter that it was strange that the big door into the warehouse was on the back side, facing the driveway leading to a city highway. In a couple of years, the fast-growing pine trees would prevent people from seeing the warehouse altogether. Visitors to the zoo entered at the palace end where there was a subway stop (U – Tierpark). No attraction lured them to make the long, long walk to the warehouse.

Günter shared this puzzle with Andi one night and added: "I wish I were not just planting pines. I do love pines, but it's a shame to plant only pines. Of course, they're fast growing and they stay green all year, but woods are so much more interesting when they have both evergreens and deciduous trees. Mixed forests attract more insects and birds."

"Ha! Just another result of a planned economy," Andi said sarcastically, "planned at the top, messed up at the bottom."

As winter approached, Günter wondered what he would be asked to do once the ground froze. When November came, sure enough, he was assigned mostly indoor work. Evidently, the palace had had no permanent occupant for about twenty years prior to the war. Thereafter, he was told, a family of Jews hid somewhere inside. Once they were discovered and sent to Auschwitz, the army moved in and created offices. The dining room and ballroom were partitioned into many small spaces. At the end of the war, the palace was used for storage. Although the building had not been bombed, it needed considerable repair work: partitions had to be removed, walls plastered, and the management didn't know what to do about the flooring.

Soon, Günter found that the man they assigned to help him didn't know much and was lazy. He spoke to the manager, Herr Pfeiffer. "I know a good carpenter, Klaus Hartmann, who's young and strong. I think he would love this type of work." Although the manager didn't respond one way or another, Günter decided that night to ask Klaus if he would be interested in changing jobs. Klaus was definitely interested. He had finished his apprenticeship and was presently working in his master's furniture factory, but was finding the work boring; the same routine, over and over again. Furthermore, he didn't like always being indoors.

The next morning, to Günter's surprise, the manager asked him about Klaus. A week later, Klaus was working for Tierpark Zoo as Günter's assistant.

Back in 1946, when Andi was starting to repair Die Birken, he had to first get the holes in walls repaired and the doors fixed so they could be shut and locked. Only then could he work on the plumbing. Thank God, most toilets, sinks, and bathtubs did not have to be replaced. For decades, the two large zinc sinks in the basement had been used for washing. There were some extra tubs available for soaking, three-legged dollies for agitating the soapy water, and a hand mangle for ringing out the water. They could be used again, once the building was correctly connected to the mains. Andi decided to install a new toilet down there, for the convenience of whoever was working in the basement.

Klaus had strung wire along the outside of the stairway banisters, on which sheets could be hung. The drippings went into the courtyard. For years now, the 24 apartments followed the same washing schedule. The fifth floor washed sheets on a Monday, fourth floor, Tuesday, etc. There were wires in the basement that were reserved for the first floor apartments on Friday. On the other days, anybody could use them. This system meant that, on weekends, the courtyard had no sheets hanging in it and the building would be presentable for visitors.

This was the same system that apartment dwellers had used for decades all over Germany. Although there were electric washing machines that could now be bought in West Berlin, Andi thought he should not spend donated Quaker money on one. Besides, the tenants had gone through so many hardships at this point, they were grateful just to be able to do their laundry. The renovated dumbwaiter really helped in hauling baskets of laundry up and down, in addition to groceries and coal. It was constantly in use.

During the war, the storage alcoves in the basement had been looted and torn up. For many years thereafter, tenants had too few belongings to need storage. Once coal deliveries again became a regular feature in Berlin, people needed a way to keep their portion secure. Andi had Klaus repair the alcoves, using chicken wire for walls and a door of smaller mesh which could be padlocked shut. Each tenant could keep their coal in a small bin inside their alcove. In later years, other items were added, such as bicycles and baby buggies. Wilma kept her garden cart in Fritzy's alcove.

Andi worried about the planned economy and how it was affecting life in East Berlin. Although, he was still the manager of Die Birken, he knew it was just a question of time before the building would be taken over by the government. There were benefits to the communist regime, but they were the benefits of socialism: the guarantee of a job with a livable wage, one with which you could afford to pay your rent and buy food and other necessities. Subsidies helped to keep prices low.

In fact, Andi realized he was no longer needed at Die Birken. The building was functional and fully occupied. Actually, it had always been fully occupied. The Berlin housing shortage was still acute, even ten years after the war ended. Now there was no more AFSC money available. His job was done here. It was time to move to West Berlin and be near Mark. Furthermore, his responsibilities with the CIA had increased, and he had to devote more time to them.

Even after Andi started working at the CIA, Reni continued to drop in at his apartment after school, initially for the reason that there was nothing going on in her own apartment. Gerda didn't get home from work until 6:00 P.M., and Sabine was sometimes home, but she wasn't really company. At first, Reni wanted to see Wilma, and, it seemed, Wilma was always downstairs in Andi's apartment with Günter. Reni usually sat down at Andi's table and did homework, but she enjoyed overhearing Günter and Wilma talk about books. At times, they had different points of view, and argued those points vigorously.

Reni wished she could do that in school, but there, she had to be careful not to deviate from the usual things that she was expected to say. Class discussions weren't sincere. She rarely expressed her opinions, and she was quite sure others felt restrained too, although no one admitted it.

She heard Günter discussing things with Wilma, things that she knew were off limits. At those times, she was really interested in their conversation. Recently, Günter had started talking to

Wilma about the Russian scientist, Lysenko.

"When I was in the labor camp in Belarus, one of the men there who worked beside me cutting down trees, you know..." Günter paused. Reni thought he was getting emotional, but he soon went on, "...he was Russian. There were many Russians, being punished for all sorts of crimes. He was a Russian geneticist, who had been discredited. Many others lost their jobs and struggled to stay alive. When Sergei lost his job, he didn't take it quietly. He spoke out and said that Lysenko wasn't a true scientist, and that the man didn't know what he was talking about."

This was the first time Reni had heard Günter speak about his life before planting trees. She noticed that Wilma didn't say anything, but kept quietly listening to Günter.

"Many men there had stories of injustices," Günter continued after a pause. "This phony scientist, Lysenko, evidently had Stalin's ear. It's almost ludicrous, you see, soon after the revolution, in the early '20s, how the Party wanted to promote workers and peasants who had no formal education into leadership positions. This happened in many lines of work, I was told. Lysenko first got promoted in agriculture when Stalin collectivized the farms. Kulaks rebelled and were murdered or sent to the gulags. Stalin's excuse for collectivizing the farms was the tremendous increase in the number of men working in industry. There had to be enough food to feed them."

Reni wanted to ask what kulaks were, but she could tell from Wilma's reaction that she shouldn't interrupt. Günter started to laugh. Reni had never heard him laugh before. He looked peculiar with so many missing teeth.

"Lysenko eventually became the Director of Genetics for the Academy of Sciences, and that gave him control over the study of genetics. Yet, this so-called 'scientist' rejected Mendel's genetics findings, as well as the inheritance theories of Darwin and Lamarck!"

Günter took a deep breath and said: "A felled tree hit Sergei. It took him three days to die. There was nothing any of us could do for him. We were forced to keep on cutting trees."

Again there was a long pause. "I know you both probably don't know about those scientists."

Reni wanted to say that she knew something about Darwin, but reconsidered after glancing at Wilma. It was then that Reni realized how important a listener was in a conversation. Wilma didn't ask questions or try to change the subject so she could talk. She just quietly listened.

"I'd like to tell you about them someday, because I find their theories fascinating. I think you would too."

Günter had been rambling and Reni wasn't sure if she was following his gist. Suddenly she saw he was looking directly at her. He must have been aware that she was listening.

"I heard you tell Andi that you're taking biology."

"Yes," she answered, a bit surprised because when she had her talks with Andi, it was usually in the evening, when Günter was on his cot in the living room, fast asleep, or so she thought.

Several months later, Reni was assigned to write an essay about 'any person who has helped East Germany and deserved praise.' Her teacher expected students to choose Ulbricht or Wilhelm Pieck, etc. Reni immediately thought of the story Günter had told about Lysenko and his mistaken theory of inheritance. Lysenkoism certainly hadn't benefitted East Germany, but she wanted to write about it.

She went to Fritzy's library, to see if she had any ideas.

"I suggest you look up Lysenko and see if something occurs to you."

Sure enough, in her reading, Reni came across an East German agronomist named Hans Stubbe, who, for a long time, had doubted Lysenko's theory about heredity. This theory had led Lysenko to predict greater crop yields through a hardening of seeds, and to mandate a new system of crop rotation in Russia. But those ideas were not based on evidence. He did not use the empirical method. Applying Lysenko's theories proved disastrous. Soil became depleted, less food was produced, and many people starved. Hans Stubbe bravely stood up against Lysenko's ideas and prevented East Germany from taking the mistaken path that caused so much suffering in the USSR.

Reni made sure she never mentioned Stalin in her paper, but made it clear that Stubbe purposely avoided mixing politics or ideology with science. She explained that there was such a devout acceptance of Lysenkoism in Russia, geneticists who valued their job had to reject Mendel's discoveries. Now, under Khrushchev's premiership, the damage of Lysenkoism is being acknowledged. Khrushchev himself said: "Soviet agricultural research spent over 30 years in darkness."

Normally, Reni got As on her reports, but this time she got a C-, without an explanation of what was wrong. All she was able to see was her grade.

She would tell Andi tonight about her low grade. Even more upsetting to Reni was the fact that her teachers no longer seemed interested in her.

Fritzy often helped Ursula with her homework. The two were in the middle of a discussion about fractions when suddenly another part of Fritzy's brain lamented the fact that she was still living under a totalitarian regime. It was different in many ways from the one the National Socialists imposed, but like the Nazis, the communists wanted to control everything, even your thoughts and aspirations. She wished Ursula could be spared. Did Ursula understand what was happening?

Ursula had been going to Young Pioneers for three years. Everyone knew that Young Pioneers was a communist attempt to mold the minds of young people outside the influence of their parents. Membership was virtually compulsory, in the sense that if a child didn't join, they would be ineligible for a university education, and their career opportunities would be limited later on. The program encouraged love of the socialist fatherland.

Pioneer children wore colored scarves, hiked, sang, and crafted fun projects in their after-school time. Numerous Pioneer pageants and ceremonies were purposely scheduled to coincide with traditional church activities. The Nazis used similar procedures to indoctrinate children. Both Nazis and communists depended on these tactics and a secret police force to control people.

Fritzy tried to put such dark thoughts out of her head. She looked at the little ten-year-old sitting with her at the table, with her round face and sallow complexion. Her slightly slanted eyes sparkled with enthusiasm. Now, the school was encouraging her to get extra training in gymnastics. Fritzy knew Ursula was strong and agile. But at age ten, should she get extra training?

Suddenly, the door flung open without even a warning knock. Reni, out of breath from running up four flights, broke the news about her C- grade. Fritzy had read her essay before Reni handed it in. When the significance of what Reni was saying registered, she muttered a string of expletives under her breath. "Did you say your teacher kept the essay?"

THE BIRCHERS

The few improvements made to Die Birken after the ASFC money ran out had been paid for by some churches in Minneapolis. Finally, those churches wrote Andi to inform him that they wouldn't be sending any more money. By this time, Cold War attitudes blocked generosity from penetrating the Iron Curtain. With no more major improvements slated for the building, Andi knew the East Berlin government was likely to take control soon. It had already taken over most apartment buildings in the city. One day, he came home to find a large notice posted on the outside door to Die Birken informing tenants that from January 1, 1956, their monthly rent was to be paid to the East Berlin Housing Authority....

The basic work had been done. There were still bullet pockmarks on the outside. The stone bricks where the exterior had been repaired did not match the original. Andi could count at least five different types of bricks. In these times, a hodgepodge of surface materials made an acceptable facade. Several of the stone window frames had nicks and were missing corners, but those were trivial details. Andi was ready to let go. His CIA work was much too complicated and worrisome at this point to have the added burden of caring for the building.

A year prior, he had bought a secondhand Morris Oxford so his commute to and from West Berlin would go faster. He wasn't as much in touch with the people in Die Birken as he used to be. He supposed that was a natural development. They no longer had the mutual concern of getting the building repaired. They were going their separate ways. People seemed more guarded in what they said, sharing less about what they did. Was this due to the Stasi? Supposedly there were informers everywhere. Some probably lived in Die Birken.

Andi's thoughts switched to his friends. He noticed that Günter and Reni were now perfectly comfortable with each other. She called him 'Günter,' not 'Daddy.' And then there was Gerda. Doesn't Günter object to that female impostor? Occasionally, Günter went up to her apartment to talk with her—about what? Andi had no idea. Günter would come back down a few minutes later, perfectly calm. Does anything bother this man? When Fritzy told Günter that his wife, the real Gerda, had been executed, all he said was: "Thank goodness she was guillotined and not hanged." Had he witnessed so many horrible things in the war that one more death didn't affect him, even his wife's? These thoughts made Andi realize, once again, how lucky he was that he had avoided both military conflict and living under the Nazis.

Andi was different in other ways. He was gay. What made being gay hard was that he couldn't let anyone know he was gay. It was ironic that being gay would quickly get him fired from the CIA, yet he was a master of concealing his identity—just what the CIA wanted. Feelings of loneliness accompanied the need to suppress his true identity. Just like the others living in the building, informers forced him to immigrate inward.

Was he stupid to choose a job that required secrecy? He couldn't even tell people where he worked. He was listed as an assistant language lecturer at Free University. He did actually teach there, but only a couple of hours a week. His sixth sense told him that Günter knew he worked for "BOB." How could he know? But Günter knew. They had never talked about it. Just like Andi knew that Günter knew he was gay. They never talked about that either. Günter was so much quieter and subdued, compared to his prewar days. He could keep a secret. He acted like a fly on the wall. Damn, he'd make a good spy!

By working in West Berlin, Andi was well informed about the issues affecting Germany and Europe. Yes, his job required him to be informed, but he also had access to good newspapers, newspapers that were objective and committed to investigative journalism. He felt sorry for his friends at Die Birken. The press in East Berlin was controlled by SED authorities. Communist ideology determined what was put in print. Events that occurred in West Berlin were written about in such a way as to denigrate the Western lifestyle, its democracy, and leaders. News of the Hungarian Uprising in 1956, for example, was barely mentioned, and nothing was said about the Russian tanks rolling into Budapest to put it down.

Years ago, Andi had bought a radio for his apartment at Die Birken. Now Fritzy and Wilma had one, and even Klaus bought one, secondhand, for his sleeping area in the basement. Although the GDR didn't want its citizens to hear 'propaganda' (news) from the West, Andi knew they couldn't selectively jam West Berlin's stations and channels without jamming those from the East. The number of families owning TVs was increasing. In spite of their efforts to stay informed, whenever Andi brought home a West Berlin newspaper, his friends were amazed at the news they had missed.

Andi would see less of the folks at Die Birken going forward. They were like a family. He would miss them, but they were capable of managing things for themselves. The one person he felt still needed him was Reni, yet she herself was a puzzle to him. As bright as she was, she didn't seem to realize that Günter was her father. They look so much alike. How could she not know? They both were tall, with the same long pointed nose and square-shaped face. Andi knew their smiles were similar, too, for he could remember when Günter had a full set of teeth. Their hair was different. Günter's was brown, whereas Reni's was a light blond and wavy. She had that Nordic look the Nazi's so admired.

Reni was seventeen now and had only one more year of high

school. Like the rest of them, she had learned how to live in a communist society. Keep your mouth shut. Express your thoughts to only your closest friends. Maybe she did realize Günter was her father, and felt it best not to let on. But Andi wondered what harm could come if Günter revealed his patrimony?

Andi was concerned about Reni's academic future. For God's sake, due to one essay, the girl was ineligible for university in the Eastern Bloc. Such a bright mind should not be stifled. When Andi moved permanently to West Berlin, he wanted to take Reni with him, but how to do that? He wasn't her father.

Her 'mother' was such a lug. Once the communists took over Berlin, Gerda no longer received her widow's pension from the Nazi government. Everybody in the GDR had to work. Gerda was 'given' a cleaning job in a Stasi office building. She had no other outside interests. To Andi, Gerda had always seemed to be intellectually dead.

Sabine, now a junior at the University of Berlin, also wasn't stimulating for Reni, but for opposite reasons. Although dedicated and ambitious, she never had time for Reni or anybody else, for that matter. Sabine monopolized the apartment's one table with her books and made sure the noise level was kept to .1 decibel.

During the week, Günter came home from work so exhausted he was asleep by nine. He was up every morning at 5:30. That was plenty of sleep. It bothered Andi that Günter spent so little of his time at home paying attention to Reni.

A plan eventually formulated in Andi's mind for how Reni could get more stimulus than she was getting in East Berlin. It would be good if she could attend Free University, in West Berlin. Andi and Günter's alma mater, Berlin University, in East Berlin, had closed for a year, soon after the war. Many of its professors refused to teach in an institution that so blatantly prescribed what was to be taught, and that disavowed intellectual diversity and free speech. By 1948, a new university opened in West Berlin, named Free University. Many of the disenchanted professors from Berlin University transferred to Free University.

Over the eight years since Free University was founded, close to a majority of its students had come from East Germany.

Another part of Andi's plan was for Reni not to have to come home to Gerda each night. Andi tried to talk both Günter and Gerda into letting Reni come live with him, but neither wanted to let her go. However, Günter pointed out that Reni had only one more year of high school. "Mightn't Free University accept her now?" he asked. "You work there. Can't you put in a good word for her?"Although Günter's face was expressionless, Andi felt the intensity of his stare.

Günter was right. Andi spoke to the dean of admissions at Free University and explained why Reni had been discredited by her high school in East Berlin. The university was willing to give Reni an exam—a five hour exam! Reni's performance must have been satisfactory, for she was offered a place in its next freshman class. This pleased all the Birchers. Andi's only disappointment was their insistence that Reni would continue to live with Gerda.

One day, Klaus was reading an old copy of *Der Spiegel* that Andi had brought. "Hey, listen to this!" he addressed Andi and Günter. "According to this article, huge swastikas have been sighted in forests in East Germany. It says they're in pine woodlands. It's speculated that they wouldn't be noticed from the ground. So far, three have been spotted from planes near Braundorf, Mickelweiler, and Vogelsang. Here, look at this photo! It's a little blurry."

"Let me see," said Günter. "Very blurry, I would say. I wonder if they're like some of those henges spotted in England. Some became obvious only when planes flew over them."

"Or the Nazca lines," Andi added, "the ones that they've seen in Peru, the desert of Peru."

Klaus asked about henges and then about the Nazca lines. "People really think they might have been made by aliens from outer space?"

"Pretty preposterous, I know, but some people have suggested that explanation," Günter offered.

Andi and Günter smiled at each other as Klaus pursued the subject. "I wonder who made the swastikas. How do you think they made them?" Even though Günter had gone back to reading his book, Klaus tried to regain his attention. "I'd like to see if I could find a swastika. They're made of trees. How was it done?"

"Yes, it must be trees," Günter said. "Didn't you say they were seen in forests?"

"Yes. We could go looking with ropes and those clamps you put on your shoes to climb trees and get up high."

Andi enjoyed witnessing Günter being ensnared by Klaus' enthusiasm. "You should take a camera when you go."

It occurred to Andi that although the swastikas were sighted in East Germany, the East German news media hadn't reported them. He wondered why? Then he remembered how intent the communists were to claim that fascists were no longer to be found in the East, that they had naturally gravitated to the West where they were accepted. The CIA knew that the Stasi oversaw the desecration of Jewish tombstones with swastikas in Jewish cemeteries in West Germany. The Stasi strategy was very effective. West German newspapers highlighted this news for weeks, making the world think West Germany was a hotbed of Neo-Nazism—just what the Stasi wanted.

Andi's move to West Berlin simplified his life. He was made head of a team. Their job was to plan strategies to decipher where Russian missile sites were located in East Germany. He didn't have the physical requirements for field work. He lacked stamina and strength, but he was excellent at analysis. He could retain and recall vital information easily. Andi loved his job.

He and Mark had to keep reminding each other that getting caught in a homosexual relationship could mean a ten-year jail sentence. It was a criminal offence in Germany, East or West. Of course, under the Nazis, it had been worse. Then, it had meant a concentration camp and possible extermination. The looming 10-year sentence further intensified their feelings for each other, perhaps, but their devotion would have been intense even without such a threat.

Meanwhile, Die Birken had its own turn of events. The East Berlin city government suddenly evicted the family occupying the other first-floor apartment that faced the street. The family had no sooner moved out, when Sabine moved into that apartment. "She must be working for the Stasi," Fritzy commented. The others agreed. It was a prime location, and Sabine had not even been on a housing waiting list. Two weeks later, a telephone was installed in her new apartment. Gerda and Reni now had the third-floor apartment to themselves.

Over the last ten years, Wilma had managed to acquire three allotments. She still had the one in what had been the American sector and was now in West Berlin. At first, she disliked farming there, hearing planes landing and taking off, but once the airlift was over, there was much less noise. The other two allotments were adjacent to each other, thank God, and close by, in East Berlin. Ostensibly, they belonged to Fritzy and Klaus, but 85% of their farming was done by Wilma. Klaus and Günter had built a shed on each allotment, so it appeared that there were two different owners. Klaus also built a bird box for the allotment that was listed under his name and mounted it to the side of the shed.

Although they had avoided the worst practices of Lysenkoism, the communist policy of collectivization of farms proved just as inefficient in East Germany as it had in the rest of the Soviet Bloc. Shelves in grocery stores were sparsely stocked because food was hard to come by. Anyone who had an allotment was required to have at least one fruit tree. Altogether, Wilma planted five trees: one apple, two pear, and two plum. She also planted a gooseberry bush. The rest of the land was taken up with rows of beans, carrots, parsnips, potatoes, rhubarb, and cabbage. Her friends in Die Birken helped her with the planting in the spring and the harvesting in the fall.

To make up for the shortage of fruits and vegetables, the GDR required its allotment owners to sell their surplus produce to the state, which then passed the food along to the public at a loss. The price that the state paid was inflated so as to encourage allotment owners to provide as much food as possible. The GDR could not admit that collectivization was not as productive as private ownership, so they adopted this hidden subsidy. Allotment growers benefitted from the state's need to make amends for a faulty system.

Wilma also had her job with the postal service, which took up her time from 8:00 to 3:00. Ursula didn't get home from Young Pioneers until 5:00. Fritzy got home from the library at 5:30. This left Wilma with a half hour to be alone with Ursula. Fritzy was with Ursula most weekends and before she left for school in the mornings. In short, Ursula was blessed with two mothers, both of whom were happy with the situation. Fritzy and Ursula did not resent the time Wilma spent with Günter, which was usually a couple of hours in the late afternoons. In time, Günter spent a half day with Wilma at her allotment once every weekend, and recently, he did this on both Saturday and Sunday. He often came later with sandwiches for lunch. By this time, they had folding chairs, which allowed them to sit out on warm evenings. The previous spring, Klaus had helped them to enlarge one of the sheds on the double lot and put in a window.

Fritzy had a secret, or more a fantasy than a secret, or a fantasy that she kept secret. She had heard that the government had started manufacturing a car for East German citizens. It was called Trabant and it was designed in the GDR. The cost to buy one was 14,000 East German marks. It would be a struggle to get that much money together. Fritzy needed something to dream about, so what the hell, at work she decided to call the state-owned plant in Zwickau that had started producing Trabants. Occasionally, she had to call libraries in other cities. Fritzy hoped that whoever inspected the phone logs wouldn't notice that the number Fritzy called that day was not that of a library.

"The Trabi has a two-stroke engine in front," the salesman said. Fritzy smirked, knowing VWs were all the rage in West Berlin. Of course, the GDR wouldn't copy anything produced in the West. She was told other details: "plastic body, seats four people, a trunk, and electric windshield wipers."

"When would I be able to get one?" Fritzy asked.

"We have a waiting list of ten years or more."

"Jesus!" she said under her breath.

"And you have to make a down payment of 50%."

Fritzy had calculated what the down payment was likely to be and had already figured out she had enough for that. She had been saving money ever since her divorce. When she learned that she would have to make monthly payments until the car was paid for, she figured that would be no different than setting some money aside each month, which she was already in the habit of doing. Oh, what the hell. She ordered one.

THE WAREHOUSE

1961

Back in January, 1956, Andi had found an apartment three blocks from where Mark was living. It was also within walking distance of the Eastern European Studies building of Free University, where he taught and had an office. It took him only two trips in his car to get everything moved to his new apartment. He left his few big pieces of furniture back at Die Birken. His salary was so much higher than Günter's, he could afford to buy a new bed, sofa, and wardrobe. The move was relatively easy. Andi also left most of his books for his friends to enjoy.

For the last two years, he had visited Die Birken once a month on a Saturday. He tried to always bring something that was hard to get in East Berlin, like good coffee, good tea, canned meats, or fish. During that time, he occasionally mentioned that he had a spare bedroom if they ever changed their minds about Reni living with him.

Reni had spent her first two years at the university going home each night to sleep in Gerda's apartment. She told Günter and Andi repeatedly that it was a "real drag." Andi noted that she was sounding like an American more and more—sloppy diction, sloppy clothes. Ugh! She told him she never had time to talk to Gerda because she always had to study, but "What I do want to talk to her about are things that Mom just isn't interested in." Andi heard her once say to Günter, "She doesn't even ask me questions." Günter knew it was true. "Just when I have time to have a little fun with my friends, I have to spend the weekends here."

Immediately after that last remark, Andi noticed Günter taking Reni aside to have a long, private talk with her. What was said Andi didn't know, but when they opened the door and came out to rejoin the group, Günter thanked him for his generosity and consented to letting Reni live with him in West Berlin. "Gerda is also in agreement," he said. Reni added that she planned to come back to Die Birken with Andi whenever he came to visit. The deal was sealed.

Andi loved having Reni living with him. Her eagerness and curiosity energized him. Occasionally, they had some good late-night discussions, but he tried to give her a lot of freedom, which was what she wanted.

What Andi wanted was more time with Mark. But they were both so busy with their jobs, all they could do was to continue getting together on Thursday nights. Reni never asked why he was always gone on Thursday night. That told Andi that she probably knew what he was doing. From teaching at Free University, he knew students were savvy about gender matters and sexual orientations.

Andi and Mark found their lack of time together very frustrating. There was nothing they could do about it, though, short of going back to Sweden and seeking new jobs. They fantasized about having a small apartment in Stockholm, "close to the Quaker Meeting," Andi suggested.

"Maybe I could get my old job back with the newspaper," Mark speculated.

But as it turned out, the two of them were both willing to put up with their situation for a while longer. They both sensed that the political climate in Berlin was about to erupt.

Ever since Andi moved out, Klaus had more access to Günter. He hoped to lure Günter into new cycling ventures, like the time they had ridden to Potsdam along the River Spree and other waterways. That was a special outing. Klaus had taken the binoculars that Andi had given him. Günter had picked up a secondhand edition of a field guide to European birds. They successfully spotted herons, ducks, and grebes. Günter suggested: "Why don't you start a list of all the species you have sighted? Some people even write down the date, place, and time of day."

At first, Klaus thought that such detail would be excessive, but the more he got into it, the more he realized that it was all useful information. The time of day was even important. He often went to River Spree on his own. His list showed he had only seen a Black-crowned Night-heron in early morning or at dusk. Then he realized—of course, Night-heron—dummkopf!

Klaus started spending more time at Günter's apartment. Even though they worked together every day, they couldn't get into long conversations at Tierpark Zoo. Klaus enjoyed talking to Günter. A couple of years ago, he realized there were frequent late-afternoon reading sessions involving Wilma, Günter, and sometimes, Fritzy. He was proud that they kept the books hidden in the secret bookcase he had built behind the wall panel.

Klaus, himself, wasn't much of a reader, but he asked if he could listen to whoever was reading. The first time he joined them, they were into the third chapter of *A Sand County Almanac* by Aldo Leopold. Before Fritzy started reading, she explained to him that she was pretty sure this book had not been banned by the Socialist Unity Party (SED). Klaus wondered if that meant that other books they read *were* banned. He said nothing. He sat up, ready to listen. By the end of the week, they started the chapter entitled: "Thinking Like a Mountain." Klaus was hooked. He told them that some friends of his, when he worked at the factory, had been concerned about pollutants being dumped into the local rivers.

In the post-war years, floods of refugees, evacuees, and ex-POWs entered Germany daily. Most new arrivees went through several stages before they were fully processed for citizenship. First, they had to go to a transitional camp where they were put in a huge room with a floor covered in straw. They slept there without beds until they could be deloused. Then they were sent to a refugee camp which was like a tent city. If they were lucky, two months later, space would be found for them in some concrete slab barrack. Barracks were freezing cold in the winter and boiling hot in the summer. This was the normal naturalizing process.

The agencies involved were so overwhelmed that the relatively few arrivees who had a place to go were fast-tracked to citizenship. Once you had an address, you could be naturalized. The authorities didn't question the origins of Günter Beck because they didn't have the time to investigate. Like his Russian captors, they took him at his word that he was a Pole with German heritage.

Even in February of 1961, there were still people living in barracks who were being naturalized. Wilma, Günter, Klaus, Sabine, and Walter had all avoided these stages because a place was found for them in Die Birken.

Wilma and Günter announced their engagement on a Saturday. They had waited until the weekend, when Reni and Andi were visiting, to tell everyone together. They were officially registered as German citizens, to be married on Saturday, August 19, 1961.

Birchers and other friends were gathered in Günter's apartment, not knowing the reason for the party until Günter made the announcement. Hearing their good news, Andi couldn't help but feel jealous, while simultaneously being ashamed of having such thoughts. Of course, he wanted his friends to be happy. He kept smiling, despite feeling bitter that he could never publically celebrate his love for Mark. He chastised himself for feeling self-pity, hoping his outward smile would cover up his inner turbulence. He mustered his diplomatic training. He even cracked a feeble joke about booking a tree house for their honeymoon. He looked around. Everybody was laughing, but he caught Günter's glistening eye. His friend's smile was subdued. Was he still embarrassed about his missing teeth?

Fritzy popped a bottle of champagne and poured a little in mismatched glasses for everybody to toast: "To Wilma and Günter."

"Prosit!"

Where did Fritzy buy a bottle of champagne? Andi wondered. Nobody asked.

"We want to move to a rural area in West Germany and run a small farm," Wilma said.

Oh, oh, Andi thought. Wilma shouldn't mention any future plans if they involved West Germany. She should know better. That will be remembered. She was acting giddy, possibly due to the champagne. Günter moved next to her and added: "That's just one idea. Actually, we know we'll have to work quite a few years longer until we have enough money for that."

Wilma looked at Günter and said: "Yes, we'd be happy anywhere, and especially if we could garden, have a couple of animals, and read books together."

Oh gees, she shouldn't say 'books!' Was Andi being too cautious? He noticed Klaus popping cheese hors d'oeuvres in his mouth, commenting how good they were. "Oh, Gerda brought those," Günter informed him, giving Gerda a warm smile.

"Fritzy, thanks for the flowers," Wilma said.

Andi looked around the room while sipping his champagne. Good grief, Sabine's here! Maybe no one else knows she's working for the Stasi. She was sitting quietly in a corner, appearing to be taking in every word. In the past, Sabine would have refused to come to something so frivolous as a party, or so he thought. Who invited her anyway? She's not joining in on the banter, of course. Andi watched Klaus approach her, holding a plate of the cheese nibbles. She took one, but hardly looked at him. It was her pretty face that urged Klaus to give her more attention than she wanted. It was not the first time Andi noticed Klaus' infatuation. Try as he did, Klaus could not engage Sabine in conversation. Reni stepped up to them to divert Klaus' attention.

Fascinating, Andi thought, while putting on an appearance of casual contentment. Finally, it occurred to him that Sabine and Gerda had to be invited to the party, as Gerda's apartment had been home to both Reni and Sabine. Surely, the others must know that Sabine works for the Stasi. She's probably one of their rising stars. It seemed so obvious to Andi, but then he'd been trained to look for special behavior. There she is, trying to listen to all the conversations in the room, probably cursing Klaus for distracting her. Too bad, Andi thought, that it's too late to tell them what he suspected and warn them to watch what they say in front of her.

Wilma knew their intention to marry took no one by surprise. She had talked it over with Fritzy many times. The issue of most concern was if she lived in the West, would GDR authorities allow Ursula to visit her. She had explained this to Ursula, but the girl didn't seem to care as long as Wilma could come to East Germany to visit her. Wilma realized her daughter was definitely a teenager now. She was involved with her local friends and school. Her horizons didn't reach further than a couple of years into the future.

Wilma also had to confirm with Fritzy that she would be comfortable being solely responsible for Ursula if she and Günter moved to West Germany. Guilty as this made Wilma feel, she also knew that Fritzy would love it. There had been many, many times over the years that Wilma had left Ursula in Fritzy's care—all those weekends she spent at her allotments, to say nothing about the afternoons she was with Günter. In fact, Wilma knew that by this time, Ursula felt closer to Fritzy than to herself. Fritzy had been the better mother.

Reni was not a problem. By the time Wilma and Günter would be married, she would need just two more courses to graduate from Free University. After that, she could choose where to live. She still hadn't decided what kind of work to pursue.

VOGELSANG

By 1961, the GDR was hemorrhaging. As many as 2,000 East Germans were leaving East Germany every day. Their exit path led through East Berlin. Once in East Berlin, they went through a checkpoint, then walked, drove, or took a local train to West Berlin. Once in West Berlin, they boarded express trains or drove on a highway with no exits through GDR territory, until they reached West Germany. The Stasi tightened control and increased surveillance, but they couldn't prevent East Germans from leaving to go to the West.

Khrushchev said he wanted peaceful coexistence. He told Eisenhower he was willing to reduce Russian troops around Berlin and suggested having a summit to discuss limiting nuclear arms. What he wanted from Eisenhower was a promise that the United States would not send any more U–2 spy planes over Russia. Eisenhower made that promise, but Ike's Secretary of State, John Foster Dulles, insisted on sending one more spy plane. The Russians shot it down. Eisenhower claimed the plane was simply monitoring weather conditions and mistakenly went off course, but the Russians knew better. They had recovered the pilot, Gary Powers, and his camera. Disgusted, Khrushchev cancelled the summit and gave the Western powers six months to pull out of Berlin.

Tensions were high when Andi returned to West Berlin after the engagement party. He had to let go of his concerns for his friends at Die Birken. Trouble was brewing in Cuba. Pressure increased to locate where the Soviets had stationed missiles in Europe, the task of Andi's team at the CIA. In the next month, he learned of a possible site near the remote village of Vogelsang, located a hundred kilometers northeast of Berlin. He had received word that the inhabitants of an isolated house 15 km from Vogelsang had been relocated and were compensated 4,500 rubles. Andi asked George, his boss, if there could be some reconnaissance in that area. At great risk, the CIA had a spy plane fly over the region, but it was so densely forested that nothing could be seen.

As many spies as the CIA had, it never had enough. A year or more ago, Andi had told Günter that the West German government would like to hire someone like him to be a spotter.

"A spotter, what do you mean?"

"Oh, you know, they would like to know if Soviet troops or equipment are being moved around."

"You mean I should park myself at a strategic intersection and count the Soviet vehicles passing by? It certainly wouldn't be very exciting."

"Well, they could offer you exciting things to do, as well."

"No thank you. No spy work for me."

Andi dropped the subject, but he still kept the notion in the back of his mind. Günter would be brilliant at clandestine work.

When Andi received the tip about Vogelsang, he thought he had heard of that town before. What was it? Then it came back to him, recalling the article in *Der Speigel* about swastikas in the woods. He remembered Klaus was excited about searching for one. He didn't have the magazine anymore, so he went to the CIA library to bring it up on microfiche. Yes! One of the possible locations where a swastika had been seen was near Vogelsang.

The next visit Andi made to Die Birken was in March. He was able to take Klaus aside before he went out on his Saturday bike ride. "Do you remember the swastika sightings?"

"Oh sure. Any more news?"

"Not anything definite, but perhaps around 15 km northeast

of the town of Vogelsang, I recently heard."

"And how far away is Vogelsang?"

Andi told him, but said nothing more. Best if Klaus thinks of the details himself. Andi didn't want to appear to be pushing it. A few minutes later, Klaus had more questions.

"How do I get there?"

"Hmm, I'm not sure, but maybe a train going north might make a stop there."

"I could take my bike on the train, couldn't I?"

"Uh-huh." Andi pretended to be preoccupied with other thoughts.

"Vogelsang! Hmm, I wonder if there are many birds there," Klaus said out loud.

"With a name like Vogelsang, I would think so. Definitely take your binoculars and your notebook."

Klaus got Günter to agree to a day trip to Vogelsang. Over the next three weeks, Klaus continually asked Günter about the forest swastikas. "How could they be made with trees? "

"It's a pine forest?" Günter asked.

"Yes, I think so."

"My guess would be that other trees that look different were planted in the pattern of a swastika among the pines."

"Oh yeah, but what kind of trees?"

"I don't know. Why haven't they looked from the air?"

"I think they have, but they haven't found them."

"That's strange. You mean someone sees it, then when they go back to look, they can't find it."

"I guess."

"Hmm, maybe the swastika trees change their appearance."

"Oh yeah, maybe that's it."

It seemed to Klaus that Günter was putting off finding out about the train to Vogalsang. Klaus wasn't sure Günter really wanted to look for a swastika in a pine forest. He knew that Günter was preoccupied by his upcoming marriage. So as not to pester him further, Klaus decided to go to Fritzy for help.

Fritzy found the train schedule. "I am surprised the train would even stop at such a small community, but evidently, many people from Vogelsang now live and work in Berlin and want to return to the village they grew up in for visits."

Finally, a month later, Klaus got Günter to go on a cycling outing to Vogelsang. They left at 5:00 in the morning. Günter and Klaus rode their bicycles to Lehrter Stadtbahnhof, the central railroad station in Berlin, to catch the 6:02 train to Karlsbühl, which supposedly had a stop at Vogelsang on Saturdays. They put their bikes on the train, and two hours later got off at the small village, which consisted of about 30 homes.

Günter had brought a compass. "Now, you said the sighting was 15 km northeast of Vogelsang?"

"Yes, that's what Andi said."

"Andi?" Hearing this made Günter nervous. Did Andi have a reason to encourage Klaus to look for swastikas? he wondered.

Whenever they came across someone in the village, they asked if there was anything unusual in the area that they might try to see on their bike tour. One man said: "I saw some large trucks come through town at three in the morning. What was strange about it was that they were driving very slowly, with no lights on—just two nights ago. The trucks were huge, twice the size of a normal lorry."

Günter mulled over the man's revelation. What could those trucks have been carrying—lights off, 3:00 in the morning? The only thing Günter could think of were missiles. He wondered if the trucks were Soviet or GDR trucks, probably Soviet. He didn't share these thoughts with Klaus.

They decided to ride their bikes north on the paved highway that went through the town. Someone had told them that, five kilometers outside of town, there would be a road, also paved, that veered off to the northeast. "That road eventually turns into a dirt road, but it's in good condition and it will lead you into the forest."

When they got to the dirt road, Klaus spoke up about the extremely wide tire marks he was seeing. "Maybe they're from the tire treads of the big trucks the man was talking about." "Yes, I think you're right. Let's ride our bikes in the tread marks they made. I'll take the one on the left, you, on the right. That way, our tire tracks won't be so noticeable." Günter was worried. Klaus would be so disappointed if they decided to go home without even getting into the woods to search for swastikas. Should they leave the road now, he wondered? It was around 10:30 A.M. and they were still several kilometers away from their designated target area. What if a Soviet vehicle drives past us? They could stop us and ask questions. If they thought we were suspicious of what was going on and looking for some evidence, they wouldn't hesitate to kill us. Günter wondered if he should tell Klaus what he was thinking and leave it to him to decide what they should do.

Günter kept his eye on the side of the road looking for a place to pull off. Finally, he saw something promising. "Here's an old logging road. Let's pick up our bikes and carry them onto that logging road so we don't leave a track."

"What? Why?" In spite of not understanding, Klaus followed Günter and carried his bike off the road. Then, like Günter, he pedaled as far as necessary to be out of sight of the road. Once Günter stopped, he asked: "What's going on?"

"Let's eat half of a sandwich while I explain something," Günter suggested. Partway through the explanation, Günter noticed Klaus' eyes lighting up. Clearly he was excited.

"Cloak and dagger stuff. Who would have thought?"

But when Günter mentioned that the Soviets might be using cameras to watch the road or even have snipers ready to shoot intruders, Klaus turned pale. "If they suspect we've seen or know something about their nuclear missiles—believe me, they wouldn't hesitate to kill us. Now what do you want to do?"

Klaus was silent but managed to devour his half sandwich. "Maybe we should ride a bit further, and then walk. I'd like to do some bird-watching. And I want to use the clamps to climb a tree or two."

Günter couldn't help but smile. He loved this young man's enthusiasm. "Let's follow this logging road and see where it leads us." Günter checked on his compass. "Ah ha, it's going northeast. That's the direction we intended to go anyway." They pedaled on the old road as best they could. From its rough condition, it appeared that it hadn't been used in years. In spite of its bumps and thick mud in spots, it was easier than going through the woods on no path at all. It was a long road with some curves, but generally, it headed northeast.

After five kilometers or so, Günter was hungry again and hoped Klaus would see some birds or something so they could stop. There was no end to the kid's energy. At last, Klaus suggested that they stop. Günter insisted they put the bikes behind a bush and carry their rucksacks with them. Beside a little food and water, they each had a light load of other necessities. Klaus had two ropes, a puncture repair kit, a set of climbing cleats, binoculars, and his little notebook. Günter also carried cleats, a flashlight, a compass, a knife, and the little camera that Andi had given him a year ago.

They started to walk. When they came to a clearing, at Klaus' suggestion, they stopped and waited, motionless, at its edge, out of sight, so they wouldn't flush animals or birds, for about ten minutes. Günter didn't want to discourage Klaus, but he thought he had heard that pine forests were not good for seeing birds, because they have few insects.

As soon as he had that thought, a grouse-like bird strutted out of the brush and into the middle of the small clearing. Klaus could hardly contain himself. He whispered: "A Capercaillie!" The large black bird fanned its tail vertically and pranced around in circles. A second later, a gunshot rang out. Instinctively Günter and Klaus crouched down. The bird fell over dead. Two men wearing Russian uniforms rushed out into the clearing. One carried a gun. The other picked up the dead bird. Günter understood them to say that they would eat well tonight.

The men went back the same way they had come, still chatting, but too far away for Günter to decipher more of what they said.

"How could they kill it?"

Günter hated to see the bird killed, too, but he was scared and hungry. He convinced Klaus to remain hidden and eat more of their lunch. Klaus then wanted to continue pedaling down the log road. "After all, the soldiers came from another direction."

Günter was willing to walk, not ride, and only for a 100 yards or so. He suggested that Klaus could select a couple of trees suitable for climbing, but then they should make their way back home. They both knew the only train they could catch to get back to Berlin stopped at Vogelsang at 5:10 P.M.

Klaus chose a larch tree. "This is good, don't you think, because the trunk is straight?"

"But look up, there's not much cover up there. We'd stick out and could easily be seen. Larches are deciduous. That's unusual for a conifer. They actually lose their needles in winter. Of course, now, it's spring…oh my God, of course…," Günter stopped in mid-sentence.

"Yes, what are you thinking?"

Günter kept looking up at the crown.

"What are you seeing?"

"I'll tell you later. Let's get this climbing business over. Choose another pine."

Günter was also uneasy because Klaus had never used cleats with spikes on his shoes to climb a tree. They didn't have helmets. They didn't have an actual harness. Each had a rope around his waist to which carabineers attached to another length of rope that served as a hitch around the tree. Günter demonstrated the method. Then Klaus tried, but Günter would not let him go higher than five feet. Klaus practiced five feet up and down. He did this over and over again, until Günter was convinced he understood the system. For a fleeting moment, Günter worried about what they would do if Klaus turned out to be afraid of heights, but then he laughed at himself. What nonsense! That's actually the biggest problem of all: Klaus is not afraid of anything!

They made it up to the first strong branch in their respective trees. Klaus took out his binoculars. Not satisfied at the view, he released the hitch so he could climb up to higher branches. The whole time, Günter worried that he might slip. When he got up 15 feet higher, he had the sense not to shout out, but his body language indicated that he was alarmed. He spread out his arms to suggest a big scene, then he pretended to be shooting a gun.

Oh my God, this is it! Günter thought. He wouldn't have the chance to marry Wilma. What to do? He better try to see for himself. At least, the higher they were in the canopy, the less likely they would be spotted. Once up at Klaus' level, he looked down and saw that there was a linear gap in the trees that started some fifty feet from their position. The gap was about 10 feet wide, not wide enough to be seen from an aircraft, Günter thought. He saw uniformed men walking around. The gap was like a corridor that ran in a straight line to a distant circle. Günter could see the circle because it was an open space, void of trees. Does the circle mark where an airplane should make a drop? Or, is it where a missile silo is located?

What's Klaus doing now? It appeared he was tying a rope to the binoculars. Günter watched him hold one end of the rope and throw the binoculars to Günter, but Günter was not willing to let go of his grip to catch them. Klaus lost his grip of them at the other end of the rope and the binoculars went hurtling down. Fortunately, the other end of the rope got caught on a low branch. Klaus' grimace indicated that he realized he shouldn't have tried that maneuver. Günter signaled for him to stay put. He scrambled down and started hitching himself up Klaus' tree to the low branch from which the binos were dangling. Gingerly, he shimmied himself out on that limb and stretched to reach the rope. He secured the binos in his rucksack and climbed up to join Klaus. They should have climbed the same tree in the first place.

Now that Günter could look through the binoculars, he clearly saw that the channel led to a circular area, somewhat exposed, in the distance. Looking over a wider panorama he saw, at the canopy level, that there were four other subtle discontinuities, quite linear, and all leading to the circular center. With the aid of the binoculars, it appeared that there was a metal cover at the center of the circle. It had to be an underground missle silo!

Günter had seen enough. Now, he had to get Klaus off the tree safely. They both climbed down to where there were no more branches. Günter made sure that Klaus' spikes were firmly in place and his hitching rope was solidly attached to a carabiner. He went over the procedure. "Remember, don't drop the hitch lower than your waist." Klaus made it safely down. Günter followed. They quickly took off their clamps and put all their equipment back in their rucksacks. It was 2:00 p.m. They walked as silently as possible to where their bikes were hidden. Thoughts of an ambush kept Günter on full alert, but riding on the logging road went well.

When they came to the dirt road, they looked up and down it before going out to ride in the big tire tracks. They pedaled as fast as they could, all the time, dreading hearing the sound of approaching vehicles. They heard nothing but the wind soughing through the pine trees, and made it back to Vogelsang in time to catch the train.

Once in their seats, they could relax. Günter remembered to tell Klaus what he realized in the woods. "Remember looking up at the crown of the larch, you know, the first tree you chose to climb?"

"Yeah."

"Do you remember what color it was?"

"Hmm, sort of a pink, wasn't it?"

"Yes, that's the color it displays in the springtime when it's in bloom. Then the needles come out and it again appears green. In fall, the needles turn yellow and, eventually, they fall off because, as I said, a larch is a deciduous pine."

"Ah ha, so if the swastika is made up of larch trees, you can only see it in spring and fall."

"That's right, so, much of the year, you can't see it."

"People observe it, but then when they go back later, they can't find it."

"That's right." Günter thought, Klaus is a bright young man. They had eaten the last of their lunch while they waited for the train. Now, Günter was sleepy. His eyes were beginning to droop.

"Before you go to sleep, what do you think we should do about what we saw today?" Klaus asked.

"I think we should tell Andi. If there are missiles there, they are going to be pointed west. He'll probably know whom to tell."

"Andi is in the CIA, isn't he?"

Günter was shocked. "Why do you think that? No, he teaches at Free University."

"I know he does, in theory, but I think he does some other things, too."

"Good heavens! You've got a good imagination. By the way, I would never tell anybody what you think. True or not, it could cost him his life."

"Yes, I know. I would never say it to anyone. Andi has been terrific. He's done so much for all of us."

"Yes, he has," Günter admitted, not mentioning that sending the two of them out into the woods to look for Soviet missiles was one of those things, apparently.

"You know, Little Shit said Andi is gay," Klaus added.

"Who's Little Shit and how would he know that?" Günter asked, even though he did have some idea, since Wilma and Fritzy had told him all about the little monster, and he had known Andi was gay for many years. "Klaus, you mustn't tell anyone about Andi, or anything we saw today, for that matter. It could put all of our lives in danger." Günter thought some more, then added: "In fact, we shouldn't even tell anyone where we went today. Does anyone know?"

"I don't think so...well, except Fritzy and Wilma."

"Let's just tell anyone else we went on a long bike ride."

"When is Andi going to visit us again?"

"I think he's planning to come next Saturday."

"Can I be present when you tell him?... How could they shoot a Capercaillie?"

"I know, that was terrible, but also, it was fortunate. The gunshot let us know they were there before they could see us, or we saw them."

Minutes later, Klaus told Günter about a lek. "There probably were females watching that bird strut."

"You've certainly learned a lot about birds."

"Fritzy brings home books for me."

"Really? I haven't seen them?"

"I keep them in the bookcase with all the others."

What a pleasant young man, Klaus is, Günter thought. Too bad his parents aren't alive to see how well he has turned out. He thought of his own daughter, Reni. War does this to families. We're all like pieces in a kaleidoscope: twisted, broken up, and released to fall into a new pattern. The original pattern is gone forever. It had been twenty-two years since he'd seen Gerda, but he could still remember so much of the time they had together. They were such idealists, had so much confidence in themselves. It reminded him of how broken he became in Belarus.

Günter caught himself drifting off to sleep. He didn't want to sleep. He wanted to talk with Klaus. This was his chance to hear about Klaus' life before the war. He could tell Klaus was glad to discuss it. Günter, at times, had to fight back tears. Klaus' story told of a close, loving family until the age of 14. That was enough to keep him directed on a good path. How wonderful.

PREPARATIONS

Before she got married, Wilma had several things she had to take care of, some of which were long overdue. She wanted to determine if her refugee friend, who was killed by shrapnel, had any relatives in Berlin. From the papers she found among her belongings in the cart, she had learned her friend's name was Frieda Liebermann. A photo suggested that Frieda had a husband and two children. Were they killed? Why was she traveling to Berlin? That was the biggest mystery. Maybe she has relatives here? Maybe she lived here before the war? Wilma had heard that there were about 200 Jews still living in East Berlin after the war. Why would they stay here?

A day in late June, instead of going back to Die Birken after her postal run, Wilma took the tram to Hackescher Markt and walked to Oranienburgerstrasse, to the New Synogogue. She loved the thought that a building was called 'new,' when it was constructed in 1866. Günter told her about the synagogue as it was before the war. "It was built in the Moorish Revival style, really beautiful."

"What style is that?"

"It produced buildings with pointed domes—onion domes they're often called, and arches that look like horseshoes. They were decorated with mosaics, both inside and out."

"Does that have anything to do with the Jews being pushed out of Spain?" Wilma was proud that she now knew enough about history to ask a decent question. Over the years, Günter had taught her so much that she was no longer embarrassed about her lack of a formal education.

"Yes," he affirmed, "evidently, Jewish architects wanted to remind Jews of their golden age, which coincided with Muslims being in medieval Spain."

Once she started walking up Oranienburgerstasse, Wilma had her eye out for a magnificent building with onion domes. Günter told her it could seat about 3,000 people. When she arrived at where it should have been, she read a sign that said, "In 1938, the synagogue was broken into and set on fire during Kristallnacht. The remains were destroyed by British bombs at the end of the war. By 1953, Cold War pressures caused the congregation to split." Wilma learned that Jews still met in the two remaining small buildings. Finally, just two years ago, that small group of Jews was ordered by the GDR authorities to demolish the rest of the building, if they didn't have the money to restore it.

Wilma was directed to a man in the synagogue's small library, Aaron Siegel. He was short in stature, with rimless glasses. Wilma told him her story about Frieda. After a brief search of the records he had in his office, there was nothing documented about her or her family, but he said he would continue investigating with other Jewish agencies. Wilma was pleased that he took such interest. She asked if the synagogue would be interested in having Frieda's belongings from her cart.

"Certainly."

"May I ask…I don't understand why she would want to come to Berlin."

"You say she came from Poland?"

"Yes. I think from the photograph that she may have lived in Warsaw."

"You know, Jews were not safe in Poland after the war," Herr Siegel told her.

"Really?"

"Many were murdered by Poles who had witnessed the atrocities committed by the Nazis and had become indoctrinated in their hatred. So, it could be that your friend Frieda thought she would be safer in Germany where, after the war, the Nazis were condemned for their treatment of Jews." Aaron chuckled for a moment before continuing. "The East Germans take it one step further, by claiming all the fascists are in West Germany." He shrugged his shoulders while smiling sardonically. "So, we are safe here, but make no mistake, not because they like us. We are still pawns, but this time, to support another ideology."

After returning to Die Birken, Wilma retrieved Frieda's belongings from Fritzy's storage alcove in the basement. She cleaned out her cart, which was dirty from her work at the allotments, and placed Frieda's items atop, including the little box and notebook she had kept upstairs in Fritzy's apartment.

To return to the New Synagogue the next day, Wilma could not take the tram because she had to pull the cart. It took her two hours. As she walked, she was overcome with the memories of her flight from Poland at the end of the war—the loss of Grandpops, thinking she would never see Günter again, relishing her brief friendship with Frieda, and not knowing what was in store for her.

Other people looked at her in bewilderment. Seeing her pulling the handcart must have summoned up their own memories after the war. One woman started to cry. Another asked if she needed help. Wilma felt she was on a pilgrimage.

Leaving the cart out on the street, she went in to fetch Herr Seigel. He helped her to lift the cart gingerly down some steps, so they could wheel it inside. They took out Frieda's belongings, one by one, putting them on a table. When they got to the wooden box, Wilma opened it up to show him the pictures and letter. She took out the wooden object and asked him what it was. He said it was a *mezuzah*, and was usually hung outside on the wall next to the door. "What is its purpose?" she asked.

"It signifies a Jewish home."

When they were finished, he asked her: "Would you like to keep the cart? It looks like you like to garden." He must have noticed the dirt under her fingernails. Wilma hesitated. He added: "I imagine Frieda would like you to have it."

Günter also had some things to get done before he married Wilma. Although he was only two years older than her, he felt he looked fifteen years older. He wasn't as strong as he should be. The five years he spent in the Belarus labor camp had really taken their toll. He had recovered from TB all right, but not from the injury to his right arm from an accident that occurred at the camp. Safety equipment, like goggles or face shields, were nonexistent. Only half of the men had helmets. At one point, a group of them were logging a steep slope. That was always a dangerous situation. The supervisor's theory was that the trees should be felled in patches, starting with about five trees at the bottom of the slope. Those should be felled in the direction perpendicular to the slope, delimbed, and then rolled into a pile. Then, you'd take on the next higher patch.

On the day he was injured, a new man had just arrived who didn't speak Russian or Polish. It was likely he had not understood the supervisor's instructions. Günter was using his chainsaw to delimb and the new guy mistakenly felled a tree in the next higher patch above him. One of the limbs of that tree hit Günter's arm, knocked his chainsaw out of his hands, and pinned him down.

The supervisor was aware of what happened. When he saw Günter was injured, he still insisted that the first patch be finished. Quotas had to be met, regardless of safety issues. A guard was always at hand, ready to kill an injured worker who couldn't go on. A replacement would soon arrive. Once the supervisor finally ordered the branch to be lifted off of Günter, he had to continue working, despite the excruciating pain he felt. His arm had never healed correctly.

The pain in his right knee Günter attributed to arthritis. Should he have arthritis at age 49? He felt he looked like an old man. How could Wilma want to marry him? And, of course, missing so many teeth! Another Belarus legacy. For the last five years, he had been training himself to smile with his mouth closed. Maybe he could do something about it, like get false teeth? Andi said his dentist in West Berlin was excellent. Günter had trouble trusting doctors in the GDR. He had heard what the Russians had done to East German factories. They probably stripped dental offices, both of dentists and equipment, and shipped them off to Moscow, too. After much thought, Günter asked Andi to make an appointment for him with his dentist.

Before they left West Berlin, Günter wanted to show Wilma some of his favorite sites at Tiergarten. He hadn't been back much since he began working at the zoo, and he had never been there with Wilma. His dental appointments were scheduled at the perfect time to go, in late spring. Once through the checkpoint, they walked together through Brandenburg Gate and into Tiergarten Park. He wanted to show her the gardening technique of espaliering trees. He was fairly sure it would be new to Wilma. They walked to the lower east end of the park.

"It is lovely, but how do they get it to look like that?"

"I'd like to try to do it myself someday, if we ever have a farm again. The process takes years, as I understand it. In the spring, you prune the plant, a pear tree for example, down to say 16 inches off the ground."

"Just imagine having several years on a farm together." Holding hands, they moved closer to one of the espaliered trees.

Smiling, Günter went on to explain: "Then, in the summer, supposedly, the buds will lengthen into branches. You train one of them to grow vertically up to the next wire. The others are trained to grow horizontally, along the wires."

"So you arrange the wires first?"

"Uh-huh."

"It would look so good against a whitewashed wall."

"Yes, I think so, too. Then, I think you're supposed to remove any unnecessary buds in the fall. The side branches are lowered and tied to the wires. That would complete the bottom level.

Then, the next year, you add another level."

After listening to Günter's explanation, she asked, "I bet you're going to miss die birken."

"The building or the trees?"

"I was thinking of the trees that you and Klaus planted. They are so beautiful, especially now that the bark has turned white."

"Yes, I'll miss them."

A month before their marriage date, Günter had his false teeth. He felt they improved his looks. His mouth was filled out, his diction was better, and he looked younger. Nonetheless, he decided not to put his teeth in when he went to work. He didn't want people to take notice of him. For the same reason, he didn't tell them that he was soon to get married. Any change in his life could arouse suspicion. He might get assigned a Stasi informer. He was rather pleased to think he could disguise himself simply by growing a beard and putting in his false teeth. He remembered Andi telling him once that the photos on identity cards could easily be switched.

Günter did feel guilty for not forewarning the manager of the zoo that he would be getting married, but again, if he did that, it might trigger an inquiry. He suggested that Wilma also not mention their marriage plans at the post office.

THE WALL

1961

On Saturday, August 13th, a week before Wilma and Günter were to get married, Berliners woke up to a wall separating East Berlin from West Berlin. The GDR army had erected it overnight "to keep the fascist hoards of West Berlin from seeping into the GDR." Of course, this was more 'doublespeak.' The real reason for the wall was to keep more East Germans from migrating to the West.

Many West and East Berliners spent the weekend standing on their respective side of the wall, watching, as it turned from barbed wire to cinder block. Only a few people had suspected that a wall was going to be built. Its rapid construction caught most people by surprise. It would soon be over 10 feet high, topped with barbed wire and hundreds of armed guard towers.

The consequences for the Birchers were severe. Reni and Andi could no longer visit Die Birken. Now, Gerda and Günter would not be able to see Reni graduate from Free University, the coming January. Reni and Andi could not witness Wilma's and Günter's marriage. It also meant no farm for Günter and Wilma in West Germany. Wilma could not retrieve her equipment that she kept at her West Berlin allotment.

The day the wall went up, Günter and Wilma spent the morning discussing its repercussions on their personal lives. Their moods swung from mad, to sad, to sulking. By 2:00 in the afternoon, Günter put in his teeth to pick up his spirits and suggested that they go for a walk. A walk was always a good suggestion when total privacy was needed. It was a beautiful day, but the gentle breeze and mild temperature did little to improve their attitudes.

"We're stuck," Wilma said.

"I'm wondering if we should try to escape," Günter suggested to Wilma.

"If we could only get a farm here, I wouldn't mind staying, but what spoils that prospect is the collectivization policy. You can't grow what you want here, and whatever you do grow is really not yours, the state decides how it will be used."

"We should probably escape right away, before they really tighten up the wall. Today, it's only barbed wire and there are probably some spots that are not yet well guarded." Now that he knew he was in love with Wilma, and that she felt the same way, all he could think of was the two of them living and working together on a farm somewhere.

Wilma was surprised at how impetuous Günter was sounding. "I don't think we should do anything rash. Successful escapes probably take months of planning."

"Someone said that all the trunk lines have been cut. We can't even telephone anyone in the West."

"If we plan to escape, I don't think we should get married." Wilma couldn't believe she had just said that. "I mean I don't think we should draw attention to ourselves."

"Let's think. How about going for a cup of coffee and a pastry?" His love for her was overpowering. She was so sensible. He realized what was most important to him was just to be with her. "Could you be happy living here, knowing we can never have a farm?"

"Yes, I truly want to be with you. I don't want to risk going to prison. If I can live with you, I can be happy anywhere, very happy!"

They said their vows over coffee and a piece of apple strudel. Wilma would move into Günter's apartment. They knew none of their friends would be critical, and the other people in the building probably wouldn't even notice the change in the living arrangements. Wilma had always spent much of her time in Günter's apartment.

The beauty of a civil marriage ceremony was that if it got called off, no one's plans were affected. They telephoned the registrar's office and cancelled their appointment to be married the next week, then went home and quietly began transferring Wilma's belongings to Günter's apartment.

Late in the afternoon, Günter knocked on Gerda's door. He found that she realized that the wall meant she would have no contact with Reni. Her eyes were red from crying. He commiserated with her and tried to give her hope. "You never know, this may be only temporary."

Leaving Gerda's, Günter went downstairs. He heard someone whistling. Once on the first floor, he saw Klaus about to descend to the basement. When Klaus spotted Günter, he stopped whistling and put on a sorrowful face. Günter realized that Klaus was glad he and Wilma would be staying, but knew he shouldn't reveal his feelings. Klaus would always be a source of joy to him.

Günter and Wilma spent the evening moving the rest of Wilma's belongings from Fritzy's apartment down to Günter's on the first floor. Finally, they were ready to go to bed. Günter debated about keeping his teeth in, as his manhood was about to be tested. He caught Wilma looking at him. She went to the tap to fetch him a glass of water. "Put them in here," she said. "Remember I love you with or without."

Günter marveled that she could always read his every thought.

THE STASH

Klaus had been working at Tierpark Zoo now for six years and loved his job. He much preferred it to the furniture factory, and was happy to spend more time outdoors. He was becoming an avid bird-watcher. While tending to the gardens and doing plantings, he could whip out his 'binos' from the case clipped to his belt if he saw something interesting. He wrote down significant sightings in his little notepad. In the summer months, he put in many hours fixing fences and gates. Since going to Vogelsang, pruning trees was his favorite task. He was quite good now at using the foot spikes to climb. While up high, there was always a chance that he may encounter a bird's nest.

In the winter months, he was able to use his carpentry skills more. Most of the zoo animals needed shelter. Their compounds always required some kind of repair or new configuration. He became 'Herr Fix-it.' He hadn't told Günter yet that he would love to lead bird-watching tours through the grounds. When he and Günter had started working there, shortly after the zoo first opened, there were few trees. Now, they were numerous, and not just by the warehouse. Lovely groves separated various regions. He thought the animals felt less exposed. There was one lake and three ponds on the property. It was easy to keep them filled. Berlin's water table was very high. Günter told him once that the city's name had to do with the Slavic word for swamp. Günter seemed to know everything.

In the last couple of years, the zoo's management had decided to make an auditorium in the palace's basement. Showing movies about animals would be a way they could attract visitors in the winter months. There was little tolerance for being outdoors in temperatures below 0 °C. The auditorium would have a stage at one end and ten rows of benches in front of it—a lot of carpentry work.

Günter and Klaus were given the job of looking over the entire basement before plans were drawn up. There should be bathrooms. They had to identify where there was electricity and sufficient lighting to set up a workshop with a circular saw, where they could stack the lumber, etc. The auditorium had to be dry. So many buildings, through years of neglect, had damp walls, mold, and dry rot. With flashlights, they penetrated into the basement's deepest recesses, tapping walls as they went around, looking for dampness. A section of one wall sounded distinctly different— almost hollow. They flashed their lights around. There was no baseboard anywhere in the basement. "I wonder if it opens." Günter pushed on one side of a six-foot panel. No movement. Then he pushed on the other side. Again, no movement.

Klaus got down on his hands and knees. "What could we slide under this?"

"Maybe a hoe?"

"Yeah!" and in a flash, Klaus went up the stairs, out of the building to a shed where the gardening tools were kept, and came back with a hoe. "Gee, it's cold out there. I wish I'd thought to put on my jacket." While he rubbed his hands together to get them warm, Günter took the hoe and tried to slip the blade under the panel. It went in easily. Then he pushed down on the end of the handle, expecting it wouldn't budge, but it did, quite easily. He held the hoe handle down as Klaus got his fingers under the edge and pulled the panel up, stepping back as he did.

"Oh my God, this is scary." He had visions of rats running out. Klaus shined his flashlight inside. The space was not large and was almost completely taken up by a wooden crate that had dimensions of about 5'x4'x1'. "Gee, do you think it's a coffin?"

"No, the shape is wrong. Does it open? Let's slide it out so we can get a closer look at it." Günter got at one end and Klaus at the other, prepared to pull hard. To their surprise, the crate moved easily.

Klaus ran his fingers around the lid. "Ah, on the back side, I think I feel two hinges which should mean...." He tried to lift the lid from the front side, and with a little effort, he pushed it up and leaned it against the back wall. He flashed the light so they could see what was inside.

"It seems to be holding several items, each wrapped in a sheet."

"Let's take one out. We should probably be very careful. It looks like whoever put these things in here wanted to make sure they wouldn't get damaged."

Günter took one side and Klaus the other, together lifting out the first object. Again, they were surprised by how light it was. They removed it slowly, so as not to bang it against the sides. Then they gingerly removed the sheet.

Günter gasped: "Oh no. It can't be. Jesus Christ! Jesus Christ!"

Klaus was not particularly religious, but he didn't like to hear Günter swear. It was just a painting of a bare-breasted, brown-skinned woman.

"I think it's a Modigliani. We need to be careful with this."

"What is modoliani?"

"Modigliani—he's a famous artist. Let's cover it again, very carefully. Is there another?"

They leaned the painting against the wall and took out something else, also wrapped in a sheet. It, too, was lightweight. Once uncovered, they could see it was another painting. Günter asked Klaus to shine the light on it. "I don't know this one, but isn't it lovely?" They rewrapped it in its sheet and took out another. Altogether, they found four paintings in the crate.

Klaus noticed Günter was shaking. "Are you alright?"

"Yes, my gut feeling is that these are extremely valuable."

"Really? What should we do?"

"Let's not do anything, yet…." Günter was out of breath. "We need to think about this, carefully…."

"Why are they being kept here?" Klaus asked.

"Yes, exactly; why? They are being hidden, don't you think? Hidden from whom? The authorities, the Stasi, the Russians? If found, they will probably be sent to Russia."

"But would the Stasi allow that?"

"They don't have a choice. Ultimately, the Russians control things in the GDR. Anyway, I don't trust the Stasi either. They're desperate for money."

"From the dust on the outside of the crate, I think they've been here for a very long time," Klaus surmised.

"The Nazis stole art from Jews and from museums in the countries they invaded. They could have been hidden here since the war."

"Or, maybe the owner hid them so they wouldn't be stolen and then was killed, so now, no one knows about them." Klaus was enjoying playing detective.

"Oh, my God!" Günter started trembling again. "Let's put these back, close the crate, and return everything to just as we found it." When this was done and the wall panel closed, Günter went on to say: "Let's keep this between you and me."

"What should we do about it?"

"I don't know yet. A way will open, I hope."

Klaus wasn't sure what 'a way will open' meant exactly, but he trusted Günter's judgment. This time he wore his jacket to go out in the freezing cold to put the hoe back in the shed.

SABINE

Andi enjoyed the benefits of being in 'the land of the free' in West Berlin. He got up every morning to find a newspaper from a free press outside his door that he could read with his morning coffee. And he looked forward to reading his mail when he came home after work. He just wished he could read mail from his friends at Die Birken, especially Günter. Thank goodness Günter had been able to meet with him before the wall went up, while getting his teeth fixed, and relay the evidence he and Klaus had found of Russian missiles possibly being located near Vogelsang.

George, Andi's boss, told Andi how important that bit of spy work was. Andi corrected George. "Günter was not a 'spotter,' just a friend."

"Really!" George wanted to know more about Günter. "Can he be recruited?"

"I've tried, but he refuses." Andi explained that Günter had spent five years in a gulag.

"So, he speaks Russian."

"Oh, yes."

"All the better," George said. "Please keep trying!"

Andi stopped his daydreaming diversion and concentrated on the day's mail. Günter had his address, in case of an emergency, but Günter knew better than to write. Even before the wall went up, it was common knowledge that the Stasi read all letters that left the GDR. In the four years since he had moved to West Berlin, Andi had never received a letter from East Berlin.

Yet, right now, there was just such a letter. It was addressed to him, on high-quality paper with the hammer and compass embossed on the back. What the hell? Inside he found an invitation to the wedding of "Sabine Christiane Baum to Helmut Karl Müller." Sabine was the last person Andi could imagine who would choose to marry. Why am I invited? I'm also invited to the reception. Another piece of paper slipped out of the envelope onto the floor. He picked it up and was surprised to see it was a personal note, handwritten on ordinary paper:

> *Your pass over the border is arranged, just show*
> *this invitation. I hope you can come.*

Why would Sabine invite me? That was very nice of her, but I was never close to her. Then it occurred to him that she had no family. They were all dead. Tears started forming. He remembered all the snide things he had thought about Sabine over the last fourteen years. He had been so focused on Reni, he had failed to see that Sabine needed nurturing as well.

These guilty thoughts consumed him for a minute or two, before he wondered how they knew his new address. Then his CIA training kicked in. If they know his address, they probably knew he worked for the CIA They might be planning to tag him with a radioactive tracer. In a calmer moment, he wondered who else would be invited. He assumed Gerda and Reni would be, since Sabine had lived with them for thirteen years or so. Sure enough, the next day, Reni's invitation to Sabine's wedding arrived in the mail.

Over the last year and a half, the Birchers had noticed a handsome man, in his early forties, coming to the building to pick up Sabine. Sometimes, he was in his Stasi uniform, but usually, he came in casual dress: "Casual dress?" Klaus challenged Fritzy. "Casual, but expensively casual. Did you see the crease in his slacks and his fine leather shoes?"

"The last time he picked her up," Wilma commented, "I heard her laugh. In all these years, I have never before heard her laugh."

At first, just getting the invitation made Klaus feel he had
some importance. By this time, he was over his crush on Sabine.
Now, he knew himself better. She wasn't a good match for him.
He honestly felt happy for her. But as the days passed, he started
to worry about what he should wear. He had sneakers and work
shoes, and two sets of trousers, none of which were suitable for a
wedding. He went to Fritzy for her advice.

"I've never had to dress a man before. But let me think about
it. I'll ask around." She had a library friend who used to be an
actress in a small theater company that made all the costumes for
its cast. In a week's time, Fritzy and Klaus walked to The Cellar to
speak to Herr Jürgen Schröder, the theater's director.

Descending steps from the sidewalk, they opened the door
fronting the street. They entered a dim, short, entrance hall. A
girl approached them. She introduced herself as Mila Schröder.
"Father is busy with a dress rehearsal. Would you mind waiting?
It should be over in less than half an hour."

Klaus had never been in a live theater before. He didn't know
they could be this small. There were only 18 folding chairs, set
out in three rows of six. He assumed Herr Schröder was the man
in the front row. The girl, Mila, continued to sit at a little table in
the entrance hall. A goose-necked lamp lit up the area where she
resumed her sewing. Her smooth hair glistened in the lamplight.
He thought her hairstyle was called a 'pageboy.'

Herr Schröder was willing to outfit Klaus for the wedding.
"My daughter can tailor anything to make it fit. You say you're a
carpenter?"

"Yes." Klaus smiled, happy to be recognized for his trade.

While they talked to the girl's father, he noticed Mila looking
him over. She brought out a tape measure and wrapped it around
Klaus' waist, then returned to her desk to write the measurement
down. Klaus was glad he had taken a bath a day ago. She returned
to measure his arm length. He felt breathless, but took the liberty
to examine her while she was close. She had smooth skin, darker
than other girls he knew. Oh dear, her father had asked him a

question. He looked at the man. Herr Schröder was smiling.

"As I said, I wonder if you could help us by making a few sets, in exchange for the tailoring?"

Klaus wasn't sure what a set was, but he said he was willing. On the way back home, Fritzy reminisced about Berlin's pre-war theater scene. "During the Weimar Republic, there were lots of theaters and cabarets. Many satirized the Nazis—so witty and clever. Of course, the Nazis shut most of them down. And these clowns that run this city today, their polemic dampens creativity—so dull. But this was fun, wasn't it?"

Klaus agreed, but wondered about 'polemic'—what does that mean, and more importantly, what is a set?

During the next week, Klaus spoke to Gerda about the wedding. She didn't know what she could wear either, so when he went to The Cellar the following weekend, he asked if the theater would be able to find a dress for her as well.

Mila's smile faded: "Sure, is she your girlfriend?"

Klaus felt himself blushing. He explained who Gerda was. "Hmm," Mila deliberated, "blond hair, white skin, and blue eyes. I think Carole Lombard—perhaps a black dress, scoop neckline, a long strand of pearls. She'll have to paint her nails. I can curl her eyelashes and apply black eyeliner and lipstick, if she doesn't know how." Another big smile: "And for you, I think, the Gatsby look: white shirt and jacket, dark trousers. The shoes I have, I think they will fit. You can wear spats to cover up their shabbiness."

For that care and attention, Klaus was glad to help with an additional set. Mila told him the clothes would have to be returned. That was fine with Klaus. When he saw what spats were, he was sure he would never wear them again.

That night, Klaus told Fritzy of their plans, thinking she would be delighted. She was not. "Carol Lombard is an American actor, and Gatsby has capitalism written all over him. The hosts will probably ask you to leave the reception. You want to blend in, not stand out, don't you?"

The next week, Klaus tried to explain Fritzy's concern to Mila. He was afraid of how she would take it and didn't want to appear ungrateful, but Mila quickly understood. "Improvisation's my thing. No, seriously, I'm sorry. I got carried away," she told Klaus. "I'll tone the costumes down and make them contemporary. Don't worry."

Klaus started spending a couple of evenings a week at the Schröders' tiny theater. Evidently, Mila, in addition to being the seamstress in charge of costumes, was the box office, the usher, and the makeup artist. He never saw Frau Schröder. One night, he asked Mila about her mother.

Her eyes glazed over: "She was trapped in West Berlin when the wall went up. We miss her so much!"

Without her saying so, Klaus realized Mila was trying to help her father by doing the work of her mother.

The day of the wedding, Mila came to Die Birken to help her clients dress. She brushed Gerda's hair to one side, partially covering her left eye. The brown dress, of ordinary cotton, had a brown hat that matched. They both were slightly dowdy in style, but Gerda had kept her figure after all these years and stood erect.

Mila examined her subject with pride. "She may be middle-aged, but she's still a 'looker,'" she told Klaus.

Klaus had other thoughts. He wished Mila could apply makeup to him, just to get close to her. The day of the wedding, he made sure he was scrubbed, freshly shaven, with clean underwear. Mila had given him black slacks, black shirt, and a light green jacket, which had worked for The Cellar's performance of Noel Coward's one-act play, *This Was a Man*. She handed Klaus a white tie.

"I don't know how to tie a tie."

"I'll help you." Mila said, flashing him a smile. "That's part of the service." Klaus thought her crooked teeth animated her smile and reflected her whimsical spirit.

An hour before the wedding, Andi drove up to Die Birken carrying Reni in his Morris Oxford. They all gathered in the courtyard, hugging, and finally, applauding Reni for graduating from university. She announced to them that she had just been hired by the German delegation to the United Nations in New York City to help with public affairs. Her job would start in September. In a month's time she would no longer be living with Andi in West Berlin. Günter was proud of her, but at the same time felt she was growing up and slipping even further away.

The Birchers tried not to show their surprise to see her wearing a skirt above her knees. Her bangs and hair were perfectly straight. It was the style of the day. Maybe the half-inch-wide black elastic band around her head, holding her bangs in place, was also the latest in the West. This must be the 'American Indian look,' Günter thought with some amusement. Instead of the iconic feather, Reni had attached a large pink camellia.

They all needed much more time to catch up. Andi promised a longer visit when they returned from the wedding. He handed Günter a big envelope. "Hold this safely, please, until we get back. I have a lot to talk to you about. We have to be back at the border checkpoint no later than 10:00 tonight."

Andi tried to steady his nerves while driving to Karlshorst. He knew that the venue for Sabine's wedding and reception was in the compound out of which Berlin's Soviet Intelligence operated. George, his boss, had shown him the map. Andi had memorized it. He knew that the headquarters for Soviet staff was in Marshall House, at the center of the complex. Radiating out from it, like spokes of a wheel, were various other sites: the Soviet officer's club, the stadium, the swimming pool, gym facilities, officer's mess, officer's quarters, an apartment building, and a hunt club for military and civilian personnel. Karlshorst was huge. Its function was generally unknown by East Berliners, but being surrounded by a six-foot fence and well-patrolled by Stasi guards put people off of inquiring.

Andi was supposed to drive to the gate at Waldow Allee. Each of them in the car would have to show their invitation and identity card.

"What is this place?" Klaus asked.

"Good God!" said Reni.

"This is just the home of the Soviet's Berlin Brigade…" Andi delivered his explanation of the place as casually as though he were saying they were going into a park. His boss, George, had told him not to take a camera or try to leave a bug of any kind. "It just may be that they don't know you are with the CIA. After all, they did send the invitation to your apartment, the address of which they could have gotten from Free University, where Sabine probably knows you teach."

So, Andi made sure his car was clean and that he carried nothing incriminating in his pockets. Once through the gate, they were escorted by a uniformed soldier on a motorcycle to the officers' club.

"That's a Stasi officer!" Klaus exclaimed. "I mean, he's not wearing a Soviet uniform, is he?"

"That's right. Let's save our questions and comments for when we get back to Die Birken." When they arrived at the officers' club, a young Stasi soldier asked Andi for his keys so he could valet park his car. Thank God, Andi had taken all his other keys off his key ring. They were back at Die Birken with Günter, in the manila envelope.

They walked into a spacious, high-ceilinged entrance chamber. A chandelier hung down over a round table in its center, holding a vase of copious white lilies. Another young Stasi soldier stood by the table and asked them to please sign the guest book.

From there, they were guided into a large room with many chairs around two walls. Just as Andi expected, they were directed to specific seats. This room was lit by three chandeliers. A walkway down the center was bordered by red rose petals. The path ended before it reached the opposite wall. Andi had just figured out that Sabine would enter and walk down that path when a soldier approached and asked him to please follow him. He smiled at his companions and followed the young man. Relax, Andi said to himself. They wouldn't go through all this show just to start torturing you.

"Please come with me, sir. You have been asked to walk the bride in," the soldier said.

"What an honor!" Andi replied. He waited outside in the entrance chamber while other guests arrived and were seated, a number of whom were soldiers and Stasi, in dress uniforms. Then a side door opened and Sabine walked out wearing a white sleeveless dress that came to her mid-calf. The skirt was very full. She looked lovely, holding a bouquet of pink roses—no veil. This was to be a civil ceremony.

Sabine smiled at Andi. "Thank you so much. I knew I could count on you. Thank you, not just for this, but for everything else."

Andi was quite taken aback. He had never heard her express gratitude or any other emotion. This is what love can do, he thought, wishing Mark was with him. He walked her down the fragrant path, where a strikingly handsome soldier took her hand. Andi returned to his seat. Gerda was wiping her eyes with one hand and holding Reni's hand with the other.

The ceremony was over in ten minutes. The married couple led the way to another room of equal size. It had several tables formally set for dinner. There were place cards. Once again, Andi was honored by being seated on Sabine's left, at the head table. I'm like the father. I'll probably have to dance with her alone in the middle of the floor. He knew all the traditional dance steps, so that didn't worry him. The conversation he had with himself in his head helped to calm his nerves. The dinner itself was truly delicious as well as exotic. One course that Andi would always remember was 'Deer with Pfifferlingen Mushrooms.'

While he was eating, Andi looked around to find Klaus. He saw Gerda first. She was seated next to an old soldier who, from the looks of things, was doing his best to engage her in conversation while not taking his eyes from her ample bust.

Ah, there's Klaus. Who's that he's sitting next to…? Oh my God, is that Walter, the Little Shit? For a moment Andi couldn't breathe. Oh, how he wished he could hear their conversation.

No surprise, Walter had grown into a very handsome man. Klaus looked uneasy, as though he was listening to something unpleasant. Andi's attention was drawn to a noisy area of the room. The boisterousness all came from one table; eight young people loosened by drink. They punctuated their loud talk with outbursts of uproarious laughter. Oops, there's Reni. Well, at least she's having fun. That's good.

There were toasts, speeches, and more toasts. After a dessert of mousse au chocolat with Belgian pralines, a three-piece band started to play. Everybody watched Andi dance with Sabine. Their eyes were on Sabine, of course, who looked absolutely beautiful.

Klaus was trying to put up with Walter, who was on his fourth glass of something intoxicating, and explaining (rather loudly) to the three people opposite him about his 'import business.' He gave them each a card. "I can get you anything you need: radiograms, freezers, just let me know what you want."

"What's a radiogram?" one woman asked.

"It's an entertainment console with a radio and a phonograph built in, with slots to hold your record albums, made from the finest wood."

Later on, he tried to engage more people by raising his voice. "Let me introduce you to my friend, Klaus, here." He used his glass to direct all eyes to Klaus. "We were orphans at the end of the war—Sabine, too." That caught people's attention. "She's obviously done well for herself, Sabine has. I'm an importer now as I've already said." Klaus witnessed the body language of his table companions; strained smiles, glancing down at the tablecloth, shrugging of the shoulders. "My friend here, Klaus— it's Klaus Altmann, isn't it?" Walter asked, emphasizing the 'Alt' (meaning 'old' in German). "You've become a carpenter. That's OK, the world needs carpenters." He laughed.

"It's Hartmann," Klaus corrected him. Should he try to put Walter in his place? He felt like complimenting the jerk for raising his reputation from Little to Big Shit.... No, scoring a point wasn't worth making their dinner companions even more uncomfortable than they already were.

On the drive back to Die Birken, both Reni and Klaus were mindful of Andi's warnings not to talk until they were back home, but if Gerda understood that warning, she simply couldn't hold back her good news. "Sabine said that she has arranged for me to move into her apartment on the first floor. I didn't quite understand it all. She said something about a lower rent for being a watchdog. And I'll be able to keep her telephone."

Andi gasped.

Gerda went on: "She's even going to give me some of her furniture. The movers are coming tomorrow." Turning to Reni she added: "If only you could come back to live with me, dear."

"I know, it's such a shame."

Andi was quite sure Reni didn't mean what she said. They drove out of the compound at 6:00 o'clock, and had a good twenty-minute drive before they would be back at Die Birken. August was the best time of year in northern Germany. The sky could stay light until 10:00 P.M.

Andi knew that the Stasi had a watchdog in every apartment building whose job it was to record the daily schedules of the tenants, who visited whom in the building, which children wore Western clothes, who liked popular music, etc. Soon, it would be Gerda's job to ensure that tenants were following prescribed Party behavior. Any deviance would be reported to the authorities. Gerda was to be a spider in the Stasi's web. How fortunate! Andi was fairly sure she didn't have the mental capacity to do the job justice. Great! Did Sabine arrange this on purpose as a present to her Bircher friends? No, that doesn't happen in the GDR, but just maybe....

When they got back, Reni announced that she would spend an hour with Gerda so they could catch up, and then she would come looking for Günter and the others. That gave Andi an hour to perform some tasks he had planned to do. When Günter and

Wilma opened their door, he and Klaus went inside to talk, shutting the door behind them. Andi immediately indicated the need for discretion. He rapidly walked his fingers up his arm, then, put his index finger to his lips. His friends began engaging in light conversation about the wedding. Message received!

Andi had two of them hold a white pillowcase flat against the wall as a backdrop to the head shot he took of the third. He repeated this routine until he had pictures of all three: Günter, Wilma, and Klaus. His camera was no bigger than a cigarette lighter, and was just one of the items in the manila envelope that Günter had guarded for him during the wedding. Next came close-up shots of their ID cards.

He started to show Günter and Klaus a map that he brought of the Vogelsang area. Günter abruptly suggested they go for a walk, since it was still such a beautiful night.

The four of them strolled leisurely down Hoffmannstrasse. Günter and Klaus retold the story of their Vogelsang adventure. Klaus went into a detailed description of the Capercaillie shooting.

When there was a break in the conversation, Günter asked: "What should we do with the map?"

"Please go back, see if you can mark the exact spot on it of the missile installation." That was not what Günter wanted to hear.

"We have something else to tell you," Klaus said. "Günter and I discovered this crate…in the palace basement."

Andi listened to this new story without interrupting. When they were finished, he said: "My God! Oh, my God! How should we handle this?" He was at a loss for what to say. "I'll see what can be done. I agree with you, don't tell anyone. It may take awhile, even a year or more, before there is an opportunity to act. Just hold tight."

Before Andi and Reni headed back to West Berlin, Andi gave his friends two newly published books. "They're by American authors, so be careful. I think you'll like them." He handed them a copy of *To Kill a Mockingbird* and *Catch-22*.

The next morning, Fritzy was dressed and ready to go to work. On descending the stairs, she overtook Gerda, gingerly stepping down while holding on to a lamp and some pillows. Fritzy offered to help and thereby learned that Gerda's 3rd-floor apartment would soon be vacant.

"Did you enjoy yourself at Sabine's wedding yesterday?"

"Oh, yes. Sabine was so kind to think of giving me her apartment."

"Yes, but also you gave her a home for many years."

"I suppose you're right. You know Sabine also made me the building's watchdog."

"Is that right? That's quite an honor."

Fritzy started helping Gerda with the entire move. When Gerda went back up for another load, Fritzy made a quick call to the library on Sabine's (soon to be Gerda's) phone saying she was sick and would not be able to come to work today.

By early afternoon, she and Gerda were finished bringing everything down. Fritzy stayed with Gerda and asked her if she could help her put her belongings in place. Around 4:00 P.M, when things were in order, Fritzy asked: "Would you let me move into your old apartment?"

"Oh, I don't know if I have the authority to let you."

"But you are the watchdog. It's your job to see that things are done right."

"I suppose you're right. Well, yes, if that will help you. Here's the key. You must be exhausted."

"No, I'll be fine. Ursula will be home soon to help me. Is there anything else I can do for you?"

"No. I think I'll lie down and take a nap."

By midnight, Fritzy and Ursula were moved and settled into an identical apartment to theirs, only one floor lower.

WILMAS'S DISSENT

1962

The four Birchers left in the book group still met, but now only twice a week, on Mondays and Thursdays, at 5:00 P.M. The location was the same—Andi's former apartment, now occupied by Günter and Wilma. It was on the first floor facing the street, just like that of the building's new watchdog, Gerda. They discussed their good fortune to have the intervening entranceway.

"Thank goodness for that," Wilma commented.

"Exactly! That means we don't need to worry about the camera I heard about," said Fritzy.

"What camera?"

"Evidently, they can drill a small hole in the wall and observe what you are doing by inserting…something…, I thought it was a camera." Fritzy then pointed out that their watchdog probably had a set of keys to get into any apartment she wished. One afternoon, they quietly searched the two rooms of Günter and Wilma's apartment for a bug, but couldn't find one. Although they still didn't feel secure, they decided to continue their practice of reading and discussing books.

"Do we still have any banned books?" Klaus finally had the nerve to ask.

"Sure, but we always put them in the hidden bookcase you built behind the panel."

"It's not just banned books we have to worry about. They also don't approve of any books by Western authors."

Klaus suggested that he make a false bottom to the dumbwaiter.

"We could store the book we are actually reading in that. Then it would be available to any of us—I mean then Fritzy or I could pick it up to read when you guys aren't home."

Günter was leery, "That sounds like a good idea, but someone may see us put the book in the dumbwaiter. Fritzy has a key to our apartment, so if we don't answer the door, why don't you see if you can get the key from her?"

"Or better, still," chipped in Wilma, "Why don't we make a copy of our key for you, Klaus?"

"Yes, that's best."

Klaus didn't read every book, but he always participated in the discussions. He arranged his now-routine evenings working at The Cellar so they didn't fall on Monday or Thursday nights. He asked Fritzy if she could bring home *The Great Gatsby*. "Mila's read it and I'd like to know about it." Fritzy explained that that book was on the forbidden list, so it was not likely she could bring it home.

Klaus and Mila had started to go out together. He had little money, but being in the theater business, Mila knew places to go that were inexpensive and fun. Eventually, Klaus asked the group if they would mind if Mila joined them, every now and then.

Fritzy was reluctant, only for security reasons. Günter thought it would be fine. "I've been thinking," he added, "that's what this government wants. They want us to be so afraid that we won't express our thoughts. Eventually, each of us will lose our identity and be only a body—superfluous, easy to control, easy to kill. Those are some of the points Hannah Arendt makes in her book, *The Origins of Totalitarianism*."

"When did you read that?" Wilma asked.

"When I first got here. Remember, I was treated for tuberculosis. That book did more to cure me than anything else. I'd love to be able to read it again. Would you believe that was thirteen years ago?"

"I've never heard of the book," Fritzy commented.

"It had just come out at that time, and the doctor in the hospital was the one who loaned it to me." Günter's thoughts drifted back to that doctor. Sadly, he couldn't remember his name, but clearly, the man knew it took more than medicine to cure a person. "Now I remember. You were treated for TB in the West." Frizty went on: "Positively, we're not going to find a book critical of communism in our library system on this side of the wall."

"It is highly critical of both Nazis and communists. Arendt, the author, says totalitarian regimes use fear to keep people from thinking for themselves, and to get them to accept the regime's ideology. She maintains that it is important to keep your identity, to think for yourself, and to discuss your ideas with others. Don't let yourself 'migrate inward.' You have to express yourself publicly, so your ideas bounce off others. She believes that having meetings like ours helps to reveal who we are and can initiate opportunities for change."

Günter's argument persuaded them. A week later, Mila came to their gathering, wearing a beret and cape. That was the afternoon they started talking about *To Kill a Mockingbird*, now Klaus' favorite book.

Wilma had grown up in an isolated valley in southern Poland and had never gone anywhere else, until she came to Berlin. Before then, politics and history rarely occupied her thoughts.

News in GDR papers and magazines had to be compatible with Party ideology. In 1957, East Berliners heard on the radio about Sputnik, then about the Soviet rocket hitting the moon, and then that Soviet astronaut Yuri Gagarin was the first man in space. In 1960, Fritzy bought a TV. Quite often, other Birchers would ask to watch it in her apartment.

Andi had told them that the GDR wanted to scramble the broadcasts from the West, but when they did so, they found their own broadcasts, containing vital propaganda, were also blocked. So, scrambling stopped. Instead, the Stasi checked the direction of antennas on buildings. If they pointed to the west, one could get in trouble. Teachers were to note if children in school talked about TV shows from the West.

After the wall went up, the Birchers could no longer rely on Andi to correct misinformation from local media. Wilma became especially alarmed when the Cuban Missile Crisis occurred in 1962. People everywhere worried that World War III was about to begin. It was this threat that got Wilma hooked. From then on, she paid close attention to current events.

After hearing Günter explain Arendt's ideas about total-itarianism, Wilma decided that she should be more proactive. She began to look at her job differently. Maybe a way would open to make some changes. From working inside the post office, she knew letters to certain addresses were being set aside to be opened, inspected, and resealed before delivery. Wilma could always tell when a letter had been inspected. The resealing process left telltale marks that she could easily identify.

For the last two years, she had worked in the same group of neighborhoods. Normally, Wilma didn't talk to people while on her route as it would slow her down, but when she saw Giselle Mechler at 452 Bergfriedstrasse planting a window box, she couldn't resist.

"What are you planting?" Wilma expected the woman to answer 'cabbage,' something practical, but she said daffodils. That encouraged Wilma to ask her a barrage of questions, which Giselle answered with enthusiasm. The next few times Wilma saw her, they greeted each other. Several months later, Wilma asked her if she had an allotment. The woman stopped smiling and said: "I asked for one and I was refused."

"Really? I thought there were lots of spaces."

"I thought so too, but they want to punish me." She turned around and walked into her building without a further ex-planation. Wilma felt Giselle's resentment. Does she associate me with the 'they?' All postal workers were required to wear a uniform which was the same gray color and style as Stasi officials. I hope my uniform hasn't put her off me, she thought.

The next day, when Wilma sorted mail, she checked the list

taped to the wall in front of each sorter. Sure enough, there was Giselle's name and address. Why was this woman being targeted?

Three days later, Wilma was carrying a letter in her mail bag addressed to Giselle, but with no return address. Curiously, it had not been opened and inspected, as far as she could tell, like the rest of Giselle's mail. She hesitated to deliver it before she could steam it open herself to see what was inside. Did she dare? She thought of Günter's wife. The courage she must have had to deliver resistance leaflets under the Nazis' noses. In comparison, this would be easy. If caught, she would pretend that it hadn't been sealed properly in the first place.

Wilma decided to take the letter home with her after work. After reading its contents, she would deliver it to Giselle the following day.

What's gotten into me, she wondered? She knew not to tell anyone, not even Günter or Fritzy. No sense bringing suspicion on others. In the morning, she opened the envelope with steam from the kettle before Günter rose from bed. Then she took it to the bathroom. In privacy, Wilma withdrew a piece of paper which turned out to not be a letter. In fact, it was a newspaper obituary that read:

> It is with great sadness that the family of Thomas and Giselle Mechler report the death of their only child, Karl Mechler, age 13. Karl fell off of the S-bahn train as it was travelling between Friederichstrasse and Lehrter Stadtbahnhof.

The obituary seemed to be from a Berlin newspaper, but on closer inspection, Wilma could tell it was fake. The sender must have intended that Giselle would see it as a death threat to her child. Wilma shuddered. It was so sinister it made her feel nauseous. She didn't want to deliver the message, for sure, but once she had considered the alternative, she realized she had to do it. The Stasi might be watching Giselle's home, or have hidden cameras. She had to deliver it today.

That was done, but a week later, there was another letter

to Giselle. This one, too, was uninspected and had no return address. This time, she found inside a small photo of a young boy around 12 years of age, wearing swimming trunks. Penned on the back was: "Karl, swimming in the Baltic, summer 1957." On the back side, there was adhesive at one corner. The photo had most likely been removed from an album. What was most disturbing was the 'X' inked through Karl's face.

Wilma delivered the letter the following day, too scared to do anything else, but she did begin to keep a list of names and addresses of people on her route whose mail had been similarly tampered with. The list did nothing to relieve those people of the psychological torture they were receiving, but it was her record and testimony to the injustice.

Where should Wilma keep the list? If it was found in their apartment, Günter would be incriminated. Maybe she could keep it on one of her two remaining allotments—one was in Fritzy's name and the other in Klaus'. She needed a place that would stay dry and that was easily accessible, without appearing suspicious. She remembered Klaus' bird box on the side of his shed. It had a hinge on it so it could be opened for cleaning. Perfect!

Wilma had lived in a country occupied by the Nazis, but the Bauer farm was so remote, she had been unaware of the day-to-day oppression that others in Poland endured. Poles living in towns and cities must have felt the pressure to conform to the Nazi ideology. Rationing and food shortages didn't affect her until she made her way to Berlin. By then, the fear of oppression came from another source, another ideology. Wilma wasn't beaten down by the double whammy of Nazi fascism, followed by communism, that Fritzy and other East Berliners felt. Fritzy would never have kept such a list.

VOGELSANG REVISITED

MARCH 1963

After the Cuban Missile Crisis, Günter and Klaus worried a lot more about the Soviet missiles at Vogelsang. They understood the need to identify the exact location of the site on the map. Still, the two of them did not want to return. This time, they knew they would be going into danger.

They studied the map. "My heavens, this must be a pre-WWII map. It's very detailed. Look, even some logging roads are shown. According to the scale of the map, I think the logging road we took must have been about here, but it's not marked. Then further on, about two kilometers, there's another logging road, I think. See that?"

"Yeah, if we took that one, we'd be closer to where we think the missiles are, wouldn't we?"

"Yes, that road goes directly east, and it's maybe wider than the one we took."

"Why do you think that?"

"Because it's on the map and the one we took isn't."

"But it could be that the one we took was built after this map was made."

"Good thinking."

The next morning, they started out early, just as they had done two years prior. When they turned their bikes onto the dirt road, they noticed that the unusually wide tire marks they had seen before were gone, and the road was now scored by many lorry treads of ordinary size. This didn't calm their nerves, however.

On full alert, they pedaled to reach the other logging road. Günter was trying to estimate distance in his head. Surely, we should see it by now? Thank goodness, no vehicles have passed us yet. Finally, they found a logging road that corresponded with the map, but it was in bad shape. It hadn't been used in years. Klaus had been right.

It was so overgrown it was difficult to pedal on, but its disuse could mean they were less exposed and safer. Obviously, no one was currently using this road. They wondered if they should ditch their bikes in the undergrowth and continue on foot. The decision was made for them when Klaus crashed into a hidden rock and was knocked off. He was shaken but not hurt, however, his bike's front wheel was buckled and it could not be ridden. A tire puncture they could fix, but not the broken wheel rim.

What should they do? "Once we get back to the road, I can rig my bike so it can be towed by yours. My back wheel and tire are fine. I have plenty of rope."

"We'll be going at a walking pace." Günter dreaded the thought.

"I think I can do some rigging to make it go faster. We'll have plenty of time to catch the 5:10 train back to Berlin."

Nothing discourages this kid. "Do you want to walk some more and perhaps climb a tree before we head back?"

"Sure."

He's probably hoping to see a swastika, Günter thought.

They hid their bikes, marked the spot, and continued on foot until they stopped to eat a sandwich. They thought they heard a buzzing sound. They stood absolutely still to listen. "Sounds like a saw," Klaus said in a low voice. They listened again. They both heard a man shouting. Instinctively they put the rest of their sandwiches back in their knapsacks. "Let's climb a tree and see what we can see."

Twenty minutes later, they were up a white pine. Klaus' climbing skills were just as good as Günter's now. He had been climbing at the zoo for the last two years. They stopped their ascent 40-50 feet up, where they both could rest on nearby limbs. The men's voices were louder now. They were approaching. Minutes later, they could see two men through the pine boughs— Russian soldiers, dressed in uniform. One carried a big rucksack. He was not an officer. The other was, and he carried a Kalishnikov rifle. Günter remained motionless. He looked over at Klaus to be sure he realized the danger they were in. The soldiers stopped under the next tree over to have a cigarette. That turned out to be fortunate for Günter—not only could he hear them, but he understood most of what they said.

"I'll be glad when this is over," the officer said.

"What are we to do tonight?"

"Guard the road while they pass."

"When will we get back to base?"

"Sometime in early morning, I'm guessing. We have to wait until all the trailers have passed. If that goes well, we're supposed to wait an hour before returning to base."

'How many trailers?"

"Eight. There are eight missiles."

"Why does it take so long?"

"Oh for God's sake, they have to be driven very slowly, of course."

They spent a few minutes in silence. "So why are they sending them back, Sergeant?"

"Sashinsky, you ask too many questions. Haven't you learned yet—the less you know the better?" The officer laughed. "As I understand it, we have a new missile, one with a much greater range, so we no longer need to keep any in Germany. Now, we can hit all of the European targets from Russia, but that's more than you dumb foot soldiers need to know."

That's great news, Günter thought sarcastically. The officer went on saying something about the Cuban Missile Crisis, but his voice was muffled as they walked away, …"learned our lesson," was the last bit Günter heard.

Pleased as he was to overhear all that, Günter thought they

should remain silent. He figured the soldiers were going to walk along the old logging road until they got to the dirt road. They would probably remain hidden at the side of that road, ready to attack any poor soul who witnessed the caravan. An hour went by before Günter felt it was safe to tell Klaus what he had heard.

"Do you think they will close down the base once the missiles are gone?"

"No, I don't think so. From what Andi told me, the CIA believes there are plenty of other things going on at the Vogelsang base, but he didn't tell me what they were."

"Don't the American forces have intelligence agents in East Germany that can do what we're doing?"

"Yes, but, according to Andi, there are never enough of them. They monitor roads at border crossings closely—like those between East Germany and Poland. They try to figure out what Russia is bringing into East Germany. Back in 1961–62, they thought surface-to-surface missiles were brought into East Germany from Poland, but they couldn't follow where they went."

After some silence, Klaus said: "I guess this means we have to stay up this tree, until the soldiers come back."

"I'm afraid so."

"They won't move the missiles in the day, will they?"

"No, and the caravan will move slowly…."

"OK, we'll miss our train. Our present task is just to get out of here alive." Klaus, no doubt, remembered that only one train a week stopped at Vogelsang.

After five hours up the tree, Günter had to stretch and change his position. Klaus had already done so several times. He had secured his backpack to a limb and climbed up higher, remaining tethered. Günter knew Klaus had not given up on his search for swastikas. He said that he had read up on larches. "They would be in blossom now that it's March, so the color of the swastika would be pink."

Klaus knew better than to call out, so he waited to get back to his former perch before telling Günter in a low but excited voice that he had found a slot in another tree that had white splotches outside, going down the trunk. He kept his eye on it from then on. "No activity, but the guano is fresh, I think." Then, twenty minutes later, "I think it is going to be nocturnal—an owl perhaps."

By 6:30, the sky was dark when they heard a loud high-pitched screech in the vicinity of the tree cavity. The squawks were persistent, about every 20 seconds. "It's babies wanting to be fed, I think." Around a half hour later, a flash of white went by and the squawking increased. There was silence for twenty minutes or so, then the high pitched sceeching started again. This was very exciting for two hours, but by midnight, Günter would have preferred to doze off.

It wasn't until morning that the squawking stopped. Daylight triggered the baby owls to sleep. Just when Günter and Klaus should have been alert to listen for the soldiers' return, they fell sound asleep. It wasn't until eight or so in the morning that Günter realized there was a new repetitive noise going on near him. He forced open one eye and was aware of Klaus snoring quite loudly, and out of Günter's reach. Günter thought he heard men coming. How to stop Klaus from snoring? Günter broke off a pine cone and threw it at Klaus but missed. He threw another. It ricocheted off a limb. A third hit, and Klaus woke up with a snort. The soldiers were clearly within sight now. Fortunately, they hadn't noticed the racket going on high up in the trees ahead of them.

As the men passed under their tree, Günter thought they looked as tired as he and Klaus felt. Günter and Klaus waited until they were sure the soldiers wouldn't come back, then descended, which in itself was hard to do because they were so stiff.

They retrieved their bikes and walked them back to the dirt road, Klaus wheeling his on its back tire. Very grateful to have reached the dirt road, their next challenge was to get to the highway as quickly as possible. Klaus took off the damaged front tire and strapped it to the seat of his bike. Then he tied the front forks just under the seat of Günter's bike. Klaus explained to Günter what he was doing.

"OK, now," he said, "you sit on the seat, let your legs dangle and I'll work the pedals standing up. We used to call this 'the two-man boogie.'" It took a while to get going, but finally, they got the hang of it and made progress. "This was a lot easier when I was six," Klaus admitted.

Wilma worried about Günter and Klaus when they didn't come back that first night. She kept looking at the clock. After several hours, she concluded that they had missed the train. Perhaps they couldn't resist watching birds. She knew there was only one train a week, but they did have their bikes, and both Günter and Klaus were resourceful. They'll figure something out, she reasoned. Klaus is probably loving the adventure. If only Fritzy had her car, they could drive there and pick them up. Although it was reported that the car would be ready soon, Fritzy told her it could still take another year.

Wilma had hoped that she and Günter would be able to work at her allotments this weekend. In the early spring, there was a lot to do. Ursula wasn't interested in gardening and never had been, perhaps because it never appealed to Fritzy. Ursula would graduate from high school in June. She wasn't interested in going to university, either. She was on another track. The school had always encouraged her to go into gymnastics. She was good at it, because she was quick and strong, but she was also chunky— not overweight, but she didn't have the svelte figure of a typical gymnast. The school was now encouraging her to take a year to learn to be a sports teacher. "That's fine," Ursula told her mother. "I have to do some type of work to earn a living."

Both Wilma and Fritzy knew that what Ursula really wanted to spend her time on were environmental issues. On weekends, she went to the local Lutheran Church, not because she was religious, but because in churches, you could get together and have lively discussions. "You know the Stasi have informers there," Fritzy warned her.

"Oh yeah, we know, Fritzy. We keep attendance: 'Today there are ten of us, including two informers.' And all ten of us laugh because no one wants the others to think that they're an informer. The Stasi want us to be too afraid to do anything, meanwhile coal is polluting our air and factories dump their waste in our rivers. What we're doing is in everybody's interest."

Wilma was proud of her daughter's strong convictions. It wasn't a big stretch to go from gardening to the environment. But the short of it was, she could never get Ursula to help her at the allotments. Finishing her last sip of tea, Wilma thought of Giselle. Maybe Giselle would like to help her. On the chance that she might come, Wilma took Günter's gardening gloves with her, an extra trowel, and her seeds, of course. She rode the tram and got off near Giselle's apartment. After ringing Giselle's doorbell, she stood outside on the sidewalk, in case Giselle wanted to see who it was.

Giselle hesitated at first, but decided to go. She wore old shoes and a bandana on her head. "Is it far?" On the tram she said: "They'll probably search my apartment or plant a bug while I'm gone. Oh well, it'll be good to get out."

Wilma decided not to respond. She didn't want to lie, so she just listened. They spent the day planting beans and potatoes. In the process, Wilma told her that she was welcome any time to help with the work and she could have a portion of what they grew.

Wilma told her a little about her own background. Giselle told her that she had a son, "But today, he's at my mother's apartment in Kaiserstrasse." Wilma remembered the note in the letter to Giselle. Were they planning to kill her son when he takes the tram home from visiting his grandmother? How horrible!

"He visits my mom every Saturday."

"Do you have a husband?" Wilma asked.

"Yes, but he's not at home."

Wilma wanted to ask more, but she thought she shouldn't

seem eager to pry into Giselle's affairs. So she waited. Giselle didn't offer any further explanation.

When the planting was done, they agreed that next Saturday might be another time they could work together, but neither of them could promise. "If I can go then," Wilma said, "I'll be here at 10:00 A.M. I wish I could be more definite than that. With neither one of us having a telephone, I can't think how else we could make an arrangement."

"That's fine. I'll take another tram line so I can go directly home. Thanks for this. It's been the best day I've had in a long time."

Gardening always brightens people's spirits, Wilma thought. Riding back home, she hoped she would return to find Günter, but he wasn't there, nor was Klaus. Now she was really worried. She went up to see Fritzy. "No, there's no other train they can take."

"What about a bus?" Fritzy couldn't answer that question until she got to the library on Monday. Wilma went to the central bus station and inquired there. A bus to Berlin did stop at Vogelsang on Tuesdays. Maybe they'd be able to take it home.

Günter and Klaus were back at Die Birken on Tuesday evening, much to everyone's relief. A family in Vogelsang had put them up for the two nights before the bus stopped at the town. Klaus and Günter did some work on their house to repay them for their hospitality. They had been very lucky. On the bus back to Berlin, they discussed the need to keep what they saw a secret. If they could get word to Andi, they would, but for now they had no way of doing so. "At least it is good news, in the sense that the missiles have been removed. They are no longer a threat."

"Except that you told me the Russians now have better missiles —missiles with a longer range that can do deadly damage."

"True." Günter didn't want Klaus to worry about it, so he didn't respond further. "You look good with a beard. Are you going to keep it?"

"Maybe. I'll see if Mila likes it."

When they went back to work after two days of unscheduled absence, the zoo manager said they would have to work the following weekend to make up for the time they missed. That seemed only fair to them.

The following Saturday, around one in the afternoon, Klaus was trimming back new growth that was encroaching on the parking lot at the warehouse's back side. A few cars and a van were parked there. Another car drove in. Klaus noticed nicely dressed women going in and out of the warehouse. Some workers brought out various items—an appliance of some sort and a big piece of furniture. Two men lifted them carefully up to put them into the van, through its rear doors.

A man came out to talk with the driver of the van. Oh my God, is that…? Yes, it is, it's Walter! He was wearing a black leather jacket that set off his light blond hair. Klaus hoped Walter wouldn't notice him. He still felt the sting from Walter's belittling comments at Sabine's wedding. What would he say this time—some disparaging remark, no doubt.

It appeared to Klaus that Walter gave the driver of the van some instructions. Then he slapped the side of the truck, and walked back into the warehouse. The van drove out of the driveway and turned onto the city highway. Klaus recalled Walter bragging about his import business. Is this what the warehouse is for? Klaus asked himself.

Knowing Walter, the operation was probably shady in some way. He related all this to Günter, who had never seen Walter, but had heard all the old stories about Little Shit before.

RADIOGRAMS

JULY 1963

On a hot Saturday morning in July, Klaus took Mila to Tierpark Zoo. Working there permitted Klaus to bring a guest for free. On this Saturday, heavy showers were predicted for the afternoon, so Klaus and Mila got there when the zoo opened. Klaus had in mind showing Mila various birds. He had already told her how he hoped to lead bird tours at the zoo, but he hadn't yet built up his confidence to broach the idea with the zoo's manager.

Since it was going to rain, Klaus thought it best to start at the far end. However, it took them longer to walk there than anticipated. He couldn't stop himself from pointing out various places he had worked on the way. When they finally got to the warehouse, they noticed several cars parked in its parking lot. Once again, some women and a couple were entering the building.

Klaus saw his chance. "Come on, let's pretend we're a married couple looking for things for our apartment."

"I have no trouble with acting." She squeezed his hand.

"But there is a man—a very good looking man with blond hair and possibly a black leather jacket—who might be in there. If so, I'll want to come back out before he sees me—just warning you."

"Really, what could be wrong with a good-looking guy in a black leather jacket?" Mila teased.

"He's a jerk!"

"What's in the building? It has no windows."

"I really don't know. Let's follow that couple getting out of their car."

When they walked through the door, they tried not to show their astonishment. Immediately before them were two leather couches, several large teak dining room tables and chairs to the right, and some radiograms on the left. Mila went up to one of those. She lifted a lid that concealed a record player turntable. On the other side was a radio. The lower half had slots for phonograph albums and built-in speakers on either side. Mila kept her jaw from dropping and put on a discerning demeanor. She turned to Klaus, taking his arm and speaking in a voice loud enough for the nearby salesman to hear: "I noticed you referred to this as a radiogram, but in my family we call this an entertainment console—or a radio/phono console. My uncle has one. He rather likes it."

Another customer came to inspect the same piece of furniture. She wore a tailored blue suit with shoes to match. "Hmm, does this come in black?" she asked the salesman.

"Our next shipment is in three weeks, but I think we would have to order that color."

"When could you have it here?"

"We have a shipment every month, so if they can produce it in black, we could have it here in two months."

"We're having a rather big party in three months time. I do want it by then."

"If you leave your details with me, I'll contact Herr Neumann, our supplier, and let you know what he says is possible. Is there something else we can help you with? We have the latest type of freezers at the far end over there."

"No, no thank you." The woman looked in her pocketbook and pulled out a business card. "Here is my husband's number where you can reach us. How soon can you let us know?"

"By Monday afternoon, I imagine. Herr Neumann places orders every Monday morning."

Klaus and Mila walked around feigning interest in a few items until a salesman started to approach them. Mila smiled but walked away to overhear another couple. When she felt they had overstayed their welcome, she slipped her arm through Klaus' and said rather loudly. "Well, we'll have to come back when we have more time." She turned to the salesman and asked: "Are you just open on Saturdays?"

"Yes," he said, "only on Saturdays."

Once outside and alone, they repeated to each other the information they had gleaned.

They had both heard that deliveries were on the third Thursday of every month. Klaus overheard a man ask if he and his wife could have the first pick if they came to the warehouse on Friday afternoon. The salesman said: "No, the deliveries are made at night and we aren't ready to show them on Friday."

Mila heard a woman comment: "This looks like it's Swedish."

Klaus heard the salesman reply in a low voice: "We try to get nothing but the best."

Mila remembered one woman said she lived in the Niederschönhausen area. "I think that is where Party bigwigs live," she told Klaus.

Later that night, Klaus suggested to Günter that they go for a walk. Günter heard the entire story of Mila and Klaus' warehouse escapade. It reminded Günter of what he had heard while working in the labor camp in Belarus. Party members lived privileged lives with a higher standard of living. Their hypocrisy was blatant: preaching socialism for the masses and reaping the luxuries of capitalism for themselves.

SECRETS

DECEMBER 1963

Ever since Günter returned from the second spying trip to Vogelsang with Klaus, he had been trying to think of how to contact Andi without arousing suspicion. Mail was opened and read by the Stasi. No one was allowed to go for a visit East to West or from West to East. All telephone calls across to West Berlin were tapped and recorded by Stasi informers. Günter could not think of a way to get a message to Andi through conventional channels.

A glimmer of hope came in mid-December that same year. The mayors of the two Berlins began talks to explore ways that relatives could be reunited over Christmas. After months of negotiations, they reached an agreement: certain residents of West Berlin could obtain a border pass to visit relatives in East Berlin between December 19, 1963, and January 5, 1964. A window opened for Günter—17 days!—until he read the restrictions: "Relatives eligible to receive visits are parents, grandparents, children, grandchildren, siblings, aunts and uncles, nieces and nephews, as well as the spouses of these persons; spouses can visit each other."

Günter read the details of the agreement to Klaus. "It doesn't do us any good, because Andi is not a relative and Reni is in New York, now."

Klaus was deep in thought, then brightened up. "Shall we go for a walk?" When they had reached the corner of Hoffmannstrasse,

Klaus told Günter: "Mila's mother can come for a visit!" Klaus explained that his girlfriend hadn't seen her mother since the wall went up.

"How does that help?"

"Well, could we get a message to Andi through her? Couldn't she deliver it for us when she returns to West Berlin?"

"I suppose you're right. Would she be willing to do that, and is she reliable?"

"I'm sure, from what Mila tells me, they all feel the same way we do."

"Another thing to consider is what if Mila's mother gets caught with the letter? She would be in trouble with the authorities. She would never be allowed to visit East Berlin again, for sure. Then they would go after the letter writers. People have gone to prison for less."

"You're right. Well, I'll talk to Mila and see what she thinks."

That night, Günter stayed up late trying to figure out how he could write a message to Andi that would not be detected. He wanted to tell Andi two pieces of information: 1) The missiles have been sent back to Russia; and 2) Swedish furniture and appliances are being delivered in the evenings of the third Thursday of the month to the warehouse at Tierpark Zoo. He formulated the simplest message possible using Hungarian words for furniture (butor) and delivery (kezbesite) and an anagram for Sweden: "spitkaputballs3rdbutorlunationgodownkezbesiteszSnedew."

The next day that Günter had off from work, he bought a copy of the Hungarian author Konstantine Gamsakhurdia's new book: *David the Builder*. The book was not on the forbidden list, nor was it likely to be in the future. He wrote a note to go in it:

In David the Builder, Gamsakhurdia has made some significant comments that I hope you find as interesting as I did. Enjoy and Merry Christmas, from your old bird-watching friend, Wolfgang Bircher 12/19/1963

Günter broke his message into three sections and put them

on page 12, 19, and 63, in small script.

The next night, Klaus washed up but didn't change out of his work clothes. It would be awkward carrying a book in public. That was something he had never done. He would feel conspicuous. So he decided the big heavy jacket that he wore at the zoo would serve as his book satchel. It had a large deep pocket in which he carried his binoculars while at work. Now, the pocket could hold the book Günter wanted to send to Andi. Having the message to Andi hidden in the book instead of a letter was smart of Günter, Klaus thought, less likely to be discovered or intercepted.

Without access to a telephone, there was no way he could let Mila know he was coming. In spite of that, she and her father always had a way of making him feel welcome, and tonight was no exception, although they were in the middle of a dress rehearsal of *The Glass Menagerie* when he arived. Klaus was glad to wait. He had the rare opportunity to watch Mila on stage. She was playing the part of Amanda. Klaus didn't know the play but he soon was captivated. She can really act, Klaus thought, on top of all the other things she can do. At times, there were moments of silence in which all that could be heard were the growls from Klaus' stomach.

After the rehearsal, Mila and her father shared their boiled potatoes and knackwurst with him. Klaus was embarrassed that he hadn't brought food. As good as the dinner was, it wasn't enough for any of them. Next time, he would bring some food with him. The conversation never flagged.

"Yes, we got a letter yesterday that Mom is coming on December 19, and staying until the fifth of January." Mila took her father's hand while they smiled at each other. She turned to Klaus and said in a low voice: "She's bringing our niece, Ute, with her."

"That's wonderful," Klaus responded, also keeping his voice practically to a whisper.

Mila looked at her father. He nodded. "But she doesn't have a niece in West Berlin." she whispered. "We've never heard of Ute before." Her eyes grew big.

Later, when he and Mila were alone, she told him about her mom. "My parents met in a circus during the Weimar Republic. They adopted a little baby born on Kristallnacht."

"That's when you were born, wasn't it?"

"Yes,…I was that baby."

Klaus was shocked. "What happened to your parents?"

"They were picked up and taken away."

"Oh my God, how horrible for you!"

"Well, not for me, I couldn't have had better substitute parents. We don't know what happened to my real parents."

"What were their names?"

"That's it. We don't know for sure. They had come from a Roma community somewhere in Poland, or possibly Hungary. Their names were Dika and Tobar at the circus. Nobody knew them by anything else. She was a contortionist and he, a juggler. They possibly weren't even married. Mom was taking care of me, their baby, the night they didn't return. The Gestapo probably didn't know about me or didn't care. Mom and Dad went down to the town hall a week later and registered me as their child. No questions were asked."

They kept quiet for a minute while Klaus digested what he had heard. "What did your Schröder parents do in the circus?"

"Dad was the manager and Mom kept track of finances."

Mila said she knew her mother would agree to deliver Andi's Christmas present when she returned to the West. "Just leave it here with us. I want you to meet her. Can you come for dinner on the 21st? That will give Mom a few days to reunite with us."

Next time, Klaus thought, he must bring plenty of knackwurst. But it wasn't guilt that kept him awake that night, rather, it was the vision of Mila's chestnut-colored hair. He kept fantasizing about running his fingers through it, in a fit of passion.

On December 19, when Frau Schröder walked through

checkpoint Charlie, Herr Schröder knew to greet her as his cousin, Emma. The letter he had received in mid-December was not in his wife's handwriting and was signed: "Your cousin, Emma."

"Emma, it's so good to see you again. Thank you for coming." When they hugged, Frau Schröder whispered: "Let's go. If I start crying, my makeup will run." She had tried to make herself look ten years younger. Everybody knew that the border guards at the checkpoints were all Stasi people. They took pictures of each person coming and going, and consulted their records.

The night of the 21st, Klaus arrived with eight links of knackwurst. He almost forgot to offer them to Frau Schröder, because he was fixated on the wonderful aroma coming from their small kitchen area. It was a delicious smell of something vaguely familiar, maybe from childhood. Frau Schröder had brought coffee and a leg of lamb with her. The dinner was so scrumptious, Klaus hardly held his own in the conversation. After the last bite of the lamb went into his mouth, he looked up and saw Mila's mother smiling at him and about to cry.

An hour after dinner, Mila's parents went into the theater, leaving Mila and Klaus alone. Mila confirmed that her mother would gladly take the book across to Andi at the Free University. Somehow, this night, they both knew that a turning point had been reached. Klaus was reminded that all his happiness with Mila could so easily vanish. He hadn't planned on asking her to marry him tonight, but it just happened. He had so little to offer her. His salary was livable but his home was just an area of the basement, without even a window to look out through. It would take them years to get an actual apartment.

They kissed. He restrained himself and only touched her silky hair. He wanted to be with her the rest of his life. "You must see where you would have to live, before you agree."

"You're forgetting, I did see the basement, the day you all went to the wedding. I could live there. I could live anywhere with you. Marrying you is all I need. "

"I want you to see it again to be sure about what you are getting yourself into."

They planned that the next Saturday he would pick her up and bring her to his place. He had spent the morning trying to clean things up. He made sure the WC was immaculate. He had built a shelf some time ago to hold his toilet articles by one of the big zinc sinks. Thank goodness, most tenants no longer washed their clothes in the basement. A few had bought little washing machines for their apartments. The washer's hoses could hook up to the sink's faucet and drain. They would dry the clothes on a folding rack. Others in the building did not mind spending some money at the laundromat, only a block away. These advancements helped to make Klaus' basement nook more private.

Klaus cooked on a hotplate. Two years prior, he had constructed a wall with a door to enclose his space and bought a small refrigerator. In order to live here with Mila, he would have to enlarge the bed and make a suitable dresser. He could do all of that with his carpentry skills. His tools and equipment were nearby in another part of the basement. In time, he would properly enlarge the space.

After he showed her his set up—he couldn't really call it an apartment—he had intended to talk about a wedding date, but the discussion didn't advance beyond the bed size. Three hours later, they resumed their conversation in close proximity. Mila's hair was disheveled. They were both hungry. He whispered in her ear that he would get her a currywurst on the way back to The Cellar. Still, they didn't want to move.

"Would you ever want to leave East Germany?" Mila asked.

He didn't know what to say. "It's not that I've never thought about it before. I mean, of course, I've thought about it, but I've never really considered it. I wouldn't go unless you came. Being with you will always be my first choice."

"That's how I feel too, but what if one of us has an opportunity to leave? What if the opportunity only allows one person to escape? Would you take it, if I promised to follow?"

He thought hard: "If you somehow were able to get out, I would definitely try to as well, but it could take a long time. It could take years before another opportunity comes."

"I would try, if you went first. I know that."

"So when should we get married?"

"It will have to be after my mother leaves. I wouldn't feel right about her spending time on a wedding when she and Dad have so little time together. Who knows when they'll see each other again? In fact, I've been thinking, I don't think we should see each other again, until we hear that Mom has made it across the border without incident with your friend's book. If something bad happens and she gets stopped, you know the Stasi will start looking into all of us. No sense in you being incriminated."

Klaus took Mila home. She handed him a black shirt and some black face paint. "I want you to have this in case you need it. You will not be easily observed at night wearing black."

Does she think that I will have an opportunity to escape, he asked himself? Does she want me to try to leave? He was restless that night, thinking about these things. It was hard to say goodbye, but he only had to wait twelve days after Christmas to see her again. She had also suggested that they not talk about their wedding plans to anyone, until her mother was safely back in West Berlin. All those precautions were typical with people's plans to cross over, but still, something did not sit well with him.

Mila's mother came to East Berlin with a plan. She had borrowed her friend, Emma Franke's, passport. Emma had a twelve year old daughter, Lena. The passport had been issued seven years previously, so Lena's picture showed a five-year-old. Her plan was to take Mila back with her. The plan had several obstacles. She didn't know how her husband would feel about her taking Mila from him. Mila was a great companion for him, as well as a vital helper at The Cellar. On the other hand, she knew her husband would want the best for Mila. Then, there was the problem of trying to make Mila look twelve years old.

What Frau Schröder didn't realize was that Mila had fallen in love and didn't want to leave Klaus. "You'll see, Mama, how wonderful he is when he comes to dinner."

"He's been a great help to the theater." Herr Schröder went on to tell his wife about the numerous sets Klaus had helped to construct.

Frau Schröder was impressed with the young man—good appetite, polite—"but they can't speak their minds here." And later: "You have to be so careful as to what plays you put on." And finally: "We'll find a way to get Klaus to the West."

After a few days, her mother started telling Mila how important it was to be able to share her thoughts and opinions with others; to vote for a candidate that she wanted, and to have her vote counted; to participate in activities of her own choosing—she went on and on. To Herr Schröder, she said how vital it was to let their daughter grow to become the person she wanted to be. Mila had spent her days in school resisting being cornered and restricted. Her protests kept her from going to university.

Herr Schröder countered: "Yes, that's true, but Mila has always loved what she does. She learns by reading and acting. And now, she has a wonderful young man that she wants to marry."

"Her prospects are to live in a basement, with a husband who works as a groundsman in a zoo! I do like him, but she can have a better life in West Berlin."

"You'd be hard put to find a better man to live with for the rest of your life," Herr Schröder said.

Her mother made West Berlin sound intriguing. Mila started fantasizing about a life with Klaus where he could have his own carpentry business. As it was now, he could only do private carpentry work informally and secretly. In West Berlin, she could take college courses; so could Klaus.

If she escaped with her mother, she would leave Klaus behind, but surely he could escape, too. It might take a while before an opportunity presented itself. The thought of leaving her father behind was almost more troubling. She couldn't imagine him leaving The Cellar. On the other hand, he was a master at improvisation, not just as an actor, but at reinventing himself. He could do it. He knew how to run a business, manage finances, and make the most out of a bad situation.

Mila's mother made it sound easy. It was like playing a new role. It felt like a worthy challenge. Three days before her mother was due to return, Mila decided to try to escape as a twelve-year-old girl. She knew Klaus would feel deceived about it, but she tried to think of it as bestowing a new challenge on him as well. Her action would encourage him to escape, too. Mila was proud of her adaptability, her facility to make changes. That was what made life exciting. Mila was young.

Her mother said they should try to cross on the last day of her stay. That would be when most people would go back. Hopefully, the guards would have to process people quickly and wouldn't take the time to scrutinize the passport carefully enough to see that little Lena had not been with Emma when she entered East Berlin 17 days earlier. Fortunately, Mila was short in stature. She acted the part perfectly. A few days later, Herr Schröder received a letter from his 'cousin' saying how much she enjoyed the visit.

When January 6 arrived, Klaus came home from work to get cleaned up. Within twenty minutes, he was out the door on his way to see Mila. To his surprise, no one answered his knock, so he tried to open The Cellar door. It was locked! They may have gone to the shops to buy some food for dinner. It had snowed during the previous night. About two inches had accumulated. None of it had melted yet as the temperature remained well below zero. He was cold just standing, so he sat down on the stone steps hugging his knees for extra warmth while he waited for them to return.

A half hour later, Herr Schröder approached. He looked glum until he spotted Klaus. "Oh God, you don't know, do you?"

Klaus panicked: "What's happened?"

"Let's go inside."

Klaus smelled alcohol on his breath. He had never known Herr Schröder to drink. The man fumbled with the key until the door unlocked. Klaus turned white, not knowing what was going on. Mila's father said nothing until they were seated at the table with a cup of tea.

"They made it safely to West Berlin."

"They?"

"Mila and her mother."

"Mila?"

"Yes." Herr Schröder explained to him how it all came about. Klaus felt as though the wind had been knocked out of him. He couldn't talk. Finally he asked point blank: "You mean, she's left?"

"Yes."

"She's gone to West Berlin?"

"Yes."

"Why didn't she tell me?" Elbows on the table, he supported his head in his hands. He felt as if his life had been taken away from him.

"She loves you very much. At first, she didn't want to go, she didn't want to leave you, but then she thought the two of you would have so many more chances in West Berlin. She thought a friend of yours, Andi, I think she said his name is, might be able to get you a fake ID."

"How could she? She didn't even discuss it with me." He was feeling utterly betrayed.

The two men sat in silence. Herr Schröder got up to pour them another cup of tea. Klaus got a whiff of the man's breath again and looked into his eyes. He realized that Herr Schröder's loss was even greater: both his wife and his daughter were gone.

It took three weeks for Klaus to smile again, but the pain from losing Mila never left him. He finally started talking to his friends in his usual way—not as eagerly as he once did, but he no longer moped constantly and wasn't as downcast. Working with Günter at the zoo helped. There, when they were alone, Klaus could divulge how he was feeling.

As time went by, his concern for Herr Schröder increased. Klaus was fairly sure he was drinking daily. The theater was black, of course. How could he put on a performance by himself? Klaus hoped he would find a new purpose. He was not so old, maybe only fifty. His hair was graying, but Klaus knew the man was capable of great outbursts of energy.

Klaus would open up to Wilma when she occasionally came down to the basement to talk to him after work. She sat at the small table where he ate his dinners while he shared with her his concern for Herr Schröder. Wilma was so good at listening. She only offered a comment after he had told her everything. "No," Klaus told her, "Herr Schröder's not the gardening type."

Finally, one night he decided to go up to the third floor to talk to Fritzy. She probably knew everything already, being so close to Wilma. As he stood outside her door, he was reminded of a happier time in Fritzy's apartment. Less than a year ago in June, he and other friends had gathered around Fritzy's new TV to watch the handsome American President John F. Kennedy give a speech. People called it the 'Ich bin ein Berliner' speech. Klaus had been amazed he could see Kennedy so clearly in front of the West Berlin Town Hall. It was exhilarating to feel he was right there with the crowd of 120,000 West Berliners.

When Fritzy opened her door to Klaus' knock, Ursula was doing exercises in the middle of the living room floor. He hadn't seen Ursula in months. Klaus knew she had graduated from high school last year and was now working as a gymnastics coach. He watched the girl practice standing on one hand, and could easily imagine that she would make a good trainer.

Fritzy handed him a cup of tea. She had been the one to introduce Klaus to the Schröders and The Cellar theater. She knew Mila had surreptitiously left East Berlin for the West. She knew all that, but what she didn't know was that Herr Schröder was deeply depressed. Klaus gave her the details of how he had been living during the last month. "He's deteriorating, and it's so painful to see."

Ursula sat cross-legged on the floor in front of them to listen. At one point she interrupted—"So there's a stage?" she asked. Minutes later she commented: "The Cellar sounds like a perfect place to have a gymnastics exhibition." Fritzy rolled her eyes. Ursula continued her fantasy: "I have about ten students that I think would like to put on a show," Ursula said to Klaus.

"It's a small stage," said Klaus.

"Can you hang a hoop?"

Klaus thought this was off the subject but, to be polite, went along with her whimsy. "There is open space above the stage. Yes, I probably could install a hanging hoop, but I wouldn't do it." Klaus was recalling Günter's concern for safety when the two of them climbed trees.

"What about a trapeze?"

"Both a hoop and a trapeze would have to be strong enough to support ten times the weight of the acrobat. That's too much responsibility. I wouldn't want to run the risk of getting it wrong."

"Don't be so ambitious, Ursula," Fritzy advised. "Your

students aren't up for such tricky maneuvers. Think about things they can do on the floor." Fritzy looked impatient. "Why are we talking about this anyway? We're trying to think of how to help Herr Schröder."

"Yes, but maybe this would help him. You know—give him something else to focus on. OK, so I guess we can't do aerial acrobatics, or hang from an apparatus. Is that it? I understand." Ursula went on, "We're working on a showpiece right now, a human pyramid." Ursula took a breath. "I've always wanted to do tightrope walking, but I guess that's out, too. OK, no matter, I think it would be the perfect place to put on a gymnastics show."

Before Klaus knew it, Ursula had talked Fritzy into driving to The Cellar so she could see the stage. Now that Fritzy had her Trabi, it didn't take much to coax her to drive anywhere. Even Klaus smiled at the prospect.

Wilma brought in a scuttle of coal. She remembered when she had to pull it up in the dumbwaiter to the fourth floor, when she lived up there with Fritzy. It was so much easier living on the first floor. The temperature outdoors was -5 °C and it didn't feel much warmer indoors.

In winter, the allotment grounds were either frozen solid, covered with snow, or soggy from a cold rain. Gardening was impossible. For these months, Wilma transitioned from gardener to knitter in her off hours from work.

She knitted a sweater or two for Christmas presents every year. By this time, she had knitted one for each person she knew well. Fritzy wore her maroon sweater almost daily. That was so gratifying. For Ursula's sweater, Wilma chose a robin's-egg blue pattern with white snowflakes. She also made her some mittens and a hat of the same pattern. For Klaus, she knitted a beige pullover and a cap to match. She added ear flaps to the cap as he spent so much time outdoors in the cold. He frequently wore both when he went to work. Günter's sweater, a cardigan, took her the longest to make. It had cables down the front and a v-neck. She knitted covers for the buttons. It was a gray color—lighter than charcoal. Once Christmas was over this year, she bought some inexpensive wool that was thick. The color was grass-green—perfect for Giselle to wear while working at the allotments in spring and fall.

Wilma hadn't seen Giselle for close to three months. It was quite understandable that she wouldn't show up at the allotments in this season, but when Wilma delivered mail at her house, once or twice a week, there was no sign of her there either. She knew it was unlikely that during the minute it took her to deliver the mail, Giselle would be coming in or out of her door, but she wondered how she was. Wilma had noticed that Giselle's mail was no longer being opened by the post office.

Giselle had never been to Wilma's apartment. She wouldn't know where Wilma lived. Previously, they had always seen each other during mail deliveries or at the allotments. So now that the sweater was finished, Wilma decided to take it with her when she delivered Giselle's mail.

As Wilma walked up to the house, she thought she saw a curtain in the window move, yet when she rang the doorbell, no one answered. That was disappointing, but Wilma was not ready to give up. The following Saturday morning, she gave it another try. This time, she took the tram. After ringing twice, a young man around twenty years old opened the door. He hesitated when Wilma asked to speak to Giselle, but finally went to retrieve her. Is he Giselle's son?

When Giselle appeared, she looked haggard. Oh, my gosh, Wilma thought, she's lost weight. Now the sweater will be too big. They barely greeted each other before Wilma blurted out: "Are you all right? What's happened?"

"Oh, Wilma! Yes, I'm all right, but..." She lowered her voice, "...my husband is home now. He was released from Hohenschönhausen a month ago."

Hohenschönhausen was the Stasi prison for political prisoners. Wilma didn't know what to say. "Prison! I'm so sorry."

"He's served his term, but it's not over. It will never be over."

"What happened?"

Giselle asked Wilma inside, shut the door, then explained in a quiet voice that her husband, Thomas, was caught digging a tunnel almost three years ago. "You may have read about it."

Wilma was completely caught off guard and didn't know what to say. Finally, she mustered: "You must be happy to have him home."

"Well, yes, of course....Would you like to meet him? I'm afraid I can't let you stay long. We never have any visitors." She looked like she was going to cry. "He hasn't met anyone new since he's come home, so I'm not sure how he'll respond. It's good that you're not in your uniform."

When Wilma entered the sitting room, Herr Mechler was in a stuffed chair. His head seemed to be dangling to one side. When he saw her, he lifted his legs and curled up, holding his knees to his chest.

"It's alright Tom. This is a friend of mine, Wilma, Wilma Bauer." He looked at her with his head to one side, seemingly too scared to look at her straight-on.

Giselle asked Wilma to sit down on the sofa. Wilma gave Giselle the sweater.

"For me? How wonderful. What a bright, happy color."

Giselle tried to keep a conversation going that included her husband. She spoke slowly always looking at Tom to see how he was responding. When they started talking about the allotments, Tom perked up and looked at Wilma. Wilma had expected to see scars or a deformity on the other side of his face. Now that he showed it to her, there was no obvious sign of physical damage.

Wilma got up to leave after 15 minutes. At the door, Giselle said: "Did you see him smile when we talked about growing beans?" His smile seemed to have given Giselle hope.

When Wilma related this to Günter, he became glum and commented: "They don't use physical torture so much as psychological torture. I've heard they never let you sleep. The lights are kept on all night and they bang on the metal door periodically to keep you awake. Some prisoners are kept in solitary confinement for over a year."

"That's appalling. How can human beings be so cruel? How do you know all that?"

"Andi told me."

"What do you think she meant when she said 'It will never be over?'" Wilma asked.

"They will probably continue to make things difficult for him. He'll need at least a year to recover psychologically," Günter estimated.

That night in bed, Wilma said: "I can't stop thinking about that poor man, Thomas. Maybe we should reconsider our own plans."

Günter didn't respond. He didn't want to tell her that he was having doubts too, but for a different reason. He wasn't sure he should discuss it with her. He was worried that Klaus would be miserable again, once the two of them left East Berlin.

KLAUS

THE END OF FEBRUARY 1964

One morning weeks later, Günter and Klaus were working in the palace basement when the attendant at the door to the palace came down the stairs to tell Klaus that a man was there to see him. Klaus went up the stairs wondering who it might be. A nicely-dressed man wearing a trilby and an overcoat approached him saying: "So, you are Klaus. My mother used to tell me about you, but the last time I saw you, you were only five years old. I'm your Uncle Kurt, Kurt Albach."

Klaus' heart fluttered with excitement to think that he had a living relative. The Kurt fellow chattered on until the zoo attendant returned to his post at the door. Then he resumed talking with Klaus, but in a quieter voice: "Show me what you are doing here." The man winked at him.

Klaus was taken by surprise. "So, you are an uncle on my mother's side?"

Once they were downstairs and alone, Kurt again winked at Klaus. Klaus led him away from the stairs over to where Günter was involved in framing off a room for the new auditorium. Klaus introduced Günter to Herr Albach, disappointed that the man, whoever he really was, was not actually his uncle.

"Do we have privacy here?" Kurt said in a low voice.

Both Günter and Klaus took a deep breath. What is all this about, they each wondered? Finally, Günter said: "Yes, there's no one around us here. No one can hear." By then, Günter had registered Kurt's accent. It sounded Swedish, yet his name was German.

"I'm an art historian from the Thielska Galleriet in Stockholm." Günter had never been to Sweden but he had heard of the famous art museum. "My coming here was arranged by Andi Szabó, a friend of yours, I'm told." He took out a card from his wallet and showed it to them both. "Andi got your message," he said to Günter. "I'm here to make a quick evaluation of the art. If I think it is of value, we will try to rescue it." Kurt paused to let them take in the significance of what he just said before continuing: "I would like to see the paintings. I have only one hour before I have to leave."

While Günter led Kurt to the backmost region of the basement, Klaus went outside to get the hoe from the storage shed. With it, he pried the panel open. Kurt kept taking pictures. Günter noticed his camera resembled Andi's. They dragged the crate out and opened it. Kurt took a flash photo of the crate.

Having removed the cloth from the painting in front, he took a picture of it. "Oh my, my, my. Uh-huh, I think a Modigliani."

Klaus went off and came back with a flashlight. They looked at the second: "Possibly a Münter, Gabriele Münter. That's exciting. Oh my goodness, two more!" They removed the cloth on the third: "Oh my God, I believe this might be 'Ulf in the Evening'— taken from a Norwegian collector during the Nazi occupation. I believe the painter is our own Carl Larsson."

He's practically foaming at the mouth, Klaus thought. The last painting Kurt thought was a Dufy. He took notes on all four paintings in a miniscule script. Then said: "Let's put these back, very carefully." When all that was done, he asked for their estimate on how much the crated weighed.

Klaus guessed about 60 pounds. Kurt estimated the crate's dimensions: "I'd say 6'x4'x1'." They pushed the crate back and closed the panel.

"Let's go out where there is some light." The men kept their voices low. "Now, about these deliveries on the third Thursday of the month," he said looking at Günter.

"Oh good, Andi, understood all of my message," Günter said. "Yes, indeed. We've been working on this. We are hoping that you two can have the crate moved close to the warehouse door, but hidden in the woods on the third Thursday in March. If there is any threat of rain, could you have it covered? Do you think you could do that?"

"Yes, absolutely, no problem." Günter said emphatically. He looked at Klaus who nodded.

"If you can do that, we'll take it from there. We have already been working on the arrangements. Do you have a way of moving the crate?"

"Yes, the zoo has a flatbed truck," Günter offered.

"What time do you think you would try to move the crate upstairs and out of the building? We don't want anybody to see you do that."

This guy seems to be more than an art historian, Günter thought. "It would have to be before closing." he said, looking at Klaus. "What do you think?"

"I think we should start the process around 3:30 in the afternoon. We have to get it to the warehouse and hide it in the woods before 5:00—when everyone leaves work to go home."

"Very good! We'll have a distraction lined up around 3:30, so you can get the crate upstairs and onto the truck. Andi tells us you both are good at improvising."

Who is this 'us', Günter wondered?

"And could at least one of you stay with the crate until the delivery truck arrives?" Kurt asked.

"Sure, we'll guard it the entire time. I don't think the delivery will come before 7:00 P.M."

Kurt corrected Günter. "It will be there between 11:30 and 12:30 that night. Make sure both of you and the crate are completely out of sight. The truck will be unloaded and, hopefully, at that point, the other people will go inside the warehouse. Then, the deliverymen driving the truck will start looking for you. That's when they hope to put the crate inside the truck without the others seeing them. You both stay out of sight, the whole time, OK?"

"Yes, we understand."

"Any questions?

"Do you know where the warehouse is?"

Kurt smirked. "Oh yes, not to worry. I have to leave, but before I go, I have something rather important for you from Andi." He pulled out an odd shaped envelope from the inside jacket pocket and handed it to Günter. "Good luck."

Kurt left them as quickly as he had come.

"I think we should open this up when we get home. We've lost an hour of work as it is. We don't want the people upstairs to become suspicious."

When they got home from the zoo, they both went into Günter's apartment to see what was in the envelope. Inside were three fake IDs: one each for Günter, Wilma, and Klaus. Their covers were somewhat worn. Klaus' was a different color and style, since it was more recent. Günter studied both his and Wilma's. They looked plausible. According to the ID, Günter's name was Wolfgang Valk and his birthday was correct, except for the year, which was listed as 1892, making him supposedly 72 years old—a good 20 years older than he actually was. He thought he could pull that one off. Just by removing his false teeth, he looked 10 years older.

He looked at Wilma's ID. She was to be Ute Valk, born in 1894, so she was 70 years old. They would have to work hard to make her appear so old. The scenario they were supposed to adopt was typed out on three sheets of paper. He started to read them when he realized Klaus was being very quiet.

Klaus had hardly looked at his passport or the typewritten directions that went with his ID. Tucked inside his passport was an additional folded piece of paper. He had walked over to sit in the chair by the lamp. Taking a deep breath, he began reading a letter from Mila.

...How difficult it was to make the decision to leave you.

How could you, Klaus thought. He felt tears welling. All the plans we had. They must have meant little to you—just another script in a play.

I was too optimistic. Dad has probably told you how we did it. I hope he's all right.

The letter was written on very thin tissue folded into a tiny square. It opened up into a large piece of paper, covered in Mila's miniscule script, just large enough to be read.

I thought you could easily do it, too.

Klaus noted that Mila avoided using the word: 'escape.'

My mother was insistent. Dad was very much against her plan. I do and I don't want to coax you to try, as well. I do, because I love you so much and will always want to live my life with you, but I don't, because I now know how incredibly lucky we were. Since being here, I have learned how many East Berliners have been killed in the attempt. Many, many more than we ever knew, because the deaths are not reported there.

This is such a mixed message. She doesn't want me to try except that she's sending me this letter with a fake ID.

I have been told that all letters from East to West Berlin are opened and read by the Stasi, but we can write each other, if you address your letters to Astrid Richter at Kellerstrasse 187, West Berlin. Astrid is a friend of my mother's who lives in the apartment next door to ours.

Mila's letter went on to say how her father could write her mother using a different name and address, which she included. She gave some details about their life together in West Berlin.

We are renting a small one-bedroom apartment. Mom is working for an accountant. I'm taking an adult education class. My monthly checkups are going well....

Monthly checkups—what the hell does that mean?

I'm told that all phone calls across the border are listened in on. Don't risk making one.

She finished the letter with words that touched Klaus:

Know that I will always love you. I will think of you as my husband whether or not we can ever marry or live together. I will be here waiting for you ten years, twenty years—whatever it takes. Just knowing you are alive gives me hope and will sustain me. I would rather know you are there and well, than have you take a chance that kills you.

Your soulmate,
Mila

THE CRATE

MARCH 1964

As the third Thursday in March approached, Günter and Klaus became increasingly anxious. They knew exactly where they would hide the crate. They had already picked out a place behind some young spruce trees, adjacent to the driveway. The crate would be exposed from the north end so they needed to put some brush there to keep it covered. Moving large branches in the flatbed truck after trimming trees was one of their typical jobs at the zoo. They thought they could have some small boughs on the bed ready to cover up the crate as they drove it from the palace to the warehouse.

At 3:15 P.M., the truck was out in front of the palace entrance. Günter and Klaus often stopped in at the palace to use the lavatory. They descended the steps to the basement and took the crate out from behind the panel, carrying it close to the stairs but out of sight of anyone who might be looking down from the floor above. They were ready to haul it upstairs once they knew the guard was being distracted.

At 3:30 P.M., Günter and Klaus heard a horn blaring. Over that racket, Günter thought he heard a woman speaking rather frantically to the guard. "I can't stop the damn horn. Could you help me?"

"That's Fritzy's voice!" Klaus said quietly to Günter.

"You're right. She must be the distraction." The two of them lifted the crate up the stairs. The horn was still going. Günter peered out the door and saw the guard with his head under the hood of a Trabi and a woman in a maroon sweater looking in with him. They got the crate on the flatbed, threw some branches over it, and started off down the road to the warehouse, driving at their usual low speed.

Approaching the warehouse, they saw some people milling about outside the door. They stopped off to the side of the road. "This is going to be harder than we thought."

"Good God!" Klaus said, ducking down out of sight. That's Walter, you know, Little Shit." Klaus was crouched on the floor of the cab. "He doesn't know you."

"OK, if he starts to get curious about the truck, I'll get out and pretend I have some work to do in this area." Three minutes later, Günter saw a man who had to be Walter: blond hair, black leather coat, point out the truck to one of two men who had emerged from the warehouse. One man, on Walter's instructions, started to walk up to the truck, but when Günter got out of the cab and walked into the trees with loppers, he changed his mind and returned to the warehouse.

Thank God, Günter thought. He remained out of their sight but he kept checking on them. Walter got into a Mercedes and drove off. The other two men waved goodbye and went back into the warehouse. Günter hurried back to the truck and drove it up close to the small spruce trees. He and Klaus carried the crate to the hiding place, threw an old tarp over it, and brought the boughs from the flatbed over to cover it up. When they got back to the truck, Klaus crouched down again, in case the men came out while they drove off.

Günter swung the truck around to drive back in the direction of the palace. He was relieved, until he saw in his rear view mirror a man step out of the warehouse door. He didn't pay the truck any attention, but pulled a pack of cigarettes out to have a smoke. Rounding a corner and out of sight, Klaus got back up on the seat. They were halfway back to the palace, where the truck was kept, when Günter realized that they had promised that one of them would continually stay with the crate.

"Since Walter is gone, I'll walk back now," Klaus offered.

"It's going to be very cold tonight. The temperature is supposed to be above freezing, but do you feel that wind? Will you have enough on to keep warm?" Günter asked him.

"Oh, sure." Klaus was looking forward to some birdwatching and had his binoculars in his jacket pocket. "I'm wearing the sweater Wilma knitted for me under my jacket, and this cap is great."

There was a gate at the palace, but Günter had a key to get in, since they often had to be at the zoo before it opened. He parked the truck and went down to the basement to retrieve the hoe and return it to the shed. He puttered around for a few minutes so he would be leaving the zoo at 5:00 P.M., the usual closing time. He walked to a small restaurant next to the subway stop and bought three knackwursts—two for Klaus—the man was always hungry. He waited until the other workers at the zoo left for the night, then he reentered and walked to the far end. It was a good five-kilometer trek. To keep the knackwursts as warm as he could, he put them between his undershirt and flannel shirt, both of which were tucked into his trousers. They settled around his tummy. Their fragrance managed to seep up through his jacket collar, making it difficult for Günter to think of anything else during the hour's walk. By the time he reached Klaus, the sky was dark.

Günter was afraid Klaus would get carried away looking at some bird or other and would forget they were supposed to remain hidden.

"I've been hearing blackbirds," Klaus said quietly. "Listen!" Günter handed him a knackwurst, which vanished in no time, as did the second. "Thanks so much. How much do I owe you?"

"No worries. What else have you heard?"

"Nothing more, yet." No sooner was that said when they both heard a mourning hoot with a falling pitch. "It's nearby... over there." Klaus pointed but it was too dark to see anything. Since the song repeatedly came from the same location, Klaus concluded that it was perched. "It's got to be an owl," Klaus said.

This kept their minds occupied until about 8:00. They still had a four-hour wait to go. Günter was seated on the ground next to Klaus. They rested their backs on the trunk of a large oak. Günter had the reassuring thought that if Klaus fell asleep and started to snore, he could easily wake him up before anybody heard.

Around 11:30, a lamp above the warehouse doors went on. Its metal shade directed the light downward. A few minutes later, a Mercedes turned into the driveway from the highway. "Walter," Klaus said. The car stopped off to the side, right in front of the spruce trees which were hiding the crate. "Damn!" said Klaus. Walter got out of his car and walked toward the warehouse. One of the double doors opened, allowing him to enter. The door quickly shut.

Ten minutes later, a large delivery truck pulled in, made a u-turn, and backed up to within five feet of the warehouse doors. The driver and another man jumped out. The double doors swung open and Walter and three men from inside the warehouse came out. There was some discussion between them. The men from the warehouse were not dressed for the bitter wind that had picked up. They went back inside and reemerged dressed in warm jackets, caps, and gloves.

In the meantime, Walter walked around the truck inspecting it. Then he took the clipboard from one of the deliverymen and looked through the papers.

Günter and Klaus could not hear well enough to pick up what Walter was asking him. "Something's wrong! Walter looks uneasy," Klaus observed.

Finally, Walter gave the go-ahead to start unloading. The truck was packed with furniture and appliances, each draped in pads of some sort, to prevent damage. The whole process took close to an hour. All the time, the men from the warehouse still looked cold. Günter and Klaus were cold, too, but at least they were out of the wind.

When the job was finished, Walter signed some papers. He

and the other men went back into the warehouse and shut the doors. One of the deliverymen looked around. Günter stood up so he could be noticed, but it was so dark, he doubted that was possible. An intense beam of light scanned the edge of the driveway. When it illuminated Günter's face, it was immediately extinguished. The driver moved the truck near Walter's car and stayed in the driver's seat while the other man, who was large and muscular, picked up the crate himself and walked through the brush to get to the truck. He stumbled and Günter heard: "Skit," but he recovered his step and walked quickly, holding the crate. When it was placed in the back of the truck, he closed the hatch door and walked around to get into the cab.

The warehouse door opened: Walter stepped out shouting: "What's going on?" Mister Muscles said with a sheepish grin: "Had to pee!" He gave a farewell wave to Walter as he got into the cab. The driver drove off, slowly.

Walter walked over to his car, sniffing. He shrugged his shoulders and re-entered the warehouse.

Günter and Klaus got home after 2:00 A.M. Günter reassured Wilma that things went well. She offered him a hot toddy to warm him up. He said he had to get whatever sleep he could before going to work the next day, knowing that, in bed, they could whisper, safe from eavesdropping bugs. He would tell her the details of their operation tomorrow night. All he managed to say before he went into a deep sleep was that he would really miss Klaus once they were on the other side.

Walter did not sleep well. He told his current girlfriend to sleep in the other bedroom. He needed to think. All she wants is sex, just like the rest of them. This new birth control pill they take is wearing me out.

Something was wrong. What was it? The deliverymen were not the same old guys he was used to. They were too sure of themselves. That was it. There may have been a reason that one of the guys needed a substitute, but both? It made Walter nervous. Should he speak to his father about it?

This kind of stuff was what his dad and he had in common. They both were connected to the Stasi. Heinz, as an employee of the CIA, was a Stasi double agent. Walter admired that in the old geezer. The "firm" probably knew his father had been a Nazi, but did they realize he still was? Would they even care as long as he covers it up? Walter knew his dad's best friend Rein, Reinhard Zellweger, had been a high-powered Nazi, ranking just under Joseph Goebbels.

Walter decided to bring up the delivery driver switch to his father tomorrow, when he went home for his mother's birthday. His mind momentarily drifted to some previous celebrations. He had executed his first prank on her when they were still living in West Berlin. She was turning 43, and had put on an equal number of extra pounds, so he hung her voluminous underpants on the tree in front of their house. His father's fury held him in check for the next few years. But when she turned 48, he could no longer restrain himself. He handed her a giant-sized cone filled with items to hide her old age, each colorfully wrapped. His favorite was the strap to hold up her sagging jowls.

Her birthday always brightened his spirits. He knew his mother hated him. I'm the last person she wants to see on her birthday, he thought. On the day prior, he always sent her a postcard saying: "Happy Birthday, Mom, looking forward to tomorrow," just to warm her up to the occasion. He chuckled. Ah, tradition! Birthdays mean so much to my parents' generation.

To add to his worries, the next morning Walter noticed the scratch on his black Mercedes as he was depositing his girlfriend back at her apartment, before he went home to his so-called family. She was pouting again and wanted to stay in the car so they could talk things over. That very morning at the breakfast table, she had left most of her blouse unbuttoned. He acted indifferent, to drive her nuts. Before going into the shower, he stripped down to his boxers and did 20 push-ups on the floor. When he stood up, he found her panting more than he was. He laughed.

But what's with this pouting? "Get out of the car. I've got to go!" She didn't move, so he got out and went around the car to open her door. That was when he saw the scratch. "Damn it!" he shouted. The girl got out of the car immediately and disappeared into her building. "What the hell!" he shouted again.

Later, at his parents' home, he was able to corner Heinz to tell him about the warehouse incident. "Why were the deliverymen different? All the items I ordered were there. Nothing was missing."

"I'll look into it."

CHOICES

APRIL 1964

Wilma and Günter always kept their fake IDs with them, in case the Stasi inspected their apartment when they were out. They took other precautionary measures, like never talking about their escape plans in their apartment. After supper, they would often go for a walk to practice and quiz each other on their new identities. In bed at night, they whispered to each other, using their new names and discussed things like: "I know you can't wear them, but will you take your false teeth with you?"

"No, you'll have to look at me for a whole month eating applesauce."

"I had better hope I don't have my period, because I can't carry sanitary napkins with me—not if I'm supposed to be 70 years old. We will need to time it right!"

This night, their after-supper walk had to be cut short. Fritzy was going to drive them to The Cellar. Ursula and Klaus were already there. It was Ursula's gymnastic students' first performance. The price of admission was two Marks per family and the house was packed, that is, all 18 seats were occupied. Fritzy, Günter, and Wilma happily stood in the rear.

Herr Schröder opened the show dressed as a clown. "Ladies and gentlemen, we are happy to introduce to you the very first performance of The Cellar Cats." He could not go on because a two-year-old sitting in the front row burst out crying, completely distracting everybody's attention. Nothing the mother did stopped the child from bawling in fear of the clown. Herr Schröder took off his fake red nose and handed it to the child, who then started laughing. Herr Schröder pulled out another nose, this one green, from a deep pocket, and stuck it on his face. Everybody laughed.

The show went on, with Herr Schröder introducing each girl as she performed her routine. The ten girls in the show covered a range of ages. The younger ones did simple movements like somersaults, cartwheels, handstands, and splits. Ursula was on stage to spot the older girls doing more advanced maneuvers such as back handsprings, front walkovers, and backflips. Their finale was a human pyramid with all ten girls participating. The audience—parents, siblings, and friends—cheered and clapped enthusiastically.

Ursula gave credit "to Herr Schröder, for providing such a marvelous place for gymnastics." She urged young people to sign up for her classes. "I'm going to have an extra one here, every Saturday morning from 9:00-11:00 A.M. Our next performance at The Cellar will be in a month."

Fritzy drove the five of them home in her Trabi. Ursula sat on Wilma's lap. The car was struggling with the added weight. "Good thing Berlin has no steep hills." When they turned the corner onto Hoffmannstrasse, they could see the seven silver birch trees Günter and Klaus had planted fourteen years ago. They were over thirty feet tall now. Fritzy said that she could see the canopy looking down from her window that faced the street.

As the car pulled up to the front of the building, Ursula looked up at the trees and asked: "What are those funny looking tassels?"

It was the kind of question Klaus loved. "Those are the tree's flowers. They're called catkins." He could have said much more, but the doors had opened and everyone was climbing out of the Trabi. Ursula's question reminded him of how much he would love to lead bird-watching tours at the zoo. If he couldn't find the birds he wanted to point out, he could talk about the trees and plants. Over the eight years he had worked at the zoo, he had learned a lot.

The next morning, he got up his nerve and asked to speak to the zoo's manager. His office was upstairs in the palace. Klaus had always wanted to go up the wide, curving staircase. Its balustrade continued on the balcony that overlooked the entrance hall downstairs. The manager had the reputation of being a recluse. Klaus had only seen him once before. He was a short man, bald on the top, with whispy hairs along the side and back of his head. Herr Pfeiffer needed a hair trimming.

"Ah, you are Klaus Hartmann." Herr Pfeiffer went to his file cabinet and brought out a folder. "Ah, yes, you came to work for us early in 1956, on the suggestion of Günter Beck." He turned around to face Klaus. "How are things working out for you?"

"Fine, Herr Pfeiffer."

"I see you and Günter are coming along on the construction of the auditorium down there in the basement."

"Yes, Herr Pfeiffer, we're working hard at it."

"Well, what did you want to speak to me about?"

"I was wondering if I could lead some bird-watching tours at the zoo."

"You're not hoping to get out of your work with Günter, are you?"

"No sir, I love working with Günter."

"Well, tell me why the zoo needs to offer such tours."

Klaus explained how different areas of the park each had different species....

"Yes, I know about the Tawny Owl. It nests in a hole in that big old oak, down by the warehouse. Have you seen it there?"

"I've only heard it at night."

"You've been down there at night, have you?"

"Yes," Klaus had to think fast. "In December, I got lucky because it gets dark before I go home."

"Well, I like your enthusiasm. You would have to give tours on the weekend, you know. We need you to work on the grounds during the week. Are you still interested?"

"Yes. Could I do it on one Saturday and one Sunday a month?"

"That's fine with me. We'll try you out for 6 months. If it seems to be popular, we'll add you to our program—you know what I mean, you'll be listed in the flyer."

"Thank you, Herr Pfeiffer."

Klaus descended the stairway a happy man. He couldn't wait to tell Günter. In fact, why not write Mila. He hadn't written her yet, and now he had something to tell her. His mood had definitely improved. Even though at times he still felt she had betrayed him, he had come to recognize, by recalling their last few days together, that she had tried to warn him about the possibility they might be separated soon.

A week later, Klaus suggested that they read another book. He asked Fritzy which book she would recommend. "*The Grapes of Wrath* by John Steinbeck would be interesting," she posited. She asked the others if they would mind having the discussions in her apartment. The rest of them realized that Fritzy wanted Ursula to be present. In spite of Fritzy's efforts, Ursula was not developing into a reader. Fritzy suggested another change. This time, she wanted everyone to have read the book before they began discussing it. That took more than two weeks.

She started their meeting by stating that the title of the book came from "The Battle Hymn of the Republic." None of them had heard of it, so the discussion that evening was spent on the American Civil War and the abolitionists. Günter and Fritzy did most of the talking.

The next time they met, Fritzy explained, with Günter's help, the Dust Bowl era and the Great Depression. At the third meeting, they talked about the book's anti-capitalism slant. "At first, Stalin wanted Russians to read the book because it was critical of the United States. But his strategy backfired. Russian readers saw that America's poorest people could still afford a car and move around the country freely. From then on, the book was banned. Fritzy told them about the author, the effects of the Cold

War, the Red Scare, and McCarthyism in the United States.

Günter and Wilma were thinking about leaving soon to go to West Germany. With the exception of Fritzy, they didn't share this with anyone because it was always best to keep plans secret. In the case of their other friends, Günter and Wilma knew they would never snitch on them, but after an escape, the authorities pursued friends and relatives relentlessly, hoping to discover one to be an accessory. Not sharing their plans was safer for everyone.

Before leaving, Wilma again approached Fritzy. "How are you feeling about taking care of Ursula, if we ever left?"

"Fine! We've been over this before, nothing has changed. I love the girl as you do." She hesitated, then continued: "To convince you, I guess I had better tell you the story about me and Bastard."

Finally, Wilma thought she was going to hear something personal about Fritzy. She had been waiting almost 20 years to hear about 'Bastard.'

"I'll make it quick. I get upset just telling the story. I married young. First mistake! He had graduated two years before me and was working for a political organization. I had always been impressed with how smart he was. Another mistake! He was given important jobs. I was still at university and was involved in my studies, and had always been naive about politics. He never mentioned Hitler's name in the first year we were married. Looking back on that now, I think it was because most of our friends saw the protoführer as a clown. Reinhard didn't want people to ridicule him, so he was quiet about the details of his work. After a year, he loosened up and began making typical Nazi remarks. He was promoted and worked in the office of Joseph Goebbels.

"Goebbels controlled Nazi propaganda, which penetrated all forms of media: newspapers, posters, radio, films, theater, literature, music, and the arts. He sold the Nazi ideology to the German people. He promoted the book burning in 1933. That was the year we married. I think Reinhard was attracted to

Goebbels's verbal agility and his intellect. The man convinced the public that Hitler was saving Germany from Jews and Marxists, who were characterized as vermin. He created the myth of the Führer.

"I said I'd make this short. Reinhard became convinced that Jews were the source of all Germany's problems. I am half Jewish. It took me a long time to become pregnant. By the time I did, in 1938, he felt he had to prove his commitment to the Nazi ideology. He forced me to be sterilized. At the same time, they took the baby. I filed for divorce three days later. He was relieved. I was an embarrassment to him, a hindrance to his career. He claims to have kept me from going to a concentration camp.

"It's odd, I know, I call him 'Bastard,' but I actually feel sorry for him. All those brains, yet he was so insecure, he willingly gave up his own child. After that, I could never have a child. That is what I had always wanted—a child—not a husband. I love Ursula as you do, but our needs are different. Ursula won't suffer being with me."

"Oh, I know she won't." They stopped to smile at each other. Wilma moved closer so she could hug Fritzy. "You were so good to me when I was raped. I'll never forget that." Fritzy poured Wilma another cup of tea. "You know the friend I knitted a sweater for, her name is Giselle Mechler. She has a husband, Tom, who was recently… How would you feel if she uses your allotment to do gardening?"

"That's fine with me." She smiled. "You know I'm not the gardening type." She became pensive. "I'm trying to decide if we should know each other, or is it better that she can't get in touch with me?" Wilma remained silent. "I mean, if she gets into trouble…. Oh, the hell with it. Yes, give her my name and address, in case she needs to get in touch with me. He's not one of those tunnel diggers is he?" Wilma hesitated, not knowing if she should reveal anything more about Tom. She was relieved when Fritzy said: "Best not to tell me."

"How difficult it will be to leave friends. I know you and

Ursula will be alright, but Klaus is the one we shouldn't leave. He's like a son to Günter. Giving up our home, our possessions, that's nothing, but leaving behind the people we love…. We feel we're abandoning you. If we could come back for a visit, or if you could visit us—but that will never happen. Crossing to the West is so final. No wonder most of the people who leave are young. They can look forward to getting the education they want, taking a job that interests them, and they haven't lived long enough to have made deep attachments. Every night, Günter and I question these things and wonder if we should go."

ESCAPE

APRIL 1964

Two days later, a disheveled old man with no teeth and an
arthritic old woman with a limp, showed up in the Language
Department at Free University in West Berlin looking for an
assistant lecturer, András Szabó. The secretary showed them into
Andi's office and said she would contact Herr Szabó. Günter and
Wilma were grateful for a chance to sit down and decompress.
They held hands and smiled at each other. "We made it," Wilma
said. Glasses and a pitcher of water were on a side table. They
helped themselves. Eventually, they asked the secretary if there
was a bathroom they could use. After directing them, the
secretary reassured them that someone would be coming soon.
    "Not Herr Szabó?" Günter asked.
    "I'm not sure, but someone will be here shortly."
    They waited another hour and a half. Finally, a tall young
man in his late thirties walked in, carrying a briefcase. He shut
the door and shook their hands. "Hi, I'm Steve," he said in a low
voice. "Congratulations on making it across."
    Günter thought he was an American, from the casual way he
introduced himself. He didn't give his last name. He assumed an
intimacy without any previous introduction.
    Steve suggested that they all sit down. He drew his chair close
to theirs without explanation and proceeded to talk in a voice
not much louder than a whisper, even though no one else was in
Andi's office. Steve spoke to them without facial expressions. He

must be CIA, Günter thought. The man opened his briefcase and took out two envelopes: one for each of them. "Please read these letters from Andi."

Günter opened his envelope. It was a relief to see Andi's handwriting, but why such clandestine behavior? Aren't we free now? This is West Berlin, isn't it? Before reading the letter, he had to ask: "Are we going to see Andi?"

Steve's mouth winced slightly. "No. If you've done something that threatens the GDR, like escaping to the West, they will come after you."

Günter interrupted Steve to say: "I haven't seen Andi in two years. I want to see him before we go anyplace."

"The Stasi have been known to kidnap escapees and take them back to East Berlin for execution. It's best you disappear from sight before they are aware that you're gone. As soon as they realize you've fled, they could come looking for you. Andi would be where they would start their search. Best not to see him. You must leave now."

Günter and Wilma exchanged glances. He was emotionally exhausted and could see that Wilma was as well. He started to read Andi's letter. Evidently, they would have to pass through East Germany right now to get to West Germany. Remaining in West Berlin was too dangerous for the reasons that Steve had just explained. The anxiety Günter felt crossing the East Berlin border resurfaced. Andi's letter was telling them that they would have to go through the whole experience again, today, now:

In this envelope is your driver's license so you can drive the Volkswagen which is parked out front of this building. The car is registered to you. For now, only Wilma should drive, and Günter, you should guide her with the enclosed maps. In the glove compartment, you will find your exit visas that were 'given to you by the East Berlin police' and some cash: both, Deutche Marks for West Germany and East German Marks. There are two small suitcases in the luggage space containing some

toilet articles and clothes.
Drive to the border crossing at Drewitz (see map).
We call this checkpoint 'Bravo.' Your persons, your car,
your suitcases, and your papers will all be thoroughly
inspected by border guards. Once you are cleared to
go—it may take some time—drive onto the autobahn,
heading for Marienborn (in the GDR) or Helmstedt
(in the DFR). You must stay on the designated transit
routes while driving on the autobahn. The maximum
speed is 62 kph. The last checkpoint, at Marienborn,
West Germans refer to as 'Alpha.'

Once you cross into Helmstedt, take the A1
(going north) in the direction of Altstein for about
20 kilometers. After passing through the town of
Kupferdorf, turn right (east) on B23 toward Metteldorf.
Just before Metteldorf, take a dirt road on the left (going
north). A sign is posted there that says: "2 kilometers
to Bronhof Hill," on top of which is a lovely view. The
driveway to your farm, Bronhof farm, is off to the right,
a half kilometer before the crest of the hill.

Memorize these directions because you cannot have
this letter on you at the checkpoints. You will have to
give the letters to Steve before you leave.

My boss, George, thanks you for the vital
information you acquired for our cause. We have
arranged for you to own Bronhof farm and the VW you
will be driving as compensation for the risks you took.

Best of luck,
Andi

Günter was grateful. He and Wilma had been very lucky, but
what about Klaus? He had taken the same risks as Günter. Klaus
didn't want to leave East Berlin. He was miserable about losing
Mila, but he had explained to Günter that he didn't think he had
the skills in deception to pass through the border undetected.

Günter would miss Klaus terribly. He tried to say goodbye

properly, but it was so difficult. When he got home from work last night, he found the doors to their apartment unlocked and the apartment ransacked. The panel hiding the books had been opened. Wilma always got home before him, but she was not there. He panicked, but then realized she could be at Fritzy's, so he ran up the stairs, two at a time. Wilma answered Fritzy's door, when he knocked. Her hair was wet. She looked strange. Oh, she's dyed her hair. The gray color did make her look older, but not old enough for 70, he thought. The fear in her eyes alarmed him. She said she didn't do anything to straighten up the apartment. She just fled up to Fritzy's and let herself in.

Wilma handed him the gray hair dye. "We've got to leave in the morning now, before they come back for us." They slept the night in Fritzy's apartment. Wilma shared a bed with Ursula while Günter slept on Fritzy's couch. The next morning, they all said their goodbyes with hugs and tears. Günter and Wilma went down at 6:30 A.M. to the basement to say goodbye to Klaus before he went to work. That was especially difficult. Klaus went to work at his usual time, visibly glum.

Around 8:00 A.M., Günter and Wilma left through the basement door to the alley, so they wouldn't be seen coming out of the front of the building. Wilma limped along with Günter to the end of the alley. Then they turned in the opposite direction from Hoffmannstrasse. At their slow pace, it took them close to two hours to reach checkpoint Charlie. They stumbled around not knowing for sure what to do, but that had been their plan. Wilma was using an old umbrella as a cane. Günter's jacket wasn't properly buttoned—again, part of the plan. They had been told that Stasi agents surveiled people, using cameras as much as two blocks before the checkpoint.

After going through all that, now that they were in West Berlin, they'd have to do it over again to get to West Germany. Normally, Günter was good at memorizing, but he was so tired, he was having trouble.

While Günter worked on learning the directions, Wilma read

the VW manual that was included in her envelope. It was dog-eared. Their car was eleven years old. She had never ridden in, yet alone driven, a VW before. Her only experience came from driving a mail truck and as a passenger in Fritzy's Trabant. In her envelope, was a small photo on the back of which was written: 'Bronhof Farm.' Wilma showed Günter the picture and smiled.

Steve took two sandwiches wrapped in wax paper from his briefcase. "You might want to eat these now, so you are not tempted to stop on the way."

Günter recognized his hunger was probably due to anxiety more than exertion. A half hour later, they were advised to take off. "You want to get to the farm before dark." Steve took their letters, envelopes, and the sandwich wrappings and put them in his briefcase. "I'll be leaving you now. Your VW is gray with a dent in the rear fender on the passenger's side. The plate number is OL 0459. Any questions?"

Wilma repeated the number out loud. Steve left them with a smile and another handshake: "Good luck." He asked them to wait two minutes, to let him get a head start before they left the building. This must be the CIA protocol, Günter thought. Now, he was even more convinced than ever that he wasn't cut out to be a spy.

He took a moment to hug Wilma. They resumed their roles as oldsters and got on their way. At Bravo, they had to wait in line for twenty minutes before the border guard was available to process them. They did what they saw others doing. Wilma shut off the engine to save on gas. Günter got out and pushed the rear of their car to keep their place in the queue.

Once their inspection began, they both had to get out of the car. The process took fifteen minutes. When it was over, the guard asked Günter why he wasn't driving instead of his wife. "I mean she is crippled, man, and you're making her drive?"

Günter acted befuddled. He mumbled something and finally spat out: "She's the driver."

The guard gave up and sent Günter and Wilma on their way,

with a disgusted sneer.

On the day after Günter and Wilma left, Fritzy had heard no news of their escape backfiring. She figured her friends had made it through to West Berlin, so she began collecting her kitchenware in piles by her door. Only after most people in the building had left for work, did she start using the dumbwaiter to bring her piles down to the first floor and into Günter and Wilma's apartment. She then collected Günter and Wilma's kitchenware into piles to go upstairs. Taking things down, then bringing other things up went on all day. There were a few things of theirs she kept for herself and Ursula. Why shouldn't Ursula have her mother's apartment? She had to have everything moved before the Stasi started investigating. That would probably begin in the next three days, or sooner. Damn their efficiency! She kept the couch, formerly Andi's couch, the easy chair and table, also formerly Andi's.

Fritzy hoped she could solicit Klaus' help to take their double bed apart and help her get it upstairs and reassembled. Then there were the two single beds that had to be brought downstairs. She had taken the day off, of course, and had told Ursula to come home from work as soon as possible. Together, they took the single frames apart and carried some parts downstairs, but had to stop when fellow residents came home. Later that night, after eleven o'clock, Klaus and Ursula carried the double bed mattress upstairs and switched locations of the remaining bulky items.

It was best not to let anyone know what they were doing. Jealousy over apartments ran strong in a planned economy. Most people had to wait for years for something that suited them. Many people gave up trying. By the third night after Wilma and Günter left, both apartments looked appropriate. Fritzy and Ursula were exhausted. They had even washed a few walls to hide the dust marks that revealed where pictures had been hung.

Klaus took the false teeth which Günter had left in Fritzy's apartment. His thinking was that no officials knew that Günter had false teeth anyway, and maybe, somehow, he could get them back to him. Ursula wanted Wilma's knitting needles and yarn. Fritzy took some books and left some of hers that she had already read in the third floor apartment.

Klaus considered moving up to the third floor so he could have an actual apartment, but then he thought better of it. He didn't want the Stasi to think that he had been in collusion with Günter and Wilma over their escape. If only Mila had stayed, they could have taken their double bed.

SUSPICIONS

The night of the third Thursday in April, Walter was at the warehouse when the delivery truck drove in. He was somewhat relieved to see the original drivers jump out of the cab, but he questioned them, nonetheless. One said he had been sick last month and the other said his mother had had a stroke. Walter didn't believe them. This order, like the last, was filled, all items were delivered on time and in good condition, but Walter's instinct told him the men were lying.

The next evening, in order to use a secure line, he went to Stasi headquarters to call his father at his apartment. "Have your men been able to find out anything?"

"We couldn't find a motive, but the deliverymen who were swapped were both Swedes."

"Do they have any connection to the wholesale people we deal with in Sweden?"

"No! In fact, there is nothing on them, which, in itself, is suspicious—too clean, too slick."

"That's scary!"

"We can only assume it's professional."

"The Sapo?"

"That's what we're thinking, but why? Why would they do it?"

"God only knows...so, is that it?"

"No, there's one more thing. There may be no relationship, but one of the zoo's employees, a groundsman, appears to have slipped over the border with a woman."

"Oh, really."

"Yes, and guess where they lived?"

"Where?"

"An apartment building known as Die Birken."

"Where's that?"

"On Hoffmannstrasse! Doesn't that ring a bell?"

"Hoffmannstrasse sure, but Die Birken—never heard of it."

"That's where we found you. Remember Andi Szabó?"

"That prick, sure! He works at the CIA, too, I think you told me. Oh my God, there's a connection. What's the groundsman's name?"

"Günter, Günter Beck; and the woman is Wilma Bauer."

"There was a Wilma, I think, when I was there. The woman I remember is Fritzy. She was a pistol." Walter remembered that it was Fritzy who called him Little Shit, a moniker he was actually still proud of.

"Fritzy, did you say? Such an unusual name for a woman! As I recall, that was Reinhard's first wife's nickname."

BIRDS

MAY, 1964

On the day Klaus led his first bird walking tour, a few people gathered outside the palace entrance—eight altogether, not including Klaus. He hadn't expected the zoo manager to join them, but was glad to see him. Klaus thought he would be nervous, but he wasn't. Of course, it helped that Fritzy and Ursula were part of the group. He had made sure to time the tour after Ursula's gymnastics class. Since there were only three binoculars among them, they would have to share. Herr Pfeiffer chose to share with Fritzy and Ursula. Klaus handed each of them a list of the 53 species that he had seen at the zoo himself.

The ground was damp, and in some places, soggy. In the future, he must remind people to wear boots like Herr Pfeiffer. The manager was wearing old leather army boots which covered his calf.

"If you can't identify a bird, but you have had a clear look at it, it's a good idea, before you leave the site, to write down what you saw: size, coloring, etc. The shape of the beak is important because that tells you what type of food it eats. If it's a cone shape, it's probably a seed eater. A thin sharp beak usually belongs to an insect eater. Then, record where you saw it: on the ground, in a tree, what type of tree. You get the idea.

"We'll go to the lake first. It's easiest to spot birds on the water. We're fortunate to have this lovely lake within the zoo. Many of the animals drink from it." He led the group through a copse on a rough path, so they were not out in the open. "Look across the lake at the far end. Do you see horses?"

"Oh, yeah."

"Those are Przewalski's horses." Klaus had to look at his notes to be sure he pronounced their name correctly. "To my knowledge, it's the only breed of horses that has never been domesticated. This is about as close as you'll get to them. Some people call them Mongolian horses. You'll see as we walk closer, they will run away."

Herr Pfeiffer turned to Ursula and asked her if she had been to Mongolia. "Not yet, I hope to go some day," she said smiling at him. Then she made a neighing sound that was quite realistic. He chuckled.

"Look, there's a duck," she called out.

"Good, now describe it."

"Oops—it's mooning us," Ursula said, laughing.

Klaus smiled and rolled his eyes at Fritzy. "It's a dabbler..." Klaus went on to tell them the difference between dabblers and divers. Then he talked about breeding plumage and a duck's vulnerability during the weeks it molts. He pointed out one specific duck on its own and asked them to describe it.

Suddenly, Klaus realized he had spent too much time at the lake, so he tried to move the group quickly to a meadow area. There was so much to see there that he didn't get to any other areas of the park. He apologized for that when he had to stop the tour because time was up. He announced future tours and walked them back to the palace. Despite the limited range, he was pretty sure that they had enjoyed themselves.

Before they dispersed, Herr Pfeiffer turned to Fritzy and asked: "So you're a friend of Klaus', are you?"

"Oh yes, for several years."

"I believe I saw you a month or so ago, when your horn wouldn't stop blaring."

Fritzy hesitated, so he added: "You were wearing that nice maroon sweater then, as I recall."

"Yes, I'm so sorry for the disturbance."

"Well, I'm glad our doorman was able to stop it for you."

"Do you work at the zoo, too?"

"Yes, I'm the manager."

"I'm glad Klaus can give tours like this. I thought it was excellent."

"I did too."

Fritzy enjoyed the bird tour and was pleased for Klaus' success. When she spoke to him that night, she asked him how he liked the zoo's manager.

"He seems fine, really smart."

"There's something about him that makes me shiver."

Klaus laughed. "To me he looks like the eagle-owl. His eyebrows sit immediately over his eyes, making them seem like piercing blue spotlights. Kinda scary." Then Klaus laughed. "I've really got it bad. Now, I'm seeing people as birds."

Fritzy didn't go on, but thought there was something about the manager that was indeed frightening. In fact, she thought she had seen him before. That Mongolian question he asked Ursula bothered her. Was that it? Maybe a face she knew long ago. His boots! I bet he was a high-ranking Nazi. Which one? Reinhard would know. A short man with such piercing eyes!

Ordinarily, Heinz would not personally investigate anything in East Berlin as it could jeopardize his double agent status. Furthermore, investigating an escape was a job for a mid-ranking Stasi officer, but he had learned long ago the importance of speed when mitigating damage involving Walter. He walked up the stairs in the palace's entranceway and knocked on the open door to the manager's office. Herr Pfeiffer was sitting at his desk in plain sight.

After brief introductions, Herr Pfeiffer offered Heinz a seat. As he explained briefly who he was, Heinz was thinking that Herr Pfeiffer looked vaguely familiar—those razor thin lips. He let that stray thought go and concentrated on the purpose of his visit. "I thought you might be able to tell me something about

Günter Beck," he finished.

"Oh, yes. Well, sadly, Günter's been gone a week now, and the work is piling up—a nice man though, a hard worker, seems intelligent. Why are you asking?"

"We now know he has left East Berlin and is in West Germany."

"So, we have lost him. Oh, dear, that's too bad. I wonder why. He never complained—oh, except once. That was when he was a relatively new employee. A man we had hired to assist Günter didn't do much, so he asked if we'd hire a friend of his: Klaus, Klaus Hartmann." Heinz wrote the name down. "He's a carpenter."

"Is Klaus still working here?"

"Oh yes. He's good, too."

"So, do you have any idea why Günter Beck would leave East Berlin?"

"No. I'm afraid not. Can Klaus shed any light?"

Heinz tried to concentrate on what Herr Pfeiffer was saying, but he continued to be distracted by the thought that he knew the man from somewhere. Then it came to him. Oh my God, he suddenly remembered, Pfeiffer is Heinrich Mueller, head of the Gestapo! "We'll be looking into that."

He tried to recall what had happened to Mueller. Heinz himself still believed in Nazi ideology, so he looked on Mueller with both awe and apprehension. He finally mustered himself to get to the point of this interview: "Can you recall anything special about a particular Thursday, the third Thursday in March?"

Between the two of them, they came up with the exact date of that Thursday. "Good, now I can look it up," Pfeiffer said. He thumbed back a page in his record book and started laughing. "Well, the only unusual thing that day was a woman's car horn went off. Our doorman had to go outside and help her to get it to stop. Why are you particularly interested in that day?"

Heinz hesitated, but then he realized that as manager of the zoo, Pfeiffer had to know about the operation going on in the warehouse, and must actually be involved in it closely. So he explained to him that both drivers had been switched for the March delivery, yet all the goods that arrived were what they should be.

Pfeiffer interrupted him to ask: "Did you check to confirm that the truck took the ferry back to Sweden?"

"Yes, it did." Heinz caught the sharper tone of Pfeiffer's voice. His eyes were piercing.

"Did the same truck make it back to Stockholm?"

"Yes."

"On time? I mean, did it go straight from the ferry terminal to Stockholm?"

"Yes, that's right. Nothing was suspicious."

Heinz continued, telling him that the regular drivers made the most recent delivery, in April.

Then, out of the blue, Pfeiffer asked: "Do you know a woman named Fritzy—who is she?"

"Fritzy?" Where's this man going? Beads of sweat were collecting on Heinz's forehead. "A woman named Fritzy?" Heinz repeated to give himself more time. "Such an unusual woman's name!" He knew it was the nickname of Reinhard's first wife— the half-Jew. Heinz recalled that it was Mueller who had ordered 30,000 Jews to be arrested on Kristallnacht. He took out his hankerchief to wipe his forehead. Good God, he wouldn't still be after her for being a Jew, would he?

"There is a Fritzy who lives in the same building as Gunter and Klaus: Die Birken," Pfeiffer stated cooly. "But you must already know that...."

"Oh yes, yes we do," Heinz stumbled, "of course, that's right. As soon as Gunter went missing, a woman named Frau Fritz immediately moved into Günter's apartment. I do remember now hearing that they call her 'Fritzy'...."

"What?... Did you confront her about that?"

"No, we were advised by her former husband to let it go."

"Why, for God's sake? We can't have squatters choosing the best apartments."

"I know, but he said not to mess with her."

"How spineless! What kind of a man.... Who is he?"

"Reinhold Zellweger." Pfeiffer didn't respond, but Heinz sensed that he knew who Reinhold was. "Reinhold said it is best not to put Fritzy on alert."

"It was Fritzy's horn that wouldn't stop blaring that day. I'd say get an undercover Stasi man to investigate Klaus, Günter's assistant. Can that be done?"

"Yes, yes, I'll get on that."

"And I'm planning to go on Klaus' next bird-watching tour. It's worth trying to get to know that young man. If we handle him carefully, we may just needle some important information from him...."

Herr Pfeiffer rose from his chair, signaling to Heinz that the discussion was over. "I'm sorry I have a meeting in a few minutes.... How may I get in touch with you if I discover more information about Gunter's escape?"

"I'll be calling on you in a week or so," Heinz said, backing his way to the door.

"No business card?" Pfeiffer asked, with a slight smile.

"No. Thank you for your help."

Heinz hurried down the stairs to get out into fresh air and gather his thoughts. He was annoyed by the way Pfeiffer (Mueller) had wrested leadership of his own investigation from him. At the same time, he found the man very intimidating. How long had he been the manager of the zoo? To his recollection, the zoo opened in 1955. Could Mueller have been hiding here the whole time since the end of the war? He thought the Americans, in particular, had been looking for Mueller since 1945. Hmm.... If they were ever to discover my double agent status, I might be able to bargain for a pardon if I disclose Mueller's whereabouts to them....

ANDI'S OUT

JUNE 1964

A month and a half later, Andi went into work as usual. He was immediately told that his boss, George, wanted to see him in his office.

"I have good news and bad news," George said. "I don't know which I should tell you first." Andi noticed George looked haggard. He was almost slumped on his desk. He pressed a button on his intercom. "Mary, could you bring us some coffee?"

"That's your third cup, sir."

"I know."

Oh my God, Andi thought. It must be really bad news. "I guess I'd like the bad first."

"I have to let you go."

"You mean dismiss me?"

"Yes."

"Oh my God! What's happened?"

"I received this last night." He pushed a letter across the desk. It took Andi three seconds to realize what had occurred. He recognized the handwriting. Little Shit, he thought, has finally played his joker.

"I've known you're gay for ages. Probably, everybody you work with knows. This letter was seen by brass higher than me. They have to fire you, because of the regulations. I argued and argued your case, all night long. Fucking rules! Some little shit cares more about rules than people."

Before the gravity that he was being fired fully sank in,

Andi couldn't help but laugh, which took George completely by surprise. Andi told George the story about Little Shit stealing the letter from his apartment. "...So, all these years, I knew this was coming. What brought him to do it now, I wonder?"

George laughed, "How did you get someone to adopt that little monster?"

"Well, I'm not proud of this part of the story."

Andi reminded George about the time he was fixing up Die Birken with Quaker money, and told him the story about trying to save the three orphans. He explained how Walter looked like a perfect, handsome child but was making everybody in the building miserable with his bad behavior. Suddenly it occurred to Andi that George knew Heinz. Should he go on? "I used a Nazi university acquaintance named Heinz's partiality to Nordic features to lure him into adopting the little monster."

"Heinz? Heinz Mayer?"

Oy. Andi had hoped George wouldn't notice. "Yes."

"Hmm, interesting. So Walter must be Walter Mayer. And Heinz was formerly a Nazi?" George paused to think that over. "They are all around us, I'm afraid. We live in complicated times."

Andi realized how much he was going to miss George, miss his work at the CIA. Where was his life going? Will this affect Mark and his work in the mayor's office?

When they got to the good news, Andi knew it wouldn't be good enough to compensate. Unexpectedly, he realized he was tired. He didn't want to yawn, but couldn't help it. What had come over him? George was yawning too, but he was justified, not having slept much last night.

"The good news is that the capture of the paintings went off like clockwork. Thank you for planning that. Evidently, the paintings are extremely valuable. They have been evaluated by international experts. The word has not gone out yet, because of the difficulty of explaining where they were found. That would create a political incident. Even if it does, I have no regrets. If 'they' had discovered them, the paintings would be in Moscow by now. We have an agreement with the Swedish government that each painting should go back to the owner from whom it was stolen. We are waiting for things to cool down, so no one will realize that they came from the zoo."

"Well, that is good news," Andi said to be polite. He already knew much of what George was telling him.

"Actually, there is more." He hesitated, then went on: "Sapo tells us that they would like you to work for them, if you're interested."

Andi really perked up at this news. "Sapo! That would be great," He hesitated. "Are you sure they really want me? Do they know I'm gay?"

"Yes, you know the Swedes, they've got their heads screwed on correctly."

Andi was overjoyed at this prospect. He couldn't help sharing with George: "Now Mark and I can live together."

"Don't tell me. Jesus, I don't want to have to fire anyone else. Mark isn't in the CIA or the military, I hope?"

"No! He works in the mayor's office." There was a pause.

"Mark Brant?"

"Yes, Mark Brant."

"Good God! Mark Brant's your...." George started to cry. "Excuse me. I haven't had much sleep." He recovered himself, but then Andi started choking up.

Two months later, Mark and Andi were living in Stockholm. They were able to purchase an apartment with the help of the severance package Andi received from the CIA. They chose one close to the little Quaker Meeting house, to which Andi walked most Sundays. Working for Sapo, Andi learned even more details about how the agency had captured the paintings.

Mark became a journalist for the same Swedish newspaper he had worked at years before, but he didn't get his column back. He had to go to the bottom of the ladder and become a reporter again. Yet, he was free to choose what to investigate. He no longer had to pursue items exclusively in support of the mayor and his agenda.

At the time that Mark became a Swedish journalist again, few people knew that the paintings had been stolen from their hiding place on GDR property. Stealing anything is a crime, but during the Cold War, such maneuvers were constantly going on, by both sides. Mark knew he couldn't speak about the theft or about what was stolen, but there were other aspects of the case that could be revealed to the public.

It was not illegal for Swedish companies to do business with GDR firms. After all, Sweden was a neutral country, but the GDR itself had to cover up such trade for two reasons: theoretically, luxury goods had no place in a socialist society, and secondly, the GDR was going out of its way to provide them for its elites (and only for its elites). There was no way for the general public to find out that there were freezers, high-end furniture, and radiograms for sale. Buyers only discovered the sales by word of mouth. So much for the brotherhood of equality!

Mark wrote an article exposing the hypocrisy of the GDR government. "A Party member can buy these items by going to a warehouse in an obcure part of the Tierpark Zoo in East Berlin." It was discussed on both radio and TV news programs in Sweden. Eventually, word got to the West German media, which was how some East Germans became informed.

Back in March, when the paintings arrived at the Thielska Galleriet in Stockholm, Kurt Albach started the process of having them evaluated as to their authenticity and value. Art experts from several countries came to the museum. Each swore to secrecy, to prevent the information being leaked to the general public. They reached consensus by the end of June. Meanwhile, other art experts worked with Sapo to identify and locate their previous owners. The painting "Ulf in the Evening" did belong to a Norwegian collector, as Kurt had thought. The owner of the painting by the Swedish artist, Carl Larsson, was easily found. The Dufy had belonged to a Jewish couple from Katowice, Poland, who had been killed in Auschwitz. Their painting was given to the couple's nearest relative.

Who had owned the Modigliani was a complete mystery. After much deliberation by art authorities, it was decided that the Modigliani should be auctioned off, with the proceeds going to the United Nations High Commission for Refugees.

In every case, except for the Modigliani, it was established that the paintings had been stolen by the Nazis and hidden in the Tierpark Palace during World War II. This revelation was a relief to Andi, George, and Sapo, because it confirmed that, although the paintings were recovered by thievery, they had been stolen goods to begin with, and those involved in recovering them had not profited from the operation.

The date the Modigliani was to be auctioned off was set for Saturday, August 25. The sale would be held in Stockholm's Auktionsverk, the world's oldest auction house. Notice of the pending event was announced all over the world, even in East Germany.

Mark wrote another article explaining how it was found with three other paintings that had been returned to their rightful owners (he didn't say where, or when):

> It is speculated the paintings were hidden by Nazis and have been in their hiding place since the war ended in 1945. Were they forgotten? Were they hidden by people who were subsequently killed, or by people who can't now get to them? Or did they have to be left in hiding because they were still too recognizable to be sold?

There was great interest in Mark's article. He had photographs and described each painting in detail. The owners, however, were not revealed. He closed his article with publicity for the upcoming auction of the Modigliani.

REVELATIONS

At the beginning of June, Heinz went back to Pfeiffer's office. He did not look forward to the meeting, but he wanted to report, as promised, whether Klaus had helped Gunter and Wilma escape. He began with what he had learned about Wilma. A post office official said they were sorry to have lost Wilma. She had been a good worker.

"What about Klaus?" Pfeiffer asked. "Do you think he was in collusion with Günter?"

Pfeiffer listened without further comment as Heinz continued: "My sources tell me that Klaus isn't intelligent enough to be of help to Günter." Heinz noticed a slight upturn at the outer edge of the man's thin lips. He went on to tell Pfeiffer about the latest article in a Stockholm newspaper. "The article revealed the function of the warehouse in terms not flattering to GDR policies." Surprisingly, Pfeiffer still had no comments or questions.

Finally the man spoke: "Could you arrange for your friend, Reinhold Zellweger, to come here to see me tomorrow some time?"

"Certainly." Heinz knew better than to ask why. How did Pfeiffer know that Rein was his friend, anyway? This man scares me. When Heinz was outside the palace, he decided to go straight to a Stasi office so he could make a secure phone call to Rein.

"I don't know why he wants to see you."

"And who is he, again—the manager of the zoo?"

"Rein, I'm telling you, make sure you go see him tomorrow. This is important. I can't say more."

Klaus frequently checked in with Fritzy when he got home from work, very conscious that his family had been reduced to her and Ursula, although Herr Schröder was quickly becoming family, too. He went to The Cellar for dinner a couple of times a week. The last time, he found Mila's father practicing juggling, with no trace of alcohol on his breath.

"I wish I had paid more attention to some of the acts we had during my circus days," Herr Schröder told him. "A couple of the magic tricks would be good here, between acts." He was referring to the acts of the acrobatic performances at The Cellar. "I just ran the business."

Klaus was always hoping to get a letter from Mila. Her letters to him were enclosed in Frau Schröder's letters to her husband. He and Mila were corresponding now on a regular basis. When he wrote Mila, he only signed "Love, K," and never put his return address on the envelope. The intensity of his feelings for her was as strong as ever. He had accepted their situation, sad as it was. Yes, he was still upset with her for leaving him, but he couldn't deny that he loved her.

One night, he went up to see Fritzy and mentioned to her that his bird-watching tours were becoming more popular. He was happy that more people were showing up for each one, and that the zoo manager continued to attend every time himself. He was hopeful that the tours would soon be added to the official zoo program, since Herr Pfeiffer was always polite, attentive, and usually complimented him on some aspect of the tour when it was over. Klaus was surprised at her response.

"Let's go for a walk. I've been sitting too much today." She's afraid Big Brother is listening, Klaus thought. It was a beautiful moonlit night and the temperature was warm. Klaus always found it a pleasure to be outside. Once walking down the sidewalk, Fritzy continued: "I have looked into the zoo manager, and I urge you to be careful." She explained that she had recognized him as a familiar Nazi leader during the war. She looked up information about top Nazi officials at the library to verify her memory. "Despite being called Pfeiffer now, he is actually Heinrich Mueller. Herr Mueller was the head of the Nazi's secret police, the Gestapo." She paused to let this fact settle into Klaus' mind.

"After the war," she continued, "the Western forces searched for him. They turned the home of his mistress upside down, but found no clues as to his whereabouts. For some reason, they thought he was hiding out in Berlin. But after a few years, they stopped their search. At that point, the Cold War had become more important to them than finding war criminals.

"Then, do you remember three years ago, hearing how the Israelis found Adolf Eichmann in Argentina and took him to Israel for trial? He was eventually executed."

"Oh, yeah!"

"Well, Eichmann was one of Mueller's subordinates."

"You're kidding! Herr Mueller was Eichmann's boss?"

"This encouraged the search for Mueller again. They still haven't found him, but I think we have."

"Oh no," Klaus sounded disappointed. "I was getting to like him." He thought for a few minutes. "I suppose we should tell someone?"

"Who can we tell? We can't get any information to anybody from here."

"I'm sorry. He's been very nice to me."

"That's what I was afraid of. Just be careful!"

"He's growing a beard, you know." She wouldn't know, because she hadn't been on another bird walk—only the first.

"Really?"

"He's talking about adding an aviary at the zoo."

"Really?"

"Yeah, you know the zoo in West Berlin has one, although I've never seen it. Have you?"

"Probably, when I was a kid, but I don't specifically remember."

Klaus thought a bit, and went on to say: "He's thinking of going to the zoo in Stockholm. He says their aviary is supposed to be spectacular. He said it would be good to have my opinion, especially since I would probably be asked to do the carpentry work." Klaus got excited. "Our aviary will have nets for the walls and ceiling, and double doorways, so the birds inside can't get out when people go in and out."

"Sounds big and expensive."

"There will be trees inside...."

"What kind of birds will be kept?"

"That's the only thing that bothers me. Birds should not be confined, so I suggested they be birds that have been injured."

"What did he say to that?"

"Nothing really; his lips suggested a smile."

Fritzy didn't sleep much that night, mulling over what Klaus had told her. In fact, she was so restless, she was afraid she would wake up Ursula. Tomorrow was Saturday. Her gymnastics performance was scheduled at The Cellar at 10:00 in the morning. Ursula needed her sleep!

The beard, Stockholm—why Stockholm? It would be so much easier to arrange to see the aviary in West Berlin. Sweden had continued its neutrality during the Cold War. Border security was less stringent there than elsewhere in Europe. In fact, Sweden was known to be a popular meeting place for Eastern Bloc spies. She had read that intelligence agencies from Iron Curtain countries had offices in the capital city that were well known. Once in Sweden, you could travel freely anywhere. It came to her in a flash: the man is planning to escape!

Fritzy dragged herself to Ursula's show the next day. She didn't see Klaus again, to talk privately, until Sunday afternoon when he came home from another bird-watching tour. Ursula had gone out with friends, so Fritzy went down to the basement to wait for Klaus. He descended the stairs whistling, stopping short when he saw Fritzy.

"What's wrong?" he asked.

"Nothing at all, I was wondering if you would help me with something heavy to bring in from my car."

"Sure. I have some good news to tell you," he said as they walked out the building. "Which way is your car?"

"Over there down the street. Come on tell me, what's the good news?"

"Herr Pfeiffer wants me to go with him to Stockholm. He says he can get us travel permits. Imagine going to Stockholm!"

"How soon does he want to go?" she asked.

"He didn't say exactly when, but that I should be ready to go any time within a week or two. He said we would just be in Stockholm for the day and will fly back the same night, so no suitcase will be needed. When I told him I didn't have a passport, he said he would make the necessary arrangements."

"Klaus, I very much suspect that he, Mueller, is planning to escape."

"That crossed my mind too, but why would Herr Pfeiffer— I'm sorry I keep thinking of him as Herr Pfeiffer—why would he want me to go with him? Does that make any sense to you?"

"I don't know. Maybe he has to give the Stasi an excuse for his needing to make this trip. You are going to make the structure and are the bird expert. It makes sense that you should go with him. You'll know what kind of questions should be asked."

"You don't really have something heavy in your car for me to carry in for you, do you?"

Fritzy laughed and said: "No."

"I'm going to Stockholm!" Klaus said with a grin all over his face.

"Just keep in mind, this all may be a ruse. An aviary at Tierpark Zoo may not be what this is all about."

"True, but it could lead to other things," he said raising his eyebrows and giving her a meaningful stare.

"I will give you some money so you can get yourself to some other destination that appeals to you. Take the other ID, in case you need it."

"And Günter's false teeth!"

"Oh, for goodness sake!" She laughed. "Remember there's an American Embassy in Stockholm where you could claim asylum, if you get into trouble. Hopefully, Mueller will concentrate on his own escape and won't care about you. But don't get your hopes up. This may all fall through."

The next day, while on his lunch break, Klaus was told to report to Herr Pfeiffer's office at 3:00 P.M. He wasn't sure what to expect. He climbed the stairs slowly. At the top, he could see into the office. There was another man in there. He hesitated to go in. Herr Pfeiffer rather impatiently beckoned him to enter, and didn't introduce him to the man. Klaus took that as an ominous sign.

"Please stand with your back against this wall, so your photo can be taken," the man said. Klaus remembered Andi taking their photos after Sabine's wedding. But this time he was given orders from a stranger, without any explanation. After the photo was snapped, the man asked him for specific information, writing it all down: Klaus' full name, that of his parents, baby sister, where he used to live before they were bombed out, his address at Die Birken, schooling, and of course, his date of birth. It crossed Klaus' mind that they could be collecting information for his obituary.

Five days later, Klaus was asked again to report to Herr Pfeiffer's office. This time, the manager was alone.

He actually smiled at Klaus. "Well, everything has been cleared. We are leaving from Schonefeld Airport. We must board the plane at 6:30 A.M. on Saturday, August 25th. How does that sound?"

"Very exciting," Klaus said, smiling.

"Here's your passport."

Klaus took it and checked the information. It all seemed correct.

"One last thing," Herr Pfeiffer said, "do you think your friend, Fritzy, could drive us to the airport? She would have to pick me up here at the zoo at 5:30 A.M. We are at the far north end of the city here, and the airport is at the south end, but that early on a Saturday morning, there shouldn't be much traffic."

"I'll have to ask her, but I'm sure she'll be glad to do it."

"I'll get our airplane tickets. Do you have any questions?"

"When do you think we'll get to Stockholm?"

"A couple of hours after we take off. It's only a short flight."

Now, the shoe was on the other foot. Klaus was leaving, not knowing if he'd ever be back, not being able to say goodbye, except to Fritzy. He knew what it felt like to be deserted and yet, he was about to do that to others, to people he loved: Fritzy, Ursula, and Herr Schröder. Klaus was fond of his basement home and his carpentry shop. It was unique. He had shaped it to be his own.

There were many other places on which he had put his stamp. Before the departure date, he wanted to visit these sites, to fix them in his memory. He went to his allotment and was shocked to find a couple gardening there and looking quite at home. They were harvesting a healthy crop of beans. Some nerve! True, he hadn't been there since Wilma and Günter left. And, he had to admit he almost never went there on his own, rather his visits had always been prompted by Wilma needing help. Wilma was the gardener, but these people were not Wilma. "Who are you?" he shouted. Their smiles quickly vanished and they seemed frozen in fear.

Then he noticed that more than beans were being harvested. There were also peas, cucumbers, and squash in baskets.

Klaus thought he heard the woman say, "Giselle and Tom." He wanted to be polite, but he had to let them know that they were working on the wrong allotment. "I'm Klaus Hartmann and this is my allotment."

The smile returned to the woman's face: "Oh, you made the bird house?"

"Yes, that and the shed. This is my allotment."

The man crouched down and wrapped his arms around his knees. The woman said timidly: "You're a friend of Wilma's?"

"Yes." Klaus started to feel better. He still kept his eyes on them, but felt less suspicious.

"Wilma said we could use these two allotments: yours and the one over there that belongs to Fritzy."

Klaus became embarrassed. He vaguely remembered Wilma saying something about his allotment around the time they left for good. He must not have taken it in properly. He stood there thinking that Wilma had done the right thing. He apologized. "You are Giselle, the woman she knitted the green sweater for?"

"Yes, that's right." She went over to the man and put her hand on his shoulder.

What's wrong with him, Klaus wondered? He seems so afraid of me. Klaus apologized again. "It all makes sense now. I think Wilma told me and I had forgotten. You are very welcome to use my allotment." He went into the shed he had built to see if there was anything inside he should remember. "You're welcome to anything in here, as well. There are some good tools."

"Would you please take some vegetables home with you? We are very grateful." She waited until she had Klaus' eye to add: "Gardening is so therapeutic."

He understood her point. "Thank you. I'm glad you are getting so many vegetables." The man looked at him. "Please forgive me for being so gruff. Goodbye. I hope you have many more successful crops here." Klaus hurried off, still embarrassed.

He went to visit Herr Schröder that night. "You know these kids make me feel twenty years younger. I think I'll start offering theater classes for children fourteen and younger. It won't be anything professional, but together, we can have a lot of fun. There is a young girl, Christiane, who wants to get involved. Her younger brother Karl wants to help, too."

Klaus noticed a box on the table. "A care package from my

wife arrived just this morning: coffee, cans of meat and fish, jellies, and a tin of cookies. Have dinner with me tonight."

"Yes, I will, but why don't you save those delicacies for another day? I've brought us some currywurst and fresh vegetables."

When it was time to say goodbye, Klaus gave Herr Schröder a long hug. There was so much he wanted to say, but he only allowed himself the hug. He went back home to Die Birken, feeling sad and excited. He was leaving so much of himself behind.

His last Thursday at work, he tried to visit special spots at Tierpark Zoo that he loved. A particular grove of trees that he and Günter had planted several years prior was one of his favorite areas. The oak, beech, and juniper trees were growing beautifully. He knew that, in future years, it would be treasured by visitors. There were favorite animals he also had to say goodbye to: the angora goats, the ring-tailed lemur, and so many birds.

He had been down to the warehouse end of the park a few times recently. He knew that Walter's business was still going. After Mark's article, there were a few people who came to the zoo asking where the warehouse was. Most got distracted on the way and decided not to bother. If they did make it all the way, they found it was closed, with no one around to answer questions about it. The building was always kept locked except for Saturdays and late-night deliveries.

THE AUCTION

Anxious about how the next day would unfold, Klaus had trouble sleeping. Fritzy had given him quite a bit of money in East German marks. She hoped it would be enough for him to catch a ferry from Stockholm to West Germany.

The next morning, Fritzy also found herself without much sleep and nervous about driving Klaus and Mueller to the airport. She had spent hours in bed trying to think things through. Did Mueller ask for her taxi service so he would leave no record of his escape? But then, would he want to eliminate her as well? One thing she was clear about: she was determined to get Klaus to Sweden, so she would take them to the airport. After that, she would need protection. The only people capable of protecting someone were the Stasi. Ha! How to pull that one off? Such thoughts continued all the way to Schöenfeld Airport.

If she saw trouble coming, she could cause a scene, but not until their plane had taken off. Then it occurred to her, if they felt it necessary to kill her, wouldn't they also think they should kill Klaus? Oh God, what to do?

Fritzy drove up to the main gate and dropped Klaus and Mueller off at the terminal entrance. They already had their tickets, and no bags to check. She waited in her car until they were safely inside. This gave her a chance to reconsider what she should do.

The Stasi could use her presence at the airport to prove that she was helping a war criminal escape. Maybe that was Mueller's trap for her. She laughed at herself for such paranoid thoughts. First of all, the Stasi never had to prove anything. They just did whatever was expedient at the time. And secondly, Klaus and Mueller had permission to leave, so she had done nothing wrong by helping them catch their plane. She reminded herself that she just wanted to see that Klaus got on the plane. She wished she had told him to ditch Mueller as soon as they were in Stockholm.

She was about to start the car and go back home when she saw a man who looked familiar walk up to the terminal entrance. Oh my god, that's Heinz Mayer, Rein's best friend! Why in hell is he coming to the airport at 6:30 in the morning? He must be helping Mueller escape. One bastard helping another! Without thinking further, Fritzy got out of the car and locked it, knowing full well that she was illegally parked. Almost twenty years after the war and there are still jerks loyal to the Nazi cause—despicable!

She started walking quickly to the terminal door, but realized, just in time, that it would be unwise to be recognized. She reached in her pocketbook for the bandana she always carried in case of rain.

Once inside the terminal, she forced herself to walk slowly as she made her way to the kiosk of postcards and souvenirs. Even though the temperature was still pleasant this early in the morning, Fritzy found that she was perspiring. Her mouth was dry—out of fear, no doubt. There were not many people flying at this early hour.

Peeking out from behind the kiosk, she spotted Klaus and Mueller sitting on metal chairs. Each chair was flimsy, but strengthened by being attached to a row of ten others just like them—a perfect symbol for the GDR, she thought. The men were not talking, but she could tell Klaus was nervous. His hands went in and out of his pockets. Mueller's mood was impossible to read because he had so much facial hair. It was almost boarding time.

An announcement was made over a loudspeaker: "Would the owner of a white Trabant, license plate number…, please remove your car immediately or it will be towed." Fritzy froze. She knew

Klaus and Mueller probably didn't know her plate number. They appeared oblivious to the announcement. 95% of the cars in East Berlin were Trabants, and most of them were painted white. She noticed two men in an adjacent lounge area stand up. They exchanged a few words and one headed toward the kiosk. My God, that's Rein! God help me! Abruptly, her ex turned to go out the terminal door. Oh my God, he'll come back inside to look for me. She walked calmly over to the lady's room. Inside, was an attendant wearing a uniform with a white cap. Her job was to keep the toilets clean and dispense hand towels and toilet paper.

Fritzy flashed 40 marks at her and lured the woman into a stall. After a few minutes of Fritzy explaining her plan, the attendant agreed to exchange clothes with Fritzy for the promised 40 marks. As Fritzy had asked, she left the stall and called her boss from an airport public phone to say she was sick. The attendant then left the airport to go home, wearing Fritzy's clothes.

Fifteen minutes later, Fritzy walked out into the lobby wearing the attendant's clothes and carrying a small broom and dust bin. She ditched those at the terminal door and made her way, slowly, to the underground. Once she was back in her apartment in Die Birken, she dressed for work. She woke up Ursula and asked her to deliver a shopping bag with the attendant's uniform to the woman's address before teaching her classes at The Cellar. Fritzy then exited Die Birken, walked up and down the sidewalks a few times, re-entered visibly flustered, and knocked on Gerda's door to ask if she could use her phone to report that her car had been stolen.

Klaus was excited about travelling. He had to remind himself to be alert for all the reasons Fritzy had warned him about. Herr Pfeiffer showed the tickets to the clerk when they checked in. The clerk said, "One way to Stockholm." Klaus figured Herr Pfeiffer just kept the return tickets in his pocket for that evening, when they would fly back to Berlin.

They sat in the lounge, waiting to board. Should he try to make conversation with Herr Pfeiffer? That may be presumptuous. He better remain quiet. He looked all around. Few people were in the terminal. His hand went in and out of his pockets, checking to feel for Günter's false teeth and the scrap of paper on which he had written Mila's address.

As they were boarding, Herr Pfeiffer picked up a newspaper from those in a display rack outside the plane's door. Klaus didn't know if he could do that too—just pick up a newspaper, without paying for it. He wouldn't risk it. He was too nervous to read anything anyway.

Herr Pfeiffer started reading the paper as soon as they were settled in their seats. The paper was in German, but Klaus didn't dare try to read even the headlines over Pfeiffer's shoulder. He saw that the woman seated in front of him was also reading a newspaper, but hers was in Swedish. Oh my God, the picture on the front page! He tried not to gasp. It was one of the paintings they found at the palace: the first one they pulled out, in fact, the one Günter had recognized and identified the artist.

Looking through the space between the seats in front of him, gave Klaus a good view. His height was an added bonus. Under the picture was the word Modigliani. That was what Günter had guessed. Later, Kurt Albach said that name when he looked at that painting in the palace basement. At the top of the article, there was a word that was similar to the word in German for auction. It occurred to Klaus that maybe the reason Herr Pfeiffer wanted to go to Stockholm had nothing to do with an aviary for the zoo. Maybe, just as Fritzy had suggested, he and the aviary were part of a ruse to allow Pfeiffer to leave the GDR. Maybe his plan is to expose me as someone who helped steal the paintings from the palace.

When they emerged from the airport in Stockholm, Herr Pfeiffer led Klaus to the taxi stand. "Before we go to the zoo, I want to show you something."

The cab took them to Stockholm's Auktionsverk. Oh, my God, this *is* about the painting, thought Klaus.

The building was large, with an arched entrance. The walls were made of a pretty green and black marble. The windows were also arched, with shiny metal frames, maybe polished brass or bronze. Klaus spotted a TV truck with a team, setting up outside the entranceway. Oh my goodness, this is a big deal!

There was a steady stream of people entering the building. Without delay, Herr Pfeiffer led Klaus directly inside. He chose seats in the middle section. He sat on the aisle and he offered Klaus the seat next to him. Klaus was very aware that there were armed guards everywhere. Herr Pfeiffer's gray beard changed his looks. He doesn't want to be recognized. Fritzy is probably right. He is that Mueller guy, former head of the Gestapo. I am in way over my head. Mueller's baldness might also help to disguise him. Twenty years ago he probably had a full head of hair, dark, more the color of his bushy eyebrows.

Armed guards were not only at every door, but some also stood next to the stage, facing the audience. There was a podium with a microphone attached positioned in front of the high, small stage. Klaus figured that behind the drawn, green velvet curtain would be the painting on an easel.

Herr Pfeiffer must know I helped to steal the paintings. Were they his? Had he been the person who hid them in the wall? Klaus had heard that the man had directed the zoo since it opened.

A lot of people taking seats were dressed in fine clothes. They'd have to be wealthy to consider bidding on the painting. He noticed Herr Pfeiffer looking around. Some people were not in seats but milling about, in front of the stage. Again, Herr Pfeiffer scanned the audience. He seemed nervous. Is he looking for someone? Klaus instinctively started surveying the crowd himself. Only about half the seats were taken, at this point. He saw the back of a man standing close to the front of the auditorium who looked like Andi, but of course, it couldn't be. Andi was in West Berlin. Nonetheless, Klaus kept his eyes on the man. Wouldn't it be wonderful to see Andi again!

The man whose head Klaus was staring at eventually turned

around. It was Andi! Klaus stood up and called to him,waving his arms. Herr Pfeiffer pulled on his arm and told him to sit down. Klaus took his seat again but sat on its edge. His tall frame made him stand out.

Andi got up and went to speak with two men in a side aisle. A very distinguished-looking man came up the aisle and asked Klaus politely to please follow him. Klaus stood up. Herr Pfeiffer flashed a look of alarm, then immediately resumed a façade of composure. Klaus stepped around the zoo manager to get into the aisle so he could follow the man who had summoned him.

Some new arrivals brushed by Klaus; no doubt trying to get to good seats. Klaus looked down the aisle and saw Andi looking at him. Klaus' spirits lit up. He gave Andi a broad smile as he tried to walk down the aisle amidst the crowd. Many people were rushing in to get seats. Klaus continued to try to make his way through them to get to Andi. A man knocked into him. Klaus felt a sharp prick on his neck. He couldn't stop himself from falling.

When he saw Klaus fall, Andi used his radio to order the doors shut. Immediately, armed guards moved in front of each exit. Andi pushed people aside to get to Klaus' slumped body. He yelled: "DOCTOR!" No one stepped forward. Andi yelled again: "DOCTOR, HERE, NOW!" The place went silent. Again, he yelled: "DOCTOR, PLEASE!" Andi was down on his knees, next to Klaus' body, which hadn't moved.

Two men rushed up. They knelt down to check Klaus' pulse and heartbeat. The crowd remained quiet. Andi held his breath. The doctors murmured to each other and then, looking over at Andi, said the young man was dead. "There is no pulse, no heartbeat, nothing. Death was instantaneous."

Andi stood and yelled, "NOBODY MOVE!" to the crowd. He then used his walkie-talkie to be sure the doors to the outside of the auction house had also been closed, as ordered. The building was absolutely locked down. Even those people in the lobby could not leave the building.

The doctors continued examining Klaus' body. They noticed a pink spot on Klaus' neck. It appeared to be a puncture wound. It had not scabbed over, so it was fresh. They speculated that the man had been injected with a poison, probably cyanide, to produce such an instantaneous death. Of course, there would have to be an autopsy.

Andi, the guards, and the owners of the auction house suspected that Klaus' death might well be a calculated distraction to enable the painting to be stolen. It was swiftly removed from behind the curtain and secured in the auction house's safe.

In questioning the doctors if they could determine what direction the needle went into Klaus' neck, they agreed that it went in perpendicular to the surface of the neck. "Klaus was tall," Andi told the doctors, "close to six feet. How tall would the person who injected Klaus likely be?"

"I would think someone of about the same height or taller," one doctor answered. The other nodded his head in agreement.

Andi turned to the well-dressed man who had summoned Klaus, who was actually one of Andi's assistants from Sapo, "We will start by investigating tall men, selecting those from the middle of the auditorium, going to the back, and out into the lobby."

One of the Sapo undercover men in the lobby noticed a tall, middle-aged man who kept one hand in the pocket of his linen jacket. He snuck up behind him and grabbed his arm. The man swung around with his left fist and knocked the Sapo man down. It was no easy feat to bring down the hulky Swede in one punch. The commotion the fracas caused was the tall man's downfall. Two guards leapt on him and had him pinned to the ground in seconds. In his pocket, they found a syringe with its needle retracted into a casing, which protected him from being stabbed himself. Later, Sapo agents surmised that the man must have been looking for an opportunity to discard the syringe in the lobby.

An hour later, people still remained seated as they had been ordered to do. There were quiet conversations going on, but the sound, a general hum, was not distracting. One man had been captured, but there must be more to this, Andi thought. Why was Klaus the victim? Andi took a moment to remember Klaus' eager smile, walking down the aisle. He couldn't help but be disappointed in himself. He had always taken pride in his acute observations and his ability to notice details overlooked by others. I must have seen the murderer, but I was fixed so intently on Klaus, he thought.

Andi recalled the image of Klaus waving his arms to get his attention earlier. Who was that person sitting next to Klaus? He had seemed embarrassed by Klaus' conspicuous behavior. Hmm, where is that man now? Andi went to the stage and turned around to look at the audience. He remembered where Klaus had been seated, but the man sitting next to him on the aisle was no longer there. He had a big gray beard as Andi recalled. What else should he look for, he thought? Oh yes, there was not much hair on his head. He scanned the audience in the center section, but couldn't find a match. Then he looked down the sides. There he is, sitting in the front row, closest to the exit. How did he get so far from his seat? He had shown no concern for Klaus when he was killed, in fact, he had moved far away and close to an exit. Why?

Andi asked another Sapo agent to accompany him. They went over to ask the man some questions. The man looked familiar in some way. They asked him to stand while being interviewed and empty his pockets, Andi saw a GDR passport. Unusual! Did he come with Klaus? He pretended he didn't understand Swedish, so Andi asked the question again in perfect German. No answer. His name was Alfred Pfeiffer. Where did he work? No answer.

The man refused to say anything more, but by midnight, Sapo agents had the police arrest both men. It took three days to positively identify Heinrich Mueller as a major Nazi war criminal, now acting as the manager of Tierpark Zoo in East Berlin. Over the next two weeks, Sapo, with the help of the CIA,

traced Mueller's whereabouts after the war. Mueller confessed
that he had been part of the Wehrmacht's think tank that set up
offices in the palace.

It was well-known that Mueller had been present when Hitler
committed suicide. Mueller said he returned to the palace to go
into hiding, taking with him four paintings he had 'acquired'
during the war. He confessed to making a crate in which to
store them. He hid the crate behind the basement wall. When
the Russians arrived, he posed as the groundsman for the
Tierpark estate. The Russians believed him to be of humble
origin and uneducated, so they kept him at the palace working
on maintenance. He rose in their estimation as years went by. It
had been Mueller's idea that East Berlin should make Tierpark
into a zoo, to rival the one in West Berlin. By the time the zoo
opened in 1955, Mueller was offered the position of manager. He
had been hiding out at the site since 1945.

The other man arrested was more difficult to pinpoint. A
week later, they were able to determine his true identity: Karl
Weiss, formerly one of Hitler's SS. They never could get him to
say he was working with Mueller, or there to help him escape.
Nevertheless, he was sentenced to life imprisonment for Klaus'
murder.

On the same day Klaus was killed, the East Berlin police had
brought in for questioning a man who was found trying to break
into a car that was illegally parked in front of the entrance to the
airport terminal. If he wasn't, as he claimed, dropping someone
off or picking someone up, why was he at the airport at 6:30 in
the morning? Eventually, it was discovered that the owner of the
Trabant was the man's former wife, Frederica Zellweger, who
lived in the same building as the man who was murdered later in
the day in Stockholm.

Because Sweden was a neutral country, Sapo could ask the
Stasi for help. This was especially appropriate, since both the
murder victim and the war criminal were East German citizens.

It was then that the Stasi uncovered Reinhold's Nazi background. Both Sapo and the Stasi concluded that Reinhold must have been an accessory to the crime. It was assumed he was helping Heinrich Mueller escape. In East Germany, there was no trial (there didn't have to be). Reinhold was simply sentenced to three years of imprisonment at Hohenschönhausen.

The GDR, always strapped for hard currency, quickly accepted 3,000 Deutsche Marks to allow Herr Mueller to be extradited to West Germany, where he was tried for war crimes. Mueller was sentenced to life in prison.

It took more than a year for all the pieces to fall into place. When matters were finally settled, Andi wrote his former boss, George:

"Although the Stasi cooperated with Sapo on the Mueller case, they never mentioned investigating how Mueller and Klaus obtained the paperwork to leave the GDR for Sweden. At first, I thought they didn't want to admit that such a transgression could happen; professional pride, etc. But, when I saw a picture of Reinhold in the Mueller case files, I knew I had seen him before. I looked into it and discovered that Heinz Mayer and Reinhold Zellweger have been close friends for over 30 years. I know from my university days that Heinz was a committed Nazi. Somebody on the inside had to procure the paperwork. I think it may have been Heinz. This is a long shot, but perhaps Heinz is a Stasi double agent."

A week later Heinz no longer worked for the CIA.

An autopsy was performed on Klaus' body. His death was found to be due to a lethal dose of cyanide as the doctors had suspected. Andi debated about what to do with Klaus' body. Andi thought Klaus was like so many others whose deaths came from trying to escape the GDR: unreported, uncommemorated, and unrecognized. The GDR always tried to avoid bad publicity, but Klaus' murder, the disruption of the Modigliani auction, and the capture of a Nazi war criminal in Stockholm were so highly publicized that Andi knew East Berliners would eventually hear the story. Still, the GDR would not want that story remembered. It would never allow Klaus' body to be buried at Tierpark Zoo, which Andi was sure would be Klaus' first choice.

Should Klaus' body be sent to Bronhof farm for Günter and Wilma to bury? But Klaus had never been there. To Die Birken? The only ground available for a burial there was where the birch trees were planted along the sidewalk in front of the building. Everybody loved those trees, and Klaus would not want one removed to make way for his body. He thought about perhaps mounting a plaque there in Klaus' memory, at least, but knew the Stasi officials would not allow that to happen.

In Klaus' pocket, Andi found what had to be Günter's false teeth and a scrap of paper with a West Berlin address, but no name. He knew of Klaus' relationship to a young woman, Mila, who had brought Andi the book from Günter that contained the information about the Russian missiles while he was in West Berlin. She had given him an unsealed letter that she begged to have delivered to Klaus, if he could manage it. He realized that the address on the scrap of paper might be Mila's, but because he was in Sweden, investigating that would have to wait.

He decided to have Klaus' body cremated and to send the ashes to Bronhof farm. Their arrival was preceded by a small package containing Günter's teeth and a long letter from Andi, explaining what had happened. He enclosed newspaper clippings.

A few weeks later, Andi received this reply:

> *Thank you, Andi, for taking Klaus from the piles of rubble into Die Birken. He was both a friend and a son to me. We formed a family, didn't we? By holding on to each other, we held on to our humanity.*

You know, this is the second time I have been sent the ashes of someone I loved. In 1940, the Nazis sent me my wife Gerda's ashes—she was executed for the crime of passing out leaflets! I couldn't fight in the war after that, so I deserted.

I regained my will to live on Wilma's farm in Poland. We are going to work Klaus' ashes into the ground of our vegetable garden. One couldn't ask for better fertilizer.

Again, thank you,
Günter and Wilma Beck

THE END

EPILOGUE

Dear Klaus,

Your wonderful bird sketches have inspired me to try to draw, so here is my attempt to capture Bronhof Farm, where Gramma Wilma and I live. Do you remember your visits here with your mother? You probably don't. You were so young at the time. The birch trees we planted then are doing well—beautiful in all seasons. Now that it's winter and there's snow on the ground, we are blessed with the stunning pattern of their variegated bark.....

We are so looking forward to you and Mila visiting us again in the spring.

Love,
Grandpa Günter

January 11, 1974

ACKNOWLEDGEMENTS

To my knowledge the historical events mentioned in *Die Birken* are accurately described. There is one exception: West German's visitation rights to East Berlin from December 19, 1963 to January 5, 1964 were limited to one day—actually for only 17 hours, from 7:00 A.M. to midnight. The characters portrayed are my creations except for Andi Szabó. There was an Andy Szabó, now deceased, who was a fellow Quaker at San Diego Friends Meeting. The Andi in *Die Birken* is based loosely on my friend Andy's life.

I owe special thanks to Christiane Kniel-Jurka and Adrian Kniel. Their revelations about German culture and lifestyles gave me the confidence to formulate the story of *Die Birken*. In addition, Christiane taught me some German which helped me in my research for the book. Then there were the readers: Martin Kropat, Gary Fairbourne, Mark Heinz, Sandy Hayes, Elizabeth Bills, Doc Burke, and Philip Shafer, all of whom gave me pertinent suggestions. Their encouragement, along with that of my docent friends at the San Diego Natural History Museum, was only surpassed by that of my husband Ken, who regularly supplied me with cups of coffee.

And once again, I have been blessed with outstanding publishers—Plowshare Media of La Jolla, California. I am grateful for their diligent editing and holding me to their high literary standards. All these people helped to make the process of writing *Die Birken* a joy.

ABOUT THE AUTHOR

Pam Barratt lives in San Diego with her husband Ken and cat, Dickens. *Die Birken* is Pam's fifth historical mystery novel. The others include: *Blood: The Color of Cranberries* (2009), *An Ostentation* (2011), *Gray Dominion* (2013), and *Malheur* (2017).

Without Dickens' persistent lap-sitting and head-butting the computer, *Die Birken* would have been published a year earlier.

For additional information, please visit her website at:
http://pameliabarratt.com/

Made in the USA
Monee, IL
14 January 2020